THE HOTTEST SUMMER EVER KNOWN

by

VALENCIA R. WILLIAMS
SIXTH EDITION

The Hottest Summer Ever Known

Jones and Williams Publication, LLC

P. O. Box 210460

Lake Orion, MI 48321-0406

E-mail: joneswilliamspublishing@yahoo.com

Bookworld Distributor 1-888-444-2524 EXT 505

Written

by

VALENCIA RENAY WILLIAMS

Cover design sketched by Kimberly Henderson
Computer Graphics by F. Alan Young
Editing by Donna L. Lopez-exhortations.literary@yahoo.com

Sixth Printing January 2006

Printed in the United States of America

ISBN
0-9740132-1-8

In Loving Memory of my Mother, Margie N. Williams, Father, Gilbert Williams, brother, Darryl Mitchell Williams and My Daughter's Father, Markel K. Jackson

"…I believe that the fear of the blood test is one of the biggest reasons why more people don't get tested."
Earvin "Magic" Johnson, April 2003
www.calypte.com

"I would like to turn my own problem into something good that will reach out to all my homeboys. I want to save their asses before it's too late."
Eazy E as reported by his Attorney Ron Sweeny, March 1995
www. eazy-e.com

"I don't think you see enough of this story in your face. There are millions and millions of people dying and a lot of it's because…..it's black people that are dying at this high rate."
Sean "P. Diddy" Combs as told to BET.com, November 2002

"I would continue to educate youngsters about the dangers of HIV and AIDS."
Alicia Keys as told to BET.com, November 2002

"I feel that AIDS is something very detrimental. It's very scary that with all the knowledge we have about it, people still don't do the right thing."
Ashanti as told to BET.com, November 2002

"If your not AIDS aware here in America, you're living on another planet. There's no excuse anymore."
Rosie Perez as told to BET.com, November 2002

About the Author

Valencia R. Williams was born January 29th in Detroit, Michigan to Margie and Gilbert Williams. She was the youngest of three with two older brothers, which led to a rather protected childhood. When she found her confidence and esteem, it was through her love for basketball. Standing at 6 feet 2 inches tall, she was one of the highest ranked high school women basketball players.

Although she had opportunities to receive a higher education and a career as a ballplayer, she made other choices… instead, prison was where she found change and education.

Within four years of incarceration, Valencia became the author of several novels. The Hottest Summer Ever Known is the first to be published, thus far.

Valencia is also a well-known and accomplished singer in the Metro-Detroit area, showcasing her talent by performing in various locations. Although she enjoys music, her aspirations are to continue publishing her novels.

Valencia's proudest accomplishment and greatest joy is being the mother of two beautiful children.

"Action is the enemy of thought."

THE
HOTTEST
SUMMER
EVER
KNOWN

A Novel By Valencia Williams

Valencia R. Williams

THE *NAKED* TRUTH

The first official report on AIDS, appeared in June 1981. Since its outbreak over twenty years ago, HIV has infected more than 60 million people, and AIDS has caused the death of more than 20 million people worldwide.

The estimated number of AIDS cases through 2002, in the United States alone was 886,575, and 9,300 AIDS cases were estimated in children under age 13.

In Africa, 5,000 babies are born HIV positive every month. One for every two babies, that means *half*, will die of AIDS.

AIDS is Real. There are a lot of people who *don't know* they are infected because they have no symptoms. Anyone, no matter how healthy they appear to be, could be infected. It comes with no name or social status attached.

This is why you MUST protect yourself.

*For a more detailed outline on how AIDS is dominating our environment, see the reference section in the back of this book.

1

PROLOGUE

A PREDATORY WOMAN

*****

SUMMER

Some might call me scandalous. Others might consider me a ho... ask me do I care. My family claims my attitude is what's wrong with me. Hey, this is me; the one they love to hate.

I know I got it honest...growing up in a violent, drug-infested neighborhood, the crack-heads and thugs ruled. It was ruthless in Detroit's most dangerous area, the low-down dirty East Side, where living was day to day.

And my peeps were the most embarrassing. I couldn't go nowhere with them dope fiends, shooting up that shit, making *me* look bad.

Even under my own roof, it was all about survival. I can't remember when I didn't live in fear. ...fear of the terrifying life of drug addicted parents. All breeds of bums stepping in and out of our space in the wee hours of the night led to a bad case of insomnia. It was all an ongoing nightmare.

Unfortunately, I wasn't the only one suffering in that hellhole...there was my sister, Treasure.

The name Treasure speaks for itself, she was once all I had...my only hope in surviving the struggle, but things are different nowadays; she's become more like a thorn in my side. After Pops was brutally killed, and Moms followed close behind him, dying from AIDS, our relationship ain't worth a damn now. She straight up just doesn't exist in my life.

I mainly fault the next of kin for that. They spoiled her, treated her like she was the only one that existed. I couldn't deal with all that favoritism and shit so I rolled out. Miss Big-shot

2

attorney! With her fancy suits and her little piece of paper! She can have all the love and stress that comes with living under my Grams' roof, I'm straight on that shit.

My family was plastic as hell. My Grams tripped on me about college. I had to let her know up front, I ain't Treasure. I graduated from high school and I damned sure wasn't about to spend another four precious years of mine to end up in the back of some unemployment line. Ain't shit out here for a black woman but her hustle. A college degree is just that...a college muthafuckin degree. I'm on some real shit now. Of course I didn't curse when I was expressing my emotions to Grams, but that was how I felt. Hell, keep it real. I went on ahead and let them believe the front Treasure put up, talkin' 'bout she's a virgin. Ho please. Her ass was open like 7-eleven!

They're so busy watching me, expecting me to fail. I just tell them, "Don't watch me, watch my moves." I don't have no time to be hangin' out with a nigga ballin' backwards! These cats out here have to pay to play, and that's the bottom line. I'm gon' do the damn thang...make it one of these days. I might not become an attorney or a neurosurgeon, but I bet whatever big fish I catch will be ballin' out of control.

*****

TREASURE

When I chose to become a defense attorney, it was for all the wrong reasons.

Let me get straight to the point. I despise drug dealers! I consider them a threat to the population. They killed my parents, selling that poison to their souls.

It was easy finding a law office to carry out my plan. I teamed up with the most prestigious firm in the city. They secretly had the same objective as I did; we handle nothing but drug cases. We shake their hands, take their money, and then send them up the river without a paddle! It would be easier if I could just click my heels and wish them all gone, but that would be too simple. I wouldn't want to miss out on all the excitement of watching their reaction when the Judge says, "I now sentence you to *LIFE*". They have no idea that I am the one that makes that all possible. Hey, my clients trust me. They give their freedom to me. Why wouldn't they? I mean, I am their attorney, after all. That's the least I can do for my loss, as well as for the children enduring now, what I had to then.

No one could begin to understand the affect my parents' death had on me. From that day forward I made a commitment to lock up every drug lord and bring down every drug organization that crosses my path. Truly, I didn't believe it would be this easy. …The way I manipulate these desperate criminals keeps me motivated

At one time business slowed up for a moment, due to our firm losing too many cases. So, we created a plan to win a few high profile cases to rebuild our reputation. Now, our cases are on overload.

I receive this natural high every time I receive a case of a young man responsible for distributing large quantities of drugs to our communities. I can't explain the feeling. I look into his eyes, silently crying out for help; and a vision of my Mom appears, laying on her deathbed, gasping for air, taking her last breath.

I only want one thing, your freedom, I say to myself, staring back into his eyes, half listening to him plead his innocence. My anger intensifies and I become vile. I begin to fill him with promises I have no intention to fulfill, and tell him all the ~~things he want to hear.~~

l me, "Ms. Lewis, why didn't you
ıs that your desire is to lock

ıg me, but I wasn't offended at all
ing the right thing. You see, a
ıt I wore a disguise. I thrive off
im wouldn't understand. This is

f Treasure. I know that it seems
ng with my pain. Not only am I
arents, but I also have to wake up
ıot hear the sound of my sister's
me. She can't let go of mistakes
~~from the past, while I've grown~~ past our differences. I wish she would do the same, but that would be something only she could change. She just doesn't know that I'm here for her. I'm not perfect like everyone seems to think I am, and I'm certainly not striving for perfection. I just want us to be a family. My life has been so incomplete without her. I worry deeply about, Summer.

I guess to keep a lot of this stress off my mind I hide behind my work. I'm hurting so bad, the pain sometimes seems hard to bear.

I can remember a quote I read somewhere that went something like, *"Hurting people, hurt people…"* Wow, now that's deep.

ONE

THE NIGHTMARE

***

SUMMER

People say death comes in threes. First, my Dad, then Mom, and now me...

Here I am lying in bed with my sister's husband, preparing to do the most vindictive, spiteful thing I've ever done! This is all her fault! None of this would have happened if she weren't so damn perfect! Now they both have to pay, in more ways than one...

It was the first day of summer and I was hot as hell. I could barely breathe in this stuffy room that my sister called her solitude, but I was able to tolerate the heated situation. ...Especially, if it meant destroying the bitch!

"Mmm," I moaned.

I like that.

The sensation I'm feeling from him right now is kind of hard to describe. He had my arms pinned over my head, caressing all my weak spots. Hubby knows what to do when it comes to pleasing a sista..

"You're a freak," I teased, watching him.

"Humph, I know," he crooned.

He was gentle in every way. I love a man that practices gentleness with my sensitive spots, especially my tits.

"There," I whispered, guiding him into the right direction. "Let me see what you can do with this," I whispered, leading him down to my hot lava. He was leaving a trail of moisture from my neck...to my navel...to my...

Sss...Mmmm... That's it Boy...right there...
He knew exactly what to do.
I was having too much fun for the moment. I needed to focus and get down to business, because Treasure should be making her way home in another hour or so.
Time is of the essence Baby Boy.
My hands pressed into his smooth bald head, pulling him deeper inside to the hive of my bitter honey, smothering him, wishing death could come and take him easily. His suffering was truly not what I wanted to happen behind my scheme. He was an innocent bystander.
W*rong place, wrong girl, Player.*
He seemed so sweet for my sister. Well, that was until he met me of course. ...No man married, gay, rich or famous can resist me. I had acquired skills in Seduction 101, earning an A+. My man, your man, whichever one wants to play. I don't hold them up; I get down to business. It's a heartless game, one that I play very well. I could give a fuck about the next bitch. I'm strictly out to get mines.
The Hubby was a little difficult at first. I suppose he had to weigh the risk and consequences of giving in to me. Yet, here I am laying here naked, ready to take his life within a few strokes from his raw flesh.
You ready ta die Baby-Boy?
I stared into the crown of his head, watching him have me for lunch.
"Take me," I demanded.
"You can't handle this girl," he said rising up on his knees exposing his erectness.
Damn...
No wonder my sister complained about stomachaches! On the other hand, he doesn't intimidate me. I've had bigger, but it's probably going to take more energy than I anticipated to pull this thing off; I'm just anxious to get this whole thing over with. It already took a lot of work to get to this point. Now's my chance to

give my sister an invitation to death. …thanks to her hubby, with his no-good-ass.

How foolish could he have been, to fall for the big butt and the smile? Humph, like most men, they trust the beauty and allow their flesh to make a decision that could ultimately cost them their lives.

So I say, FUCK the world! …And everybody in it, including Treasure.

That's right, Boo. You and Hubby are goin' with me.

"Hold on baby girl. Let me grab something." He reached over me to his wallet on the nightstand.

"What do you need baby? Let me get it for you," I said.

"I'm tight…I got this."

To my surprise, he pulled a condom from his wallet. Before I could react, he started tearing it open with his teeth, grinning at me, anxious to move on to the next level. I had to think fast! The condom idea was out of the question!

"Baby," I said, caressing his hardness. "How are you supposed to get a good feeling with that piece of rubber between your flesh and mine?" I stared seductively into his eyes.

"Humph," he chuckled. "Trust and believe, your boy is going to get his baby." He pulled the moist rubber from the package.

"But I don't want it," I whined, lubricating my finger, and then rubbing his nipple and his hardness simultaneously.

"Convince me how bad you want me inside you without it," he slurred, losing focus. I watched his head fall back, arms fall to his sides, and condom hit the floor. It was over. I won! I now own his soul. I led him to another position, me on top this time. …My control spot.

"What if you get pregnant?"

"Shhhhhhhhhh…" I placed my finger across his lips.

My warmth was sitting on top of his flesh, straddling. *Death* waits patiently for him.

Sorry boo…

I stared into his eyes.

"You win," he said surrendering.

It was time for the kill, but before I could guide him into the deep path of destruction, the door swung open!

"WHAT THE!!" He looked around me to a face that was far too familiar to the both of us.

"POP! POP! POP!!" Stray bullets scattered the room and I took cover, diving to the floor, not realizing I was hit.

I could feel something burning, something fighting its way through my flesh! "NOOO!" Was the only scream I could utter. ...The last scream to be heard. I was alone in my puddle of blood, fighting for my life.

PLEASE GOD! DON'T LET ME GO OUT LIKE THIS!!!

I fought for prayer, for a response! Silence, only silence, no one heard me. God turned his back on me. I was balled up in a fetal position, trying to alleviate the pain. Blood found its way through my air passage and I couldn't breathe! My vision became blurry. My hands and legs felt so cold.

All is lost...

Suddenly, I felt the presence of someone standing over me. This person was screaming, crying, holding her hand over her mouth.

"HELP ME!" My eyes cried out to her.

Tears plunged down the sides of my face, I couldn't move. My heart rate was rapidly rising and falling. ...The pressure from the pain forced me to ball my hands so tight that my nails punctured through the flesh of my palms.

Darkness started to settle in. The unknown cries, started to fade, and I knew the game was over. I could no longer breathe. My body would soon rest under the earth. My eyes were no longer under my control, rolling up into the back of my head; I felt pressure in my brain. I wanted to yell. I wanted to live. I wanted another chance! The only thing promised in life, finally caught up with me;

DEATH...

*****

Then I woke up...

Sweat covered my body, as I exhaled harshly; I threw the damp sheet away from me, jumped out of the bed, and raced toward the bathroom! My hands covered my naked frame, rapidly searching for wounds!

AIN'T THIS A BITCH! A FREAKIN' NIGHTMARE!!

I laughed nervously. I was still unsure whether there was something real about what I had just encountered. I stared in the mirror, glancing over my body, and continued checking for wounds. I needed reassurance. I turned the faucet on, water splashed everywhere from the pressure. I pulled a hand full of water up on my face, making sure I was awake.

"A nightmare," I sighed and sat down on the edge of the tub.

This dream was too real; the reality of it was too close for comfort.

And why the hell would I be dreaming of screwing a husband that doesn't exist? Treasure probably will never get married. Men like freaks, humph, not geeks! Her face was blurry; I couldn't see her. I wonder what that meant.

I had a disease of some kind, something deadly I assume. I didn't want to die alone. That scares me. As bad as I want to ignore this, it might be in my best interest to see a doctor. I guess...I don't know, maybe. Doctors make me uncomfortable. They give bad news. I'm not ready for bad news.

TWO

TIMBER MONTGOMERY

*****

TREASURE

Timberland Montgomery is one of my clients. Mr. Montgomery is being charged with "possession and attempt to distribute narcotics." I first took on this case having no idea what he had been through, until I met his child, Timber.

I'll never forget that day his wife came into my office to retain me. I started not to take the case. Her husband didn't meet my criteria. He was small fish, I didn't carry poles small enough to reel him in, but seeing his wife, accompanied by this beautiful little girl gave me a change of heart.

I was so amazed at how much this beautiful child reminded me of Summer. It took me back to the good 'ole days. Thoughts of the loving memories we once shared touched me deeply, so I invited Mrs. Montgomery into my office to at least hear her out.

"I'm sorry for the chaos here. Make your self comfortable," I offered.

"Thank you," she said anxiously taking a seat, sitting her child on her lap.

I made myself comfortable across from them. "I'm sorry, your name again?" I had a lot on my mind as I rattled through papers.

"Kenya, Kenya Montgomery."

"Mrs. Montgomery, how can I help you?"

Then the child spoke, "And my name is Timber Lee Montgomery!" She flashed a warm welcome smile.

I glanced at her, returning the same warm smile. Timber was very tiny with a round face and fat cheeks. I stood, walked around the desk, kneeled down to her and said, "It's nice to meet you Timber Lee Montgomery. May I ask how old are you?" I reached out my hand to her, taking hold of her small fingers. There was a feeling of *de ja vu*; I couldn't understand it. Her little touch was so familiar.

"Tell the lady how old you are, Sweety," her mother coaxed.

"I'm four years old."

"Well, let me see what I have here for such a big girl." I reached behind me on top of my desk, grabbed a jar that I had filled with assorted candy, and gave it to her. I then made my way back over to my seat and finally recovered the information that Kenya had called and left with my secretary earlier.

We went over her husband's case. Due to the fact that Mr. Montgomery wasn't a big time dealer or a drug lord, I truly didn't want to take his case. Locking him up would be less than a challenge for me, but Kenya was persistent. She wouldn't give up on her endeavor to gain my help.

"Please Ms. Lewis! I love my husband, I need him home!"

I noticed Timber looking up from the floor where she was organizing a puzzle.

"Mom, where's daddy?" Timber asked.

That did it. I at least had to look over the case, as my anger was won over by a four-year-old charmer. I also was curious to know what type of bum would leave his family in this position.

"He's away Sweety... Remember what Mommy said last night about Daddy being away for awhile?" She tapped the corners of her eyes with a tissue. Timber nodded in agreement with her mother.

"Alright Pumpkin, finish your puzzle," she said.

"Okay," Timber sighed. I could see the disappointment in both their eyes.

Timber was off doing what most children do at her age; going back and forth in my candy jar. I didn't mind, because the love that radiates from a child like her makes me forget how ugly life is. I was enjoying her company. Her mother attempted to say something to her about going back into the candy jar, but I reassured her it was okay.

Kenya Montgomery was only twenty-three; she seemed very mature and responsible for her age. She had tactfulness about herself that any man would find attractive. Her skin tone was a medium cocoa color that highlighted her tired hazel eyes. She had a look that seemed to always be serious, and a positive aura about herself. She wore her hair pulled back in a simple style that complemented her persona.

Kenya desperately wanted to see her husband come home. I personally didn't think someone of his character deserved to be a part of their lives. One of my objectives was to do all I could do to make him disappear, free of charge. This one is on me.

After my appointment with Kenya, I went to visit Mr. Montgomery at the County Jail. He looked rough, but who wouldn't after sleeping on a concrete floor in an overcrowded facility like this one. I could only imagine with whom and what he was sharing his space.

"Mr. Montgomery, I'm Treasure Lewis, the attorney handling your case.

"Sounds like a plan." His deep voice was hoarse. "I appreciate you workin' with a brotha. So the wifey came and took care of you, I see?"

Sitting there, staring into his eyes was inciting the usual anger that comes over me when facing scum like him. I didn't even bother to tell him I had taken his case without charge. I told Kenya that I insist that she keep her money, do something special for her and her daughter. She's going to need something to fall back on once I get rid of this fool.

"Well, Mr. Montgomery, let's put it this way, I'm going to do the best I can with what you two are working with." I forced out a professional, courteous tone.

"Did you meet my Shorty?"

13

"Excuse me?" I wasn't familiar with all that street lingo. I can't stand it!

"I'm sorry, my daughter."

"Oh! Yes." I managed a small chuckle.

"Beautiful, isn't she?" His voice became raspy.

Oh please... don't start sobbing!

This is the turn off point for me. These young uneducated brothers get themselves into this, and then they think a few tears can get them out.

You should've thought about that when you were selling that poison to your people!

I hoped that my expression didn't coincide with my thoughts.

"Are you okay, Mr. Montgomery?"

"HELL NAW I AIN'T OKAY!" He suddenly lost control.

I jumped at his enraged behavior.

"Listen," I made a gesture with my hands for him to back off. He was losing control.

The guard opened the door and asked, "Is everything okay in here?"

Mr. Montgomery tried to rectify the situation, but it was too late; I was ready to leave by then.

"Please, Ms. Lewis, I'm sorry, just hear me out...please."

He made an attempt to touch my hand, but I moved away, holding in my anger, trying to calm down. He pleaded with me, but my mind was made up to just leave. There was nothing he could say to me at that point that would make me stay. I stood, watching him unfold. Then I boldly said, "This meeting is no longer in session officer. You can take him." The officer came toward Timberland.

"MS. LEWIS, PLEASE! DON'T LEAVE ME IN HERE! MY DAUGHTER WILL DIE! I HAVE TO GET OUT OF HERE! BEFORE IT'S TOO LATE! PLEASE!"

I was almost to the door. I turned toward him, signaling for the guard to wait. That's when he revealed what was eating at his insides, hoping that it would gain my sympathy.

14

"Have a seat Mr. Montgomery." The only thing I could think of was the welfare and safety of Timber.

"Oh…God," he cried, trying to regain his composure.

This big overgrown man sitting here, crying like a two-year-old child amazed me. I've seen this a thousand times though, coming in here talking to these so-called *hardcore men*. Only when they're in the presence of their peers do they carry out this untouchable attitude; but in here, they're straight up Barbie dolls!

"Do you need more time to get yourself together, Mr. Montgomery?"

I sat back on the edge of my seat. I wasn't comfortable with him at all. My tolerance level at that point was very low and I'd about enough of his whining.

"No, I'm fine," he said, sniffling and wiping his eyes with his bound cuffed hands. "I'm ready to do this."

"Mr. Montgomery? Do you feel your wife and child's safety is at risk?"

"Safety? Kenya didn't tell you?"

"Tell me what?" We stared at each other for a few seconds as he searched for words.

"Timber, my love, my only child, my baby girl… got AIDS Ms. Lewis. Please help me get home to my baby girl, Ms. Lewis."

My heart dropped! His last words were like echoes from the dead.

Timber has what?

I stared in disbelief and looked away from him, trying not to get too emotional, as I rose from my seat. He started crying as I stood to leave. A part of me didn't want to go, but the cold stubborn side of me prevailed. I needed some time to digest what he just said. I stepped out of the room fanning my eyes trying to dry my falling tears. This was unexpected. Timber appeared to be a healthy child. There were no signs of illness while in my presence. This isn't fair. None of this is fair. Here I was trying to make their situation worse, knowing very little about the lives I was serving to destroy.

I have to help this man. It's the least I could do at this point.

After leaving the jail, my mind was overtaken with the thought of all the suffering that beautiful soul was about to undergo; too much for an innocent, helpless child and too young to understand that type of agony. I cried as reflections of my Mother reappeared in my mind. The way she suffered; the way the disease affected her. Timber would soon have to endure that same pain. Why? How did she contract AIDS? God, please help her....

*****

Learning more about Timberlands' case opened my eyes to the various reasons some of these young naïve men choose this destructive lifestyle. When Timberlands' child, Timber, somehow contracted HIV through a blood transfusion, Timberland was lost. With a criminal record, finding a job was difficult for him. Having made many mistakes in his past virtually destroyed any hope or opportunity to provide a decent life for his dying child. Having no means of supporting his family weighed heavily on his shoulders. He felt he had no choice but to take the first money-making opportunity that came around. That choice was the one that landed him in jail.

Because of the extenuating circumstances in Timberland's case, he was released on his own recognizance.

Armed with newly established, but temporary freedom, he was still imprisoned with the thought of losing his daughter.

Timber went into the late stages of AIDS two months after Timberlands' release…and died. Her death traumatized me. I wasn't at all prepared for this, but I had to move on.

This tragedy helped me to see beyond the surface and look at the character of the person. What I guess I'm trying to say is, you never know what a person is going through or why people make various decisions; some that can prove to be detrimental to their lives. Thinking back, I know that I've made some choices in my life that I'm no longer proud of, and this has been a valuable lesson to them all.

Now I haven't completely changed my perception of drug dealers, but I will work hard on treating these individuals as human beings.

THREE

OBLIGATED

*****

SUMMER

I am so tired.

This here is unbelievable. I can't believe that I'm allowing a nightmare to lead me into this clinic! I have other priorities that I could be handling instead of sitting here. You know what? I'm leaving! I'm out.

"Summer Lewis," a nurse called out over the noisy waiting area.

"Ain't this about a…" I sighed harshly.

I turned toward the unfamiliar voice, trying my best to ignore a bunch of welfare recipients and their ghetto kids running around here stepping on my expensive shoes! I might just have to pop one of these degenerates upside the head!

Tolerance has never been one of my virtues, which is one of the reasons why I strongly support abortions. I don't understand why women have all these damn kids! For what? A check?

I followed the nurse to the back to prepare for what I assumed would be an examination. How wrong was I to believe?

I really wasn't vibing with this wanna-be nurse at all. I knew her kind. She's the type who will examine me, then share the results with her co-workers and road dawgs after work.

"Okay, Miss Lewis. Have a seat while I check your file and ask you a few questions," she said.

I made myself comfortable up on the examination table, noticing her staring heavily at my file. Something grasped her attention.

"My name is Tawaunna Anderson. I'm the nurse who will be assisting Dr. Tice today. Has anything changed since your last visit with us?"

"No. I can't say that it has."

She cleared her throat. "It shows here you have had two terminated pregnancies in the last eight months and that you have a past history of recurring yeast infections..."

"Hold up. I didn't come here for a Bio. Just a simple pap smear, the results, and I'm out of here."

"This is standard procedure, Ms. Lewis. If you're not comfortable with it, you can take it up with the doctor if you'd like."

Is she getting smart?

I could feel my left eyebrow arching as I asked, "Where's the doctor?" My patience was wearing very thin.

"He'll be here shortly. Now as I was saying, Ms. Lewis, has anyone ever talked to you about practicing safe sex? I would recommend that you try it."

"What?"

Oh no. This trick got the game all twisted! I stepped down from the table. It's time for some gangsta shit!

"I'm just trying to warn you. You've been lucky so far to get away with treatable infections. Even they can build up a resistance to treatment and it's just as easy to contract HIV and AIDS. I think you better consider being a little more careful with who you sleep..."

"Let me get this straight. Are you expecting ME to take some advice from YOU with that big ass herpes sore dangling from your lip?"

"Oh!" She caught a case of sudden surprise.

"I recommend YOU suck it, lick it, or whatever you do with a glad bag in your mouth."

"Wait a minute Ms. Lewis. I can accept some constructive criticism. But, while I'm using a sandwich bag, you may have to get yourself a body bag."

We both stared at each other, waiting for the other one to bust a move. Then a knock at the door brought us back to reality. The doctor entered.

Damn you fine.

I secretly glanced at him, enjoying the memory snap shot. I definitely liked what I saw, and I could tell that I had an effect on him. For some reason, he seemed pleasantly surprised to see me also.

Just made your morning, didn't I? I was smiling to myself.

"Good morning, Ms. Lewis. How are you? I'm Dr. Tice," he said, reaching to shake my hand.

His warm, blush colored lips complemented his light-bronze tan. Discreetly, I checked out what he was packing.

I could work with that.

He was setting off some hot, rousing, tingling sensations in me in a way that had me plottin'.

Maybe I can bust a nut while he's checking my uterus with his two fingers. Now that would be some freaky shit right there! I thought, giggling. He glanced around at me, giving me a shy grin. I had him to the point where he could hardly concentrate on his work from looking over at me so tough.

"Tawaunna? Is everything okay?" He regained his composure.

I almost forgot about 'pimple lip'. He was noticing her discomfort as she was holding her hand over that thang. I don't blame her; I wouldn't have showed up to work! Hadn't she ever heard of sick leave?

"I'm fine Doctor," she mumbled, turning away from us.

He gave us a questioning stare. He must be new, because I'm not familiar with him being at this clinic. Either way, this is crazy, I don't even do white boys, but it was something appealing about this one. It's got to be the money. I can tell he's rich and that's enough to convince me that ain't nothin' wrong with a little jungle fever.

"So what do we have here Tawaunna?" She eased the file to him, obviously self-conscious now about her lip, hoping that he didn't notice. How could anyone not notice?

He turned to me and said, "Okay, Ms. Lewis..."

"Doctor, can I speak with you in private, please?"

"Sure, I don't see a problem with that. Tawaunna, can you please excuse us?" She gave him a cautious stare.

Let me find out their doing the damn thang!

"Sure Doctor. If you need anything, just let me know." She winked, looking like a horse with a fly in his eye, and pulled the door closed.

"All right, Ms. Lewis. What can I do for you?" He leaned up against the sink comfortably.

I admired his style. He was neat, but rough. He sported the doctors' coat, but underneath was something a bit more enticing. He wore a nicely fit black designer crew neck with a visible logo. His slacks had a nice fit and the black leather shoes brought his attire all together. The scent he was sportin' smelled like something so familiar. It was nice too.

This white man got taste, huh?

"Before we begin, let me clear one thing up," I said sitting back on the examination table, inviting him with my eyes to come closer. "I don't like this Ms. Lewis thing. Please call me Summer." He smiled, giving me a shy nod. "Why are you smiling? Did I say something that amused you?"

"No, Miss...I'm sorry, Summer. You said you needed privacy." He placed the file behind him giving me his undivided attention. "How can I help you?"

"Well, first of all, I'd like to address the fact that your assistant's behavior was very unprofessional."

"Come again?"

"She was rude and down right tacky. I felt like she was trying to humiliate me or something." I secretly glanced at his well-manicured nails that excluded a ring.

A single white man with paper? I got the vapors...

"Please allow me to first offer you an apology on behalf of my staff. I would like to assure you that the nurses here are certified and trained extensively. They are fully aware of the consequences they could face if they are not extremely careful." He proceeded to wash his hands while he explained. "My staff has a responsibility to our patients, which happens to be a major part of their job description. Please know that I don't condone, nor do I tolerate that kind of behavior. I will definitely address Ms. Anderson about this. I hope," he said, while shaking the water off of his hands and snatching a paper towel. "…that I have placed your mind at ease, Summer." The way he just slid into my name did something to me. This here is going to be interesting.

"Mind if I call you Michael? I mean, if that's no problem with *the peoplez*." He stared at me like, *"peoplez???"*

Slang Michael, slang.

I see I'm going to have to put him up on a little of this ghetto flavah.

"Sure, I don't mind." He winked.

That's all I needed to see. When his cell phone vibrated, he lifted his white coat to check the message. I admired the leather Gucci belt that hugged his toned waistline. Everything about him made the thought of doing a white man even easier for me.

"You know who you remind me of?"

"Ben Affleck?" He folded his arms annoyed.

"People must tell you that all the time."

"Pretty much."

"Don't let that go to your head, now," I said.

"Let's stick to the basics."

Was he dissing me?

Maybe I read his response wrong.

"You called earlier requesting a complete physical. Is this for a job or something?"

"Yeah," I answered quickly.

"And you would like all your results today?"

"Yes. You are a doctor right?"

"Correct. But I haven't met one that could obtain all your results this fast unless it was considered an emergency. May I ask why the rush?"

"You can make it happen, Doc. You got the magic stick, work it."

"The magic what?"

Why did I say that?

Too much Fifty and Lil' Kim on my brain, I guess.

"Never mind," I said.

"I'll see what I can do." His eyes dropped to my cleavage.

"What's next?" I lay back on the table; allowing my cleavage to squeeze through my low cut blouse. I had his attention until the tap on the door snapped him out of it. You probably guessed who that someone was... "Pimple Lip"...

"Excuse me, Doctor? Do you need any assistance with Ms. Lewis' blood work?" She stared suspiciously back and forth between the two of us.

He cleared his throat and said, "Oh, yes!"

Tawaunna made her way inside the room and walked over toward Michael.

"Okay Ms. Lewis, where did we leave off?"

Did this fool just go back to calling me Ms. Lewis?

Ohh, I see what's happening here.

I got you player.

The stare I gave him was so intense, that he avoided eye contact. Like I thought, these two *were* freakin', I could feel the intensity in the air.

May the best girl win.

"Let me fill you in on what exactly a physical entails. I will perform a breast examination, and a pap smear. According to your file here, you're due for one." Tawaunna was placing the instruments up on the tray while I continued to stare at him. I could tell that I was making him uncomfortable. "I also noticed in your file that there are no results for an HIV test. Have you ever been tested?"

For some reason Tawuanna stopped what she was doing to wait on my answer. They both stared at me like I was already a candidate for the virus. Only I knew the truth to that question.

"Yes. I was just tested in August," I lied.

"That was more than nine months ago, so I recommend that you update your file with another one." He insisted.

"I agree doctor. Ms. Lewis, like I mentioned earlier, seems to be promiscuous…"

"Excuse me!" The doctor snapped.

"No need, Michael, I got this."

I was off the table by then. Michael was in between us, demanding that Tawaunna exit the room. Our eyes grilled each other's all the way out the door.

I'm gon' whup yo' ass if I ever see you on the block! My eyes read. I never forget a face.

"I apologize for the…"

"Don't go there. Let's just get this over with. I've got better things to do," I snapped.

And like all the other men in my life, he bowed down. He called for another nurse to assist him. Regina was her name. She was older, and mature, with no cold sores.

Michael was persistent with the HIV thang, but I wasn't feelin' it at all. I don't want my days numbered! Since Mom passed, I haven't had the courage to be tested. I've had too much raw flesh to want to know.

There's no doubt in my mind that my results will most likely be positive. So, before the whole thing was over, I gave in, ran out of excuses. I felt like I had no choice, I guess. Michael made me feel obligated because I didn't want him to think I had anything to hide. Now I have to walk on eggshells 'til my results come back.

I can't even begin to count all the dudes I done slept with! I know one thang though, I should've NEVER stepped foot in this joint! A freakin' nightmare got me living on the edge now! I just had to know the truth.

The truth of the matter is; I know I'm a candidate for many reasons. One, I disdain condoms; I love the feeling of the flesh. That was one true thing about the dream. ..."Condoms take away my sensation". ...Uh-Uh, can't have that. But, all this anticipation of waiting for my result is going to kill me! Hell, if it's positive, I'm going to kill my damn self! I can't live knowing I'm going to die from that shit! If I receive a phone call asking me to come in, that's all I need to know that I'm hit! I don't want no AZT's, no advice, and no freakin' counseling! And I'm not going out by myself, neither! I'm taking me a few prisoners!

*****

One thing about Time that I've come to realize is; when you want it to slow up, it flies by; when you want it to fly by, it goes slow as hell. The day I dreaded rolled around and I was on the edge. My phone rung and the voice on the other end made me nervous. It was him, Dr. Death calling to give me bad news. I know that's what it was; I could hear it in his voice.

"Hello, this is Dr. Tice. Miss Lewis I would like to see you in my office as soon as possible. I need to go over some things with you. Please call the office at your earliest convenience."

This phone call sent me into frenzy! I was experiencing all kinds of crazy thoughts. I was trying to figure out what my results were without confirming them. So to accommodate all the "self" talk, I avoided his request and took matters into my own hands.

I'm not dying alone

25

FOUR

DIRTY

*****

"Summer, you have a minute? I need to talk to you," Treasure said with an uneasy tone.

It took a lot of courage for her to call Summer. She had dialed Summer's number numerous times before making it to this point. And just to think all of that built up courage got shot down by the one that she loves more than life.

"I know this is not you Treasure!" She could hear the phone fumbling in Summer's hold. "Didn't I tell you to lose my number?"

"I-I..." Treasure sighed. "I just wanted to call to see how you were doing, Summer. What's so hard about that? I haven't heard from you in a while now."

"That should tell you something. Have I called you? ... Huh? ...Well then!" She said sarcastically before Treasure could respond.

"You know what...?" Tears welled up in Treasure's eyes. She couldn't hide the pain that was in her voice.

"I do know this. You can call Grams with all that crying and shit! Let them cater to you. I got company!"

Summer slammed the phone down in the cradle, getting back in motion.

"Who was that baby?" The deep voice of a thug whispered in her ear.

They were in the middle of sexing when Treasure called. The sound of Treasure's voice threw her concentration off and made it even harder for her to deal with his presence. Hell! She just met dude the other day!

"Check this out," she said holding his face between her hands, and then continued. Dude slowed up his penetrating to hear Summer out. "Don't stop your flow. ...Make me cum, but never question me and my business. You got that?"

He nodded, turned on by her aggressiveness, and the feeling of her warmth around his raw flesh. He offered to use protection, but Summer refused. Without question, he went along with her and took the risk, convincing himself that she was too beautiful to have anything threatening.

Just another statistic, Summer thought, leaving him with one of the best nuts he'd ever had.

*****

After being hung up on by Summer, Treasure stared heavily at a picture she kept under her pillow of the two of them when they were young. She needed to release some tension, so she landed face first in her pillow muffling her cries. Not having her sister right now was almost as bad as loosing their mother.

No matter how Summer treats her, Treasure is always thinking of a way to somehow reach her.

I will not give up on you Summer.

FIVE

PICTURE THIS

*****
SUMMER

I got mad issues, but it doesn't change the fact that I have to live with them. Point blank, I have to do me regardless!

I'm stepping out on the scene with this lethal weapon of mine. My health is in God's hands right now. So with the little time I have left on earth, I'm about to start flaunting all the beauty I have and get what I want in return.

My body is a work of art; nice firm breast, a round ass, flat tummy, and nice legs. OH! Don't let me forget; no excessive fat under my arms jigglin'. You would have thought I lay under the knife to get the shape I have. It's *all* exceptional to the eye.

I know I sound conceited, but I can't help it! Hell, I've earned it. I work out for as long as my body can stand it. I'm in Bally's pumpin' iron with my personal trainer. My body's a beast! People think J-Lo got it goin' on! Humph, move over Jenny! Puffy, you need a girl?

As far as describing my looks, dudes wonder if I got Indian or Cuban in me. Let me set the record straight! I'm African American, dammit! ...An African American QUEEN. ...Yeah, that's me. I'm a muthafucka with my natural thick long hair flowing to the center of my back, deep ocean dimples on both cheeks, and a smile that'll make a man cum without foreplay. There's nothing fake about my appearance. If they would stop focusing on my beauty, they might be able to see me, but then, that's what makes the shit I do so easy.

28

I also do a little boxing for extracurricular. Ever since this dude took me to see Roy Jones kiss the floor after being knocked out by some new cat, I been knocking a few out myself; not to say they stay there, but I could surely give them a run for they money. Last but not least, the way I roll my hips... HYPNOTIZING! Ya heard! On the real, I watch videoz daily. I have to keep up with the hip-hop world, stay in the groove. I'm bringin' the pain! And to these cats, it's pure pleasure! Humph.

Last Saturday, I went down to this club off Woodward in downtown Detroit. I usually roll alone, but a few chickenheads I know from way back; China, Jade, and Monique accompanied me. I was sending the crowd to the sideline with every move, matching my curves so well; the peoplez just had to watch.

We had a ball that night so we returned the following Saturday to represent this rap group out of the NYC.

This broad, who I remember being there the previous weekend, was on the dance floor copying my moves! I guess she was trying to win her a one-night-stand, so I let her do her thang and didn't hate. She had obviously been practicing. All her hard work deserved something; but when they played "Get Low" by the Ying Yang Twins, I had to represent. I grabbed Jade up and we pushed our way to the floor. Before the song was over, we stole the show! I don't know where that chick went.

Then they played my cut by Lloyd Banks, "Smile". I did everything but stripped and slid down a pole off of this hit. The only thing I could hear over the music was fellas yellin', "WORK THAT SHIT GIRL!" I aced this hip-roll move that had the fellas drooling. I had me a little buzz too.

One of the rappers that was in the house that night was trying to push up on me. He wanted this juice, and I was going to give it to him; you know I was, but not that easy. Rappers get juice on the hour. In order for him to fall prey, he had to trust me. His video was hot, and *damn*, he was hot. After looking at them juicy lips on him, I knew I had to work him. He reminded me of Nelly with his wet luscious lips. All the groupies were falling to his feet, but he wasn't paying them any attention. He needed a challenge.

29

I'm a little familiar with these famous cats. One of the golden rules is, "Never give up the booty, until you receive the benefit." I'm not blinded by the bling until it's around my neck.

When it was time to work my magic, Jade and I was sitting at the bar, sippin' on some Paul Masson, feelin' good. Monique and China was somewhere getting their swerve on.

"Here he come, Summer," Jade said bumping my arm.

"I'm not sweatin' dude. You want 'um?"

"It's whatever," she said smiling.

"Wha'sup Gorgeous?" He spoke to me, sliding in between us. Jade eased away after she seen his interest was with me.

"Not a thang." I said to him and then called out to my dawg. "Yo, Jade! Where you goin'?"

"I'm going over here to see what China and Monie is up to!"

"Them yo' girls?" He said looking me up and down.

"We hang out every now and then," I said, smiling up at him. "Before I forget to mention, that was a nice performance Baby. You really rocked this joint tonight."

"Thanks Beautiful. You did too. Where you learn to move like that?" He signaled for the bartender.

"I picked up a few moves here and there. Why? You act like you never seen a woman get down. All them ho'z in your video?" I finished my drink.

"Can I get you another drink?" The bartender asked me. I nodded the answer "no". I was already high, caught up into the song that was playing by Fat Joe, *Lean Back*. Everybody was on the floor rocking back and forth like they did in the video.

"Yo Man, let me get something for the lady and me."

"I'm tight, baby," I intercepted.

"You sho?"

"Trust me. I'm already buzzin'. If I drink anymore, I'll be buggin'."

"Aight, Pretty." He ordered a drink and continued. "What's your name, Ma?"

He leaned into the bar. I kept my composure, because I really wanted him bad! I knew I had to stay relaxed.

"Summer." I responded, leaning my head against my closed hand.

"Summer? Humph, like Winter, Spring and Fall?"

"Uh-uh...more like rain, sleet and snow." I stared away.

"Sounds cold."

"I am." I stared into his eyes. My response flew right over his head.

"How old are you? Let me guess...twenty-one, twenty-two?"

"I look that young?" I asked sounding surprised. People always tell me I look younger than I am.

"You'z a pretty muthafucka. I don't see many women look as good as you without make-up. I love me a naturally beautiful woman."

"Thank you, baby. And to answer your question, I'm twenty-six."

"Auh, hell naw! Quit playin'! You know that's my age girl!" He laughed.

"So I guess we have a lot in common."

"I guess we do." He sipped on his drink staring at me.

Damn I like this girl.

Chicks were walking by calling out to him. He ignored. I had his attention and was lovin' it!

Stay cool Summer. Work Him girl!

"Let me cut the chase. My management is scouting for beautiful women that can move, and look what we have here," he gestured, as he looked me up and down.

"And what exactly do we have, here?" I smiled, flirting.

"Something I wish I had a long time ago." He sucked his teeth, continuing to scan me from head to toe. I could see he craved for what sat before him. "I could sure use someone like you on my team."

One of his boys called out to him. He just threw his hand up and said, "Hold up Chief!"

As he turned his attention back to me I asked, "Is that right? And what exactly does a girl like me have to do to be down on your team?"

"You pretty," he said staring heavily at my hair.

"It's real."

"Did I say anything about weave?"

"You didn't have to."

He focused back to our discussion. "Yo, check this out. We're about to shoot my video for my new hit. You heard of…"

"I know, I know," I said cutting him off. "I support you baby. I'm up on all your latest hits. You the man!" I teased.

"In desperate need of a lady."

"There's plenty to choose from. Look around."

"Something good doesn't come easy."

He just doesn't know what's lurking behind all of this beauty.

"You have your own style," he continued. "A rare style, that is."

"I agree."

"Well, why don't you agree to chill with me in Miami on the proposition I just offered you."

"Tell me more about this proposition." I pulled my hair around my neck, exposing the fine baby hair that lay so beautifully against my skin.

"How about us talking business over breakfast? It's going on two in the morning. What's your favorite spot?"

I'm up on this game right here. The only time brothas try to take sistas out to eat breakfast from the club at this hour is when it's a booty call.

"I'm not hungry Baby. Thanks for the offer though. Just give me an idea on what you're talking about."

"Let me cover this. You will be doing some basic shit, like gigging on a beach set with a few other chicks. You'll be rockin' the finest Burberry and Fendi swimwear, and many more of those glamorous designers you women love. It's going to be off the chain! Bring a couple of your friends, I promise I'll show ya'll some love."

While he was talking, I couldn't help but notice his bling. I liked his taste. ...Not too much, and it looks good against his skin.

"Sounds good. How much paper are we talking?"

"Damn, Pretty." He chuckled. "You don't waste no time, do you?"

"I don't mean to be rude... but'ta, I have bills, Boo."

As much as I would love to be chillin' with this celebrity, I need security. Loot. I'm not flying all over the globe spending up my change like the majority of these groupies that just want to be seen with a star. If the price is right, it's on! If not...

"Come back to my room with me. We can talk figures there." He licked his lips and almost had his way. ...Almost.

"I don't do room conversations."

"You something else girl." He nodded his head, smiling. "Rare."

"Like jewels." I smiled in agreement. "How long are you in town? Maybe we can do dinner."

"Not long, but I'm interested in knowing more about you. Dinner is on. Name the time, the place, and where I can pick you up."

I like this chick. If the pussy is as good as her flow, I might have to lock it down.

We set the time and place to grub. I was impressed, especially to be offered a spot in his video. Picture my fine ass on TV; I won't be any good after that. To think these ho'z be hatin' *now*! It's over.

I chose "Sweet Georgia Brown" to eat. He was familiar with the spot, though he hadn't been there before. He was more like a hotel-eatin' brotha. He didn't like to be around too much attention when he was on tour, so usually he'd just chill in his suite. However, he found me interesting enough to try it out.

I gave him the directions to my high-rise. It was only a few blocks away from the club; right off the water. I was kind of disappointed that he didn't give me his information; it made me feel a little insecure. I really didn't want to go back to my dawgs empty handed. I ended up pulling a fake move and wrote down a bogus number, holding it in my hand until I reached the table. Once they seen I was holding a piece of paper, I slid it in my bra.

"What did he say, Summer?" China asked anxiously.

"What kind of cologne was he sporting?" Monique interrogated. "It smelled like something familiar when he walked past me."

"Ya'll gon' hook up?" Jade pressured.

"Hook us up with one of his boyz!" They all jumped down my throat!

"Why are ya'll ho'z acting like ya'll never seen a rapper before? It is not that serious."

"What's up with the piece of paper you placed in your bra?" Monique asked jealously.

"Ya'll know he was trying to take me back to his room. I wasn't feelin' him like that. I told him to give me his hitter and I'll call him tomorrow."

"I know that's right!" China said, giving me a high-five.

"I would have taken the offer," Monique said, while sipping on her drink.

Monique began acting distant after that. She was urking me so bad, that I left her ass at the club along with Ol'Boy and friend'z. She probably wanted to stay anyway to see which one of them wanted some head. I hope whoever she got, kept the lights on. Monique has these fine little bumps around her lips that she tries to hide with makeup. It doesn't help. That shit is too obvious!

As far as China and Jade, they're yellow bus material. They ass is special. Let me find a better way to describe them; The lights be on, but nobody's home.

SIX

DON'T SWEAT THE SMALL STUFF

*****

TREASURE

"Treasure, here are the files you requested on United States versus Aaron Carlton," said the young secretary, placing the file on my desk.

I sat quietly with my back turned to her, staring out my window. I really should be in a better mood, now that I am a partner with a new firm. I had to leave Brandon & Zilx. They still practiced the same beliefs I once did, now I have some new objectives; ones better carried out with this new firm.

I wanted to eventually start up my own partnership with three of the greatest women I'd ever met. They were like sisters I never had. All of us made it through some tough times, and now three out of the four of us had all worked our way up to partners with this firm. That was enough, for now.

"Thank you Renee," I said swinging my chair around to face her.

I'm sure she was heading out of my office to get back on the phone with one of those no good men she's always messing with. I couldn't help but to become annoyed by the way she was chewing on her gum. I had to calm myself before I went there with her.

I was trying to look out for a sister when I hired her ghetto behind. It's the price you pay when you're looking out for one of your own. Black folks! It just doesn't pay off. I'm speaking of the ones that make it bad for everyone else with obnoxious behavior and rude manners. My associates warned me before I made a final decision to hire Renee, but I felt everyone deserves a chance to grow. I definitely was wrong about this one.

"Listen, Renee." She was standing halfway out the door.

"Yes?" Her mouth was on overdrive with the gum popping.

"Here." I held the Kleenex up in the air for her to take hold of.

"What's this for?"

"The gum, please get rid of it."

"Oh. I'm sorry Treasure."

Help!

*****

I began reviewing Aaron Carlton's file. It read, "Possession with intent to sell." My eyes had begun to grow tired, and my stomach growled hungrily. Another situation I was really trying to avoid taking personal. ...This client here was far from being what I considered a loser. Yet, he had this notion that he's God's gift to women. The last thing I would want in my life is a man who sold drugs.

I tossed the file to the side and prepared to leave my office. I had to grab me a bite to eat before I became sick. Tonight my Grams and Aunt Kim are throwing a celebration for my success. I'm really not in the mood for all the praise, but I accepted their offer. My Grams is so sensitive when it comes to me. Plus, she's all I have as a mother figure and I wouldn't want to hurt her feelings for anything in the world.

Grams looked just as beautiful today as she did twenty years ago. She dyes her grey hair a blue tint that highlights her youthful skin. She's truly blessed not to look as old as she is. I stay on her about her eating habits. Diabetes has been dominating our culture and she has been really lucky so far.

Aunt Kim is another story. She has so much havoc in her life with that no good husband of hers. He's a liar and a cheater! Aunt Kim has a brilliant personality and was what I once considered a strong black woman. But since Tony, all that beauty and strength is slowly washing down the drain.

As I was ordering some delicious food from a restaurant over in Greek Town, Aunt Kim was calling in on my cell phone. I didn't want her to know where I was. Grams would have a fit if she knew I ate someone's food other than hers. So, I avoided the call.

Aunt Kim mentioned earlier that Grams invited Summer to my gathering tonight. I hope she makes it. It would really mean the world to me.

SEVEN

I'LL NEVER TELL

*****

TREASURE

With all the construction going on, making it to Grams was taking forever.

My mind was rapidly moving ahead of me. I fell into deep thought, realizing how boring my life truly was. I feel lonely and sexually deprived. Here I am, a defense attorney at the age of thirty, living in a lovely condo, making a comfortable salary and the most precious thing of all, I'm still holding on to. My virginity! *Who will be that lucky man*, I wondered. I pick my dates like a four-leaf clover, so I know it won't be easy. Thinking back, most men I've dated became bored with me because I just wasn't ready to put sex on my agenda. It was tempting, but not that tempting.

In college, I was surrounded by a bunch of hungry predators that somehow sensed I was a virgin. "The class dove," they called me. It was like they could smell it. Or maybe because I had turned down a couple of offers, explaining that I wasn't ready to give it up that easy. The men knocking at my door probably were scheming on, "who can get it first."

My cell phone was going off again. This time it was my girl!

"Hello?"

"Treasure, what time are we meeting up with you at the hall tonight?"

"Is this you Jacqueline?"

38

"Don't let me find out that you still haven't caught on to my voice after all our years of being friends. Oh," she playfully acted like she was crying, "that hurts my feelings."

"Stop playing Jacqueline. I knew it was you, silly. Listen, I'm on my way now to pick up Grams and Aunt Kim. How does 8:30 sound to you?"

"8:30 sounds good." We hung up.

Jacqueline is a true character. We met in college when I attended the University of Michigan; she was my roommate in the freshman dorm. I did my four years, graduated, and continued my education at U of M's law school.

My first impression of her was that she was one of those stuck up, "A" students. At first glance, I thought her beauty was nothing other than the conceited type, but I was wrong. She was the exact opposite, and I envied her. She had a beautiful complexion that tanned astonishingly in the sun. Her eyes changed colors from shades of grey to green. Her hair was long and beautiful. She was flawless. The one thing I loved most about her was her smile. Her teeth resembled porcelain and looked as if they were made for Hollywood.

Jacqueline and I used to sit up until the wee hours of the night talking about different things. I tried to avoid the family conversations because her family was more like the "Brady Bunch," and mine was more like "Boy'z in the Hood." I found her stories interesting, although it intensified my jealousy. Her outspoken and aggressive attitude would get the best of her sometimes, but that served her well in her position as a defense attorney. She fought for her clients, no matter what the cost.

Jaqueline would always tell me how much I reminded her of some beautiful actress whose name I can't even pronounce. She showed me a picture one time in a magazine and the woman was beautiful. That was a compliment to me, but I knew better. I was what people called a *lame*. I never participated in any of the college after class parties. I was all books and homework while she went out to social gatherings with friends. At first I didn't see her making it through, but she surprised me. As I encouraged her to place education first, we became closer. She knew that I was looking out for her best interest so she took my advice, slowed down, and got busy in the books.

One day I had come in from class extremely tired. I glanced over and noticed Jacqueline was washing out something at the sink. I picked up some mail on my way in and began scanning through it. I was being distracted by her bopping up and down with headphones on; I thought that was strange because she had never listened to music with headphones before. We teased each other a lot, so I eased up on her, and reached to touch her shoulder. That's when she swung around in a karate position, ready to attack! I fell out laughing! Little did I know the joke was on me.

The look on her face told me something was truly wrong. I asked, "What's wrong? Did I scare you?" I was still kind of chuckling from her Bruce Lee move.

"Who the hell are you?" She snapped. I placed my hands on my hips at her sudden change of attitude. As much as she plays with me, how dare she!

"Okay, jokes over. I'm sorry I scared you Jacqueline. You can stop this now." She then started to laugh.

"Oooohhh…you must be Treasure," she said with astonishment.

Right then was when I drew the line. I knew how she loved to carry a joke out too far. So I turned away from her and walked toward my room, but someone stopped me in my tracks. It was the sight of her that blew me away. I instantly looked back at the woman that I thought was Jacqueline. I couldn't do anything at that point, but place my hand over my mouth in amazement. They were identical. I couldn't tell them apart!

Jacqueline interrupted my thoughts as she was making her way out of the bathroom and said, "So, I see you've met my sister, Jeraldine." They had the same smile, hair, complexion, height; the same beauty! It was an amazing sight to see. I had seen twins before, but never as beautiful as the two of them.

I stuttered, "Y-yes, I'm sorry…"

"You don't have to apologize. It's nice to have finally met you Treasure. My sister speaks highly of you." She held out her hand, clearing her throat to stop me from staring at her so hard. "You can close your mouth now," she said giggling.

I was so embarrassed. Before I could comment any further, there was a knock at the door. "Excuse me! I'll be right back." I said walking briskly toward the door.

I snatched it open, not asking beforehand who was there. What was standing in front of me is stored in my memory, forever.

The individual said, "Hello, my name is Janet. You must be Treasure..."

That's all I remembered before I hit the floor. By the time I regained consciousness, Jacqueline, Jeraldine and Janet were all standing over me. They had shifted me from the floor to the couch. I screamed and laughed at the same time. Seeing them standing beside each other was awesome! Triplets! Flawless! They were the perfect three. Absolutely gorgeous.

Like I said once before, Jacqueline loved to play; she planned this whole surprise. She'd told me that she had sisters who attended the college there, but she failed to say they were identical. For all I knew, one of them could have been there doing her homework while she was out partying. I couldn't tell.

I became a member of their family. Being a part of a real family is something that I've always dreamed of.

We'd all acquired experience working with other firms, while dreaming of eventually becoming partners. Now, Jacqueline, Jeraldine and me, had all worked our way up to partners in the same law firm. Janet ended up working on the other side of the fence, becoming a federal prosecutor.

Jacqueline was the *smoothest* one of the three. You would never know how she was coming at you until it was too late. One day we were sitting around the dorm, and I began crying because this guy had just broken it off with me.

Of course, I wouldn't have sex with him, but I was kind of used to this guy in particular; Andrew Collins was his name and unforgettable, he was. He was going for his Ph.D. I thought he was the man of my dreams with his tall masculine frame. He was model material, the kind you saw on the front of the *Men's Cosmopolitan*. I truly thought I was in love. Little did he know, if we had been together a little longer, he could have had me.

After coming out of the shower I laid across the sofa to relax. Jacqueline was lying on her stomach on the floor reading *Essence* Magazine.

She looked up at me and asked, "What's wrong with you, Kido?"

"I'm missing Andrew."

"Who? Girl, please! You did the right thing, leaving that punk!"

"He wasn't all that bad Jacqueline, he…"

"Like…I…said, he's just like the rest of them, no good dogs!" She gritted her teeth.

I was hardly paying her any attention, as she started male bashing. She acted like that whenever I would talk about my male acquaintances. I had no idea why she hated men so much until I fell off to sleep and was awakened by her tongue massaging my neck. She startled me, and I didn't know what to say at that moment. I couldn't move! It was like she was holding a gun to my head. When I tried to say something, she shushed me, untied my robe, and fell head first in between my thighs. In my mind, I was screaming STOP! But in my heart, I wanted to know what the end result would be. The feeling I received from her giving me oral sex was nice and tingly. My orgasm was so deep, like something I had been missing for so long. She was very experienced and gentle.

The next morning was hard for me. I couldn't look at her the same. I was sure that our friendship was at stake, until she broke the silence.

"Look Treasure, I have no regrets about what took place last night, but I do know one thing. I love you. I don't want to lose you as my friend. If it makes you feel any better, it will never happen again." She reached out to me and we hugged. Yet the look in her eyes told me something totally different; it wasn't sincere. If the situation was to ever present itself again, I believe she would take it. My feelings were just the opposite. I love Jacqueline, but not like that. Even though the feeling was nice, I had to stick with my original plan; marrying a man and having a family. No woman could give me that.

Presently, Jacqueline is a lesbian and lives with a woman who's also an attorney. I love her all the same and wish her well in everything she does. The only thing that I ask for is that our secret stays in that dorm room.

EIGHT

NO LOVE LOST
Summer/Treasure

*****

SUMMER

I started my day extremely early, as if I was preparing for the Grammy's. I hadn't eaten the night before, so when I hit the gym that morning, I recieved a better work out. My body felt even tighter. I had the day all set up for my "Celebrity Boo." I swung by the mall to do some shopping, and snatched up this tight designer suit that fit my body like a glove. I already had mad gear in my closet with tags still on them, but you know how it is. I had to sport something extra special for this occasion.

Before I made my way to the shower, I popped in my Blu Cantrell CD and grabbed my cordless, just in case he tried to call. After washing down with some smell good, I was preparing to step out when the phone rang. I damn near fell back into the shower trying to answer it.

"*Ouch*, hello." I answered, trying to hide the fact that I was in pain from bending my damn fingernail back.

"Summer!," said the voice on the other end of the phone.

"What?" I shook my finger, trying to ease the pressure.

I was already pissed that it wasn't who I thought it was! I hate that! You be thinking it's Brian McKnight and it ends up being your grandmother.

"What?!" Grams yelled. "Giirrlll...I will come out there and jack you up!"

"Sorry Grams, I thought you were someone else. I didn't catch your voice at first. My bad."

I usually catch the caller ID to avoid slip-ups like this one. I hope she's not about to start with the lectures. I wouldn't hesitate to pull the plug from the wall and act like it was an accident.

"Sorry!!! That word has always been so easy for you to use, Summer. Look, I don't have time for this. Are you still meeting us tonight?"

"Tonight? For what? Aww Naw, Grams, I forgot all about the party tonight. I'm sorry but I'm not going to be able to make it." I could hear her getting revved up. "My supervisor called and threatened that if I don't show up for work today, I would have to look for another place of employment. Grams you know that I can't afford that."

She must be crazy to think that I would cancel my plans with Ol'Boy to spend time with a sister I don't even claim. I still haven't gotten over her calling me the other day. The idea of me being at the party was supposed to be a surprise. I was only considering it for Grams, but now it's completely out of the question.

"SUMMER DEVYNE LEWIS! That's exactly what I'm talking about! You're always full of disappointments! It never fails! You place your family last, and it's always about you, YOU, YOU, YOU!"

Here she goes. Where's the plug to disconnect?

"You knew for weeks about this party!" I yawned while she vented. "This is special Summer! Your sister has made a success out of her career! How could you do this to us? Girl, you make my blood boil!" As she continued to bump her gums, the other line beeped.

Thank you Lord.

"Hold on Grams!" I didn't waste any time clicking over on her.

"Hello." I softly spoke into the mouthpiece as I began placing a clear coat of polish over my freshly chipped nail.

"Hey baby." The deep voice spoke in my ear.

Now, I couldn't catch the voice right off the back, so I asked suspiciously, "Who is this?"

45

"Oh so you don't know my voice no mo?"

That's it!

I was getting ready to throw the phone clear across the room! Here it is going on 5:45, and this is still not the call I'm waiting on! I clicked the bastard off!

Damn.

I couldn't believe I let that nobody and Grams tie my line up! I was hoping she would have hung up by now, but she didn't.

"Grams, again I apologize. Listen, I have to pay bills out here, but, if you'd like, I could move back in there with you and…"

"HELL NO! Keep your hot behind out there by the river where you can cool off! You just remember this, Summer Devyne Lewis!"

I hate it when she calls me by my whole name.

"I'll never forget this, (Click)."

"Old woman…" I muttered into the dial tone.

I bet she wouldn't have hung up on Treasure like that. It's so obvious she loved her more. It's all good though. I've grown past all that. I'm dealing with more serious issues than who she loves more. I'm on my own and living on a day-by-day basis.

*****

TREASURE

By the time I'd made it out to Grams to pick up her and my Aunt Kim, they were waiting patiently for me. They were into this party thing more than me. Like I mentioned earlier, I really wasn't up for all the praise, but I knew I couldn't afford to hurt anyone's feelings. They worked so hard to put it together, the last thing I would want to do is not show my appreciation.

We headed down I-94 East, going toward downtown. I noticed how quiet they both were. Aunt Kim was usually the talkative one, especially when we were all together. The only time it's this quiet was when it had something to do with my sister. So, I prepared my heart for the blow.

"Treasure, your sister won't be able to make it tonight," Grams said with disappointment.

"Why?" I exhaled with a painful sigh.

There was a big part of me that knew the answer already. Yet this little section in my heart wanted to prove me wrong. I don't know why I keep beating myself up to make things right with her. I guess I miss her too much.

"She had to work, baby. She said she doesn't..."

I cut her off. I couldn't handle another excuse for Summer. I hate the fact that Grams is always the one in the middle. She's too old for this kind of stress.

"Grams, please, don't worry about it, okay?"

"I'm sorry baby. I know how you feel about your sister..."

"Grams please." I held my hand up.

The whole thing was changing my mood for the worst. I just wanted to get this over with. I changed the subject, because I could tell that Grams was feeling my irritation.

"Aunt Kim, is Tony coming?"

Aunt Kim knew I could care less about her husband. The question was just to change the direction of the conversation.

"Yeah Treasure, he's coming. He had to take care of some things at his office. He'll be right down," she said, fixing her hair in the mirror. I'm sure she doesn't believe that lie herself.

I'm sorry but I don't think or believe that I could ever bring myself to accept Tony. He's a dog! I just tolerate him for her and my cousin's benefit. Back in the day he was *one* of my parents' drug suppliers. He kept their veins filled with that garbage! Then, when they died, he had the nerve to pay for their funeral! Grams always said, "Everything done in the dark comes to the light." He's just not right, and I don't know why Aunt Kim can't see that! Hopefully, whatever wrong he's doing to her will soon come to light. The devastation will surely be enough to make her leave him for good.

NINE

CHECKMATE

*****

SUMMER

I know this fool didn't stand me up!

I blew off some steam, kicking off my designer sandals, plopping down on my bed. I can't believe I got played this way. I really don't know how to handle a situation like this. This shit is new to me. I had the whole night planned on how I was going to work this cat, too. I guess everything happens for a reason.

When my phone rung, it caught me off guard. I usually allowed my phone to ring about four times before I answered it, but not today. I'm going to let the answering machine pick it up. I'm not pressed anymore.

"Hi." My voice came on with music by Musiq playing in the background. *"You have reached 555-3122. Sorry, I'm not in to take your call, but if you leave a brief message. ...I got you (Beep)."*

My voice sounded even sexier on tape.

"Hey Pretty." A deep scratchy voice echoed through.

It's him! It's him! YES!

I damn near sprung my ankle diving for the phone.

"Helllooo." I threw on my sexy voice.

"Ay, wha'dup? I thought I missed you." I could hear one of Twista's songs playing in the background. "I tried to call you earlier, but the line was busy." The clear bass of the music in the background faded.

48

"I apologize about that Boo; I had to go on line to retrieve some information. I'm a very busy girl." I was frontin,' trying to sound professional.

"What do you do for a livin' Baby?" He asked, sounding interested in my work affairs.

"I manage this tax company over on the westside. I do the expansion of locations all over the Metro area and close the deals. It's cool, for the pay," I lied.

"Hmmm, busy girl. So where does time become available to a player down the line?"

"How far down the line are we talkin' P-L-A-Y-E-R...?"

"Not too far. We'll set sumthin up. I like yo' fine ass."

Now that's what I'm talking about.

"Speaking of time, how can I fit into your schedule with all of the women that you have! I probably wouldn't stand a chance!"

"Trust me; I keep all my pieces in order."

"Oh, so what you're saying is that I'm just a piece of your puzzle? You playing games with me, boy?"

He chuckled and said, "Naw baby, not at all. You still hungry? Are we still on?"

"Starvin'." He has no idea what I've been through.

"Well, let's do this."

"I'm ready."

"Then let a nigga in then."

"Where are you?"

I nervously made my way over to my door and there he was standing on the other side. I felt faint. I opened the door trying to stay calm, smiling at his surprise appearance. Without entering my space, he returned the smile, reaching out to me, nodding his head for me to come with him. This kind'a shit turns me on fa' real!

"Let's go," he said.

"Okay." I flashed a sexy grin. I slipped my sandals on, grabbed my Prada bag, locked up, and was out.

We made our way to the back of his black Excursion limo. ...Black, my favorite color. I was beginning to get comfortable in his presence. I couldn't get out of my mind how exceptional he looked standing at my door. I just wanted to drop to my knees, open my mouth up wide, and say, *aaahhh*. I knew from that point the dick was gon' have me crazy in love.

Stay cool, girl.

I really admired his style and secretly observed him as he was talking on the phone. It sounded like he was having some type of disagreement. You know I was ear-hustlin', but I was more interested in him.

I was so relaxed with the way he was playing in my hair as we headed to our destination. He stayed on the phone though. It was business, nothing personal. I just grabbed his CD collection and started scanning through it. He released my hair and became really frustrated with whoever he was talking to.

"MAN, LOOK! I'LL HIT YOU BACK!" He tossed the phone on the floor.

Damn, I wonder what that's all about.

He stared out the window in deep thought. I didn't want to seem nosey, but I wanted him to know I was there if he needed someone to talk to.

I sat back beside him, laying the DMX CD to the side, and started rubbing the nape of his neck.

"You all right, baby?" I smiled when he looked my way.

"Yeah Pretty, I'm tight. These people just got a brotha stressin', that's all."

"You want to talk about it?" I tried to gain his trust by comforting him. Surprisingly, he opened himself up to me.

"It's this fuckin' record label I signed with! If I had the choice to leave this shiesty lifestyle, I would. I would go back to the ghetto where those hungry muthafuckas found my broke ass! Life is not that grand in my world, baby!" He tapped my nose, winked and topped it off with his famous lip licking thing that he does so well. "These young fools out here trying to get into the industry need to know this shit here isn't what it looks like! This here is straight up hard work and robbery. Some people turn to drugs to escape from all the pain and pressure that comes with the game. I was just trying to get my shine on, feed my family, take my people out the hood, and live in peace; but I failed to read the fine writing. I signed across the dotted line while staring at them numbers that was on the check! Now I'm stuck! I feel like I'm doing time, in the belly of the beast! It's like someone else controls my life! They're making millions while I'm spending mine on bullshit! I have to change my ways before a nigga be straight starving. ...Again."

I really didn't know what to say at this point. I knew very little about the game. I'm dealing with a different kind of stress. I'll just try to let some words of encouragement flow off the dome. I hope I don't sound stupid.

"You know baby. I've made a lot of mistakes, some I wish I never had, but we live and we learn. ...It's a part of our nature and growing process. From what you're telling me, you took a bad deal. Is that right?" Listen to me sounding like an attorney.

If my sister could hear me now.

"Something like that," he said resting his head back on the seat.

"Well, I used to hear a lot about people in this game being jacked by labels and false management. But after really taking a closer look at the situation, I see the game behind it. Think of it this way. ...Someone fronted you a hundred thousand to lay down some tracks while agreeing to sign you to their label. It sounded good, the money damn sure looked good, and instantly you took the bait."

What the hell am I saying?

"Let me stop, I don't..."

"No, no. Keep going. ...I'm listening, baby," he said attentively.

This cat is feelin' a sista. I have to make this sound real good.

"I guess what I'm trying to say is. ...Business is business. It's a heartless game. We mean nothing but dollars to them. That's why it's important to read before you sign. I don't care how much money they're flashing in your face. The bottom line is, nothing's free. And to keep it real, they really don't owe you. Ya'll sign the deals that get them greedy bastards paid. It was just game that you didn't recognize, Baby. You said, the opportunity was there and you took it. ...So, that leaves no one to blame but yourself. ...Get over it." I sat back in the seat like I had just made a point he couldn't argue.

Did I say that right?

He looked at me with an expression I couldn't read. I didn't know whether he was going to put me out on the curb or what.

"Look at you over there," he said brushing my hair off my shoulder and caressing my neck. I couldn't help but notice how exceptionally white his teeth were, behind that gorgeous smile.

YES! Coast clear.

We pulled up in front at the spot and the chauffer assisted us out the back. Ol'Boy held me close and I was lovin' it! It was like, everybody knew who he was. I could hear people saying, "That's so and so!!!" Being in the spotlight really had me feelin' good. The fun part was walking through the double doors holding hands. I was hoping that I saw someone I knew so that I could show him off. That didn't happen.

Instead, I ended up having to face some groupie waitress who was dying to get flexed on. If anyone could've seen her reaction when he responded to her offer to use the VIP section, you would have thought he'd accepted the key to her crib. She acted like I wasn't even there. She was being very disrespectful, purposely swaying her hips as we followed her to our table. She was trying real hard, but I was a step ahead of her. She thought she was a slick one, but compared to me, she was a snake competing with an Anaconda. And trust and believe; I slither a lot faster!"

I was really starting to enjoy myself, in spite of him carrying on again on his celly.

I'm gon' ask him to turn it off! ...Sike!

This conversation he was having sounded more personal. ...Possibly one of his road-dawgs. The chickenhead waitress was looking back, hungry for a chance with my Boo.

Not tonight, Ho. Bring your groupie ass to one of his concerts. I'm sure he would let you give him some head.

My mind was racing overtime. I was giggling and having fun by my damn self. HELL! I can cum by myself too!

It's just me, myself and I... I sang to myself, rocking side to side while waiting for the groupie waitress to take our order.

Here the trick comes.

I don't believe how this bitch is standing here, hovering over him, and not paying attention to me at all. I kept asking her what was up as she repeatedly ignored me.

Disrespectful Ho!

I had know understanding, because this restaurant be havin' mad celeb's off up in here. I'm sure this is not the first time she had seen someone famous up in this joint. I was fed up with the chick ignoring me, so I plucked water in her face from my glass.

"Excuse you!" She wiped the water from her face.

"Ay, Dawg! Let me hit you back!" Ol'Boy hurried off the phone.

"Everything aight baby?" He stared back and forth between the two of us.

"No sir, I was standing here..." The waitress started before I could get out a word.

"Wait, wait, wait a minute." He raised his hand up to her. "First of all, you're out of line, not only to me, but to my girl."

I was happy that he checked the bitch. Better him than me. I sat back and watched him handle the ho. He was going off and I was impressed that I had it like that.

He continued, "We came here for a meal. Now, if you don't want me to call your supervisor over here, then I would be swaying those hips over to the back to bring me and my lady some grub. ...Do we have an understanding?" His eyebrows tensed up and you could see that thug mentality appearing. It made me a little horny.

The broad just nodded, turned around, stuck her tail in between her ass and crawled behind the wall. I wanted to laugh, but I couldn't. It wasn't lady like.

After that, we ate our meal, sittin back just kickin' it. I thought about how I used to think people of his stature were different from me. I came to the conclusion that they're no different. They have problems, they hurt, they laugh, and they *shit*; ...Like I had to do right then. We'd talked a little too long. My stomach was bubbling and my butt cheeks were contracting together like prayer hands. I didn't do public restrooms, so I had to wait until we left for my crib. Besides, it was only around the way. It's going on one in the morning and he was still talking. Why did this have to happen at such a time like this?
I can't hold it!!!!

TEN

YOU'RE ALL I HAVE

*****

TREASURE

It was nice to see all my friends come out to support me tonight. I wished I had been able to enjoy myself more. I wasn't feeling merry, but again, I had to show my gratitude.

Grams couldn't sense the dismay behind the front I put up through the whole ordeal. I don't think anyone noticed, at least I hoped not. Everyone else was having a good time, and that was all that mattered to me.

At least they were happy.

I hugged and kissed everyone, as I headed out to drop off Grams and Aunt Kim. I should have known that wouldn't be easy with Aunt Kim in the car. It never fails with her, a stop here and a stop there. She needed to pick up her prescription from the drug store. I didn't question the need, being that I had an idea what it was for. After living with her for so many years, I had run across plenty of her antibiotics spread across her room. I wrote down the names on the bottles and looked them up in a medicine book. What I found out disappointed me. Kim's husband had no respect for their marriage, because he had been giving her a venereal disease! What was even worse was that my Aunt allowed him to get away with something so trifling. I never could understand that. Between that, and probably a bunch of other bacterial infections, he should have been history.

While waiting on Aunt Kim, I started a conversation with Grams. I mentioned how much I appreciated the party, and so on. I didn't notice that I was talking to myself, until I heard her snore. I couldn't help but to laugh.

I love that old woman.

I unlocked the door to let Aunt Kim back inside and headed toward our destination. I noticed Aunt Kim was trying to hide her medication.

No need Aunt Kim; I know the deal.

Aunt Kim knew all too well the consequences of sleeping with a lie. I just hope she wakes up before it's too late.

"So Treasure, did you enjoy yourself tonight?" Aunt Kim asked, while stuffing her secret into her purse.

"Yes I did. Thank you. Everything was really nice. I can't thank you and Grams enough."

"I would really like for all of us to come together as a family and do something like this again, soon. Would you like that niece?"

"That would be nice, Aunt Kim."

Dropping them off was a drained relief! I was literally tired from being phony all night. I really needed time for self right now. I was exhausted mentally, emotionally, and physically.

On the way home I couldn't think of anyone but Summer, the way we grew up, and the pain of our separation. I knew one thing, Summer was a character! I began to chuckle, just thinking about how grandiose she was. I personally think she takes things too seriously. She can hold a grudge, obviously, and that's the one thing that irritates me about her. I feel she hates me for making something out of myself, and she feels like I was treated better than her. I guess Grams did show a little favoritism at times; but it was only to acknowledge my hard work and everything I had achieved in life. ...nothing more. Summer had the opportunity to do right. She knew this. It wasn't my fault that she chose the streets over furthering her education.

Not by force, by choice, Summer.

Reminiscing on the times we'd shared; we did have some fun...until the storm came.

I can remember when we had these dolls. I named my doll Danielle. Summer named hers Nikki. We put those dolls through it; slapping tons of grease in their heads and feeding them real food! I'll never forget the time Summer took Mom's curling irons, plugged them into the wall until they became hot, and curled Nikki's hair. Nikki's hair melted all over the curling irons, making a whole mess! Mom's curlers were ruined! Summer tried to hide them from her, but she found them later and it was over! Summer denied it, but Mom knew she was guilty. When Mom found Nikki with a patch of hair missing, that was all the proof she needed to spank Summer's behind. I wasn't going to let that happen to my sister. I was very protective of her.

I heard Summer running away from Mom, screaming. That's when I ran into my room, quickly changing out of my clothes into my Wonder Woman panties. I used my bed sheet as a cape! I dashed into the living room and stood in front of Mom before she was able to hit Summer again.

"GET BEHIND ME SUMMER! GET BEHIND ME!" Mom looked at me like I was crazy! I don't blame her, because picturing myself in that panty set still makes me laugh.

I'll never forget Mom's words, while Summer was hiding behind me shaking.

"Oh...so *Wonder Woman* is here to save her sister, huh?" She held the strap in one hand while the other hand rested on her hip.

I nodded my head at her, not feeling threatened at all. My arms were folded, chest poked out, waiting for Mom to bow down like they did on TV. I honestly thought my powers were working, until Mom said, "Well, I guess you can get some of this too... Wonder Woman!"

Those were the good old days. Summer would whine, because I wouldn't play Wonder Woman anymore. Shoot! Wonder Woman was history after that! That spanking was painful! Summer wouldn't give up though, she loved our good times; the games, and everything that we did together. I miss that. It was the last time I remember Summer laughing. I really wish Wonder-Woman were still around.

Drugs and ongoing fights between our parents began to dominate our childhood. It was at that point that there was no more *Hands-up-to-eighty-five*, no more *S-L-I-D-E* and *twee-a-lee-a-leet!* We shared nothing but tears, and feared for our lives. Many nights, I would find Mom laying on the kitchen floor unconscious, bleeding, swelled up, and high. And can you imagine what it felt like to watch your father beat your mother daily?

Dad used to deal with some serious issues. I knew he had been in the army and fought in the war. Other than that, I knew very little about his past. What ever happened to him over there still remains a mystery.

He didn't care about the time or place when he lost it. He started jumping on Mom, beating her up anywhere. Summer and I were too embarrassed to have our friends over after he snapped and jumped on her in front of them. He was a sorry man.

We found out that he was the one who introduced Mom to drugs. Love is blind, and that's another reason why I'm not too pressed to find it. Mom would do anything he asked her to do.

Heroin was *his* drug of choice. There were *always* needles lying around the house for Summer and I to discard. Luckily, neither of us ever got poked. ...We would have been victims of worse circumstances.

We were even more afraid of the strange faces that lurked around, watching us like we were their next target. Summer and I lived our lives fearing that one of those crazy faces would be the death of us, not knowing. ...Death was only a few steps away...

One day Summer and I returned home from school to find our door hanging wide open. Immediately I thought something had happened to Mom! I took Summer's hand and walked inside. The complex was ram shacked! It looked like a robbery, but that was impossible. ... We were broke! I searched the complex, scared that I would find Mom dead. Luckily, there was no one in the house, just the two of us, frightened to death. Summer was shaking so badly that I had to hold her tight to try to calm her. I closed the door, straightened up a little, and sat in silence; hoping Mom would soon return. We had no phone, no lights, and no gas. We didn't know what to do. We didn't know what to expect. Then something horrifying happened!

Three men came bursting through our front door, cursing and yelling! We were bunched together and led into a corner, screaming and crying! I tried to run, but the guy was too big. The look in his eyes told me he wouldn't have hesitated using the gun he was holding in his hand. I covered Summer with my body, trying to protect her! The guy demanded that we be quiet, *or else.* One of the men was holding our helpless, blood stricken father around his neck.

"WHERE'S MY SHIT NIGGA!" I heard one of them yell.

He was at their mercy as they beat him up. He obviously had stolen something from those thugs. Within seconds, two of the men forced Dad to the back, while the other one watched over us. I could feel something terrible was about to take place. It was only a matter of time. I had to think fast! There was no doubt in my mind that if we didn't get out of there, we were going to die.

No witnesses, was all that kept creeping through my mind. I could still hear them beating my father in the backroom. Luckily, the guy who was supposedly keeping an eye on us, turned his back, and gave us our chance to get away. I grabbed Summer's hand, and we broke out the front door. The guy made a grab for us, but we were too fast for him!

We were no more than a few complexes down before we heard the gun shots that claimed the life of our father. It stopped me dead in my tracks.

Breathing harshly, Summer tugged at my sleeve, whining in her sweet voice, "Treasure! Come on!" That scarred us for life! Many broken dreams and promises resulted from that nightmare. We ended up having to relocate to live with Grams and Aunt Kim.

Mom rolled around a couple of days later, high as usual. She didn't know what was going on. While our lives were at stake, she was out on some street corner trying to make money to supply her addiction. My bitterness toward her continued until more bad news came our way...

Dad's autopsy revealed that he had AIDS. The doctor informed Grams of the results. It was extremely painful for Grams to try to tell Mom.

Mom stayed on the go after Grams finally told her. She did all she could to delay getting tested, but the day finally came when Mom had to know. She had run from the truth for as long as she could. It was Aunt Kim who talked her into getting tested; telling her she should do it for Summer and me. I guess Mom felt somewhat obligated, because she went through with it, and sure enough, she was positive. Everything seemed to move in slow motion from that point. Mom wanted to die at home, so Grams set her room up, and I never left her side.

Summer, on the other hand, wanted no parts of Mom. She wouldn't come in to the room if her life depended on it. I couldn't understand Summer for that, so I turned bitter toward her. I realize now that I should have been more sensitive to her emotions. Instead, I ignored her and acted like she didn't exist. I cared for no one but Mom and Grams.

She fanned the flames of my resentment even more when I went looking for her one night and found her in bed with the next door neighbor, Justin. She was only 14, with a 22-year-old man! Justin was like a son to Grams! I was very upset to see them engaging in a sexual act while Mom was laying on her death bed! The sight of his head in between her thighs made me sick to my stomach. I never told, and she never found out that I knew. I just focused my attention back to my dying Mother.

Then to my surprise, one night Summer appeared. I was half asleep beside Mom, in a rocking chair. Summer glanced over at me, making sure I was out before she entered the room all the way. Once everything was clear, she tiptoed over to Mom.

Summer was disturbed with Mom's setup. The only air supply Mom depended on was from a respirator. Summer didn't look like that cold, callous individual that I knew before that night. Her emotions were exposed completely. It was then that I knew why she never stepped foot in that room. She was scared to face Mom dying. Seeing Mom suffering the way she was had done something to Summer psychologically. I watched her unfold. She covered her mouth as she cried and released all the pain of slowly losing a loved one.

Our lives changed from that point. Summer went into a shell, and I've been making efforts to crack it open ever since. After Mom died, she shut me out completely, not wanting any part of me. I felt like I had lost my best friend. In many ways, I've stopped growing since we parted ways. ...Since Mom died. My inner child still rests beneath my soul.

"Lord, please make Summer see that I love her. I need my sister Lord. Life is not the same without her. Amen."

ELEVEN

TILL WE MEET AGAIN

*****

SUMMER

Finally! I thought, as we returned to the limo, getting me one step closer to my bathroom. I was still trying to play it off, and was thankful that he didn't notice my discomfort. I was relieved when he found his way back to his cell phone. I wanted so bad to lean down and grab the CD that I never got the chance to play. I needed something to take my mind off the urge in between my cheeks. I was about to explode! I had to interrupt Ol'Boy and ask him to shoot me by my spot.

"Baby, can we run by my place for a minute. I need to make sure I turned my alarm on." Any excuse will do at this point.

"Hold up, man," he said to the caller. "DRE!" he called out to the driver.

"Wha'sup?" Dre responded, rolling the inner glass down.

"Yo man, swing Shorty around her way." Dre gave a nod and disappeared back behind the glass.

Ol'Boy went back to his convo while I tried hard to sit pretty. I could just imagine how I looked, contracting my ass right about now. I was extremely uncomfortable! Again, I can't believe this is happening to me! Dre was pushing the whip through traffic so fast I was beginning to think he had the same objective in mind. I hope not.

When we pulled up, I tried to let myself out. Dre was taking too long and this was not a game! Ol'Boy was still on the phone carrying on. He didn't notice my discomfort.

Dre finally came around to my side, opened the door and reached for my hand. I literally pushed him out of the way! Ol'Boy said something, but I just walked off saying, "I'll be right back, baby!" My apartment is 21 floors high. Right about now, I'll take the stairs!

I got up to my door and I couldn't get my key to turn in the lock. I don't understand this. As much money as I pay to live in this supposedly high-class apartment, the key should be electronic! I was about to kick it in, but it opened. I stripped down while racing to the bathroom without a care in the world...

"Aaaaahhhh...."

Minutes went by and I had never felt better. I was just about to call it quits when there was a tap on the door.

Damn! I left the door unlocked.

"Bay! When you finish shittin,' I'll be out here chillin. Hurry up!" Ol'Boy laughed.

No...He...Didn't. I was so embarrassed. Facing him now would be the ultimate task. He had to know I was fighting the urge but, to intrude, and come straight out with some mess like that! Scandalous!

I sprayed a little air freshener, not really too worried about the odor. I'd flushed between drops to absorb the funk. After calming down a little, I took a thorough shower, douched, and then threw on some smell good before making my way out to him.

"Woo Wee! Damn Girl! You blew the spot up!" He teased. He had made himself at home and kicked back on the plush carpet.

"You play too much," I whined.

He was having too much fun, and I found comfort in his sense of humor. I observed the way he took his Air Force Ones off at the door and made himself at home on my floor, flippin' through my photo album.

"I thought I told you I would be right back."

"You took too long, but believe me Baby-Girl, I feel you. Don't hold that shit back on my account." He was playfully waving his hand like he smelled an odor.

I threw one of my couch pillows at him and the fun began. We started rolling on my floor, wrestling before I knew it. I was winning at first, but only because he allowed me to. He pinned me down and started tickling me, gently biting my neck. It was all that!

"Oh, so you wanna play," he said.

"Ha ha ha ha ha!!!! Stooooooop!!" I laughed and screamed for mercy. I hate to be tickled. "You win, baby! You win!"

He eased up, sitting on his knees, staring down at me with a huge smile on his face. I had something up my sleeve though. I waited on him to turn away and dove on his back, forcing him down. It didn't take long before he had me at his mercy again. I loved this play fighting thing.

Breathing hard, laying on our backs, I realized that I was really into him. I know that it was ultimately the fact that he was famous. Besides that, he was here with *me*, alone. ...A celebrity.

He picked up my photo album again and started flipping through it, staring at the pictures. That kind of disturbed my mood. I still haven't been able to face my loss, and there he was about to stir up feelings over it. It's been over a year and I still haven't been able to face that tragedy; I don't think I ever will.

"Who's this baby?" He asked about a picture of my best friend and me, chillin' at the All-Star game in LA.

"That's my girl, Vette. She really knew how to keep it real with a sista," I reminisced.

I could feel him staring at me, and I sensed him noticing the disturbance in my eyes. He went back to flipping pictures, landing on a few favorites of mine. There was one with LaVette and me hangin' out in Cancun with a few celebrities she knew.

"Humph, look at ya'll. ...Look at my man Kirk-D, chillin'!" He smirked.

I could tell that he really didn't care for the people in the photo. These cats in the industry are always beefin' over dumb shit. It is too much money to go around to be going through the drama.

I smiled as I stared intensely at the photos. I could feel tears starting to well up. I shyly turned my head to tap the corners of my eyes before he saw a tear drop.

"What happened between you two?"

"She was killed last year."

"Killed? I'm sorry to hear that."

"The wrong place and wrong dude was what claimed her life."

"You want to talk about it?"

I was silent for a moment. "No...Well, yeah... yeah we can kick it." I was comfortable with him now. I wanted to go deep.

"You two looked like you were really close. Look at yall!" He searched for humor.

He noticed that I didn't think it was funny. Then he started focusing on the picture of us in Miami chillin'. That really brought back some memories. We were high that night! "We had so much fun together," I said, smiling. "We really did. I wish I could turn back the hands of time. She didn't have to die like that. Messin' around with Donovan didn't get her nowhere but in a box next to his. I mean, he was throwing her crazy loot! She didn't want for nothin'! None of that glamour stuff was worth her life, though. Vette loved that fool, worshiped the ground he walked on. He built her a phat crib, out in the 'burbs. She had all kinds of glamourous shit. To make a long story short, dude and some of his associates were beefin' and Vette got caught in the middle. Her mother found both of them tied to chairs in the basement of Vette's home, with gunshot wounds in their heads." I lay my head back against the sofa, staring up at the ceiling. "The day before she was killed, she'd asked me to go shopping with her. I made some lame excuse so that I could chill with some player that truly wasn't worth it. What kind of friend was I to not be there for my dawg?"

"A true one, Shorty. Have you ever thought that things happen for a reason? Good or bad, there's a reason behind it. Start paying close attention to the things that go on in your life. You feel me? Like the people you meet, places you go, and things you see; little things, you know. ...Think about it, you could have been sitting in that third chair Baby Girl. Hold on to the memories and never take life for granted. Okay, Pretty?" He tapped my nose and pulled me into him, placing his nose into the crown of my forehead. What he said sounded like a verse in one of his songs. I was feelin' him for real. It made me want to reconsider having him inside of me, under my circumstances.

"Thank you, Baby. I really needed to hear something encouraging. That means a lot to me, you just don't know..." He gently lifted my chin, bringing us eye to eye.

Let him go Summer, don't make him a victim.

"Hey, a favor for a favor..."

Before I could react, he had his lips connected with mine as he softly caressed them with his tongue. It felt so right. His strokes were intense as he flowed down my neck to my chest. I felt so lucky to be in his arms. He made me feel so good. I was his! I couldn't push him away now. I wanted him. I had to have him. Thoughts of keeping him secure kept creeping in and out of my head.

Don't do this girl, tell him to leave!

He was slowly detaching my clothes piece by piece. My nipples grew attached to him with just a gentle brush of the sole of his thumb. He made his way down to my love, letting his tongue pierce my wetness. It was good. In the background you could hear Floetry's song playing so elegantly. ..."*All you gotta do is say yes, don't deny what you feel... let me undress you baby, open up your mind and just rest. Im'a bout ta let you know, you make me sooo-so-sooo-so-so-soooo-so-so... you make me sooo-so-sooo-so-so-sooo-so-so...uh.*" Floetry crooned the lyrics beautifully.

Something came over me. I couldn't let him go through with this. I had to warn him. Give him a chance. When he came up for air, "Baby," I whispered. "Where's your condom?"

"You don't have one around here somewhere?" He caressed my wetness with his fingers, followed by another kiss on the tip of my pearl.

"Nooo... Ssss," was all I could respond.

Strap it up Player! She tight and all, but you a celebrity!
Just 'cause she fine as hell don't mean a damn thang when it
comes to AIDS, his subconscious said. *Fuck that! I wanna feel this*
good shit tonight. The devil won.

"I love the way you feel. You so warm, and tight. I like
that." His fingers slid in and out of my warmth slowly. "You know
what? Don't sweat it Shorty…I trust you," he said.

Well, I tried. He obviously doesn't give a damn about life!
He doesn't even know me! How the hell can he trust me? Let me
introduce myself….

Hi, my name is death. It was a pleasure knowing you…

Waking up out of a deep sleep, I turned over to feel for my
Boo. Gone. I squinted my eyes, trying to make out the time that
was glowing on my clock in the dark. "Six forty-five?" I jumped
up, flicked on some lights, and his presence was no longer there.

*How he just gon'…*There was an envelope on the end of
the table. I walked over and picked up the package. As I opened it,
money fell to the floor! There was also a note, but I was paying
attention to nothin' other than the dead prez.

Later for that, yo. …I threw the note to the side, and
counted the doe. "HELL YEAH! Pay this lease up, buy me some
gear!" I sat down on the sofa, spending every dime before I went
anywhere. Damn, I almost forgot about the note. I opened it and it
read…

"Good Morning Pretty… By the time you read this, yo'
Boy will be on his way to Indiana, my next stop. I have to admit,
you took care of a brotha last night girl. I can still taste you...still
smell you. I'm looking forward to picking back up where we left
off in Miami, on the set, Gorgeous! My info is on the back," I
turned it over and glanced at his info, then continued to read.
"Here is a lil something for them bills I saw laying on your
kitchen table this morning. Till we meet again…One."

Damn Player, I wish things could have been different…

TWELVE

THE PLAYERS' LIST

*****

SUMMER

I swear I didn't feel like getting up out of the bed today. I just laid there, stretching and yawning. I felt so fatigued and my muscles ached to the bone. You know, I wonder if people suffering from HIV have these symptoms. Look at me starting my morning with the negative thinking, ruining my concentration. I keep telling myself that I'm going to push these wretched thoughts to the back of my mind. I had to stay focused and continue to ignore the phone calls from the clinic. Hearing their voice on my service was a setback for me. *"Ms. Lewis. This is Regina calling for Doctor Tice. Please call the office at your earliest convenience."* I was so aggravated that I'd tossed the tape in the trash. *I truly believe this discomfort is possibly from sleeping half the night away on my floor, not to exclude the good thug passion I had,* I thought in denial of the truth. I wonder what my celebrity friend is doing now…

*****

OL'BOY

"Wha'dup fellas!" I sat down in my plush R.V., chillin'.

"You wanna hit dis?" Paul passed the blunt.

"You know it my nigga." I took a pull, coughed, and continued, "Yo, we did that gig up in Detroit. That spot was off the chain! I'm glad we had the opportunity to push our shit, ya'll

68

feel me?" I inhaled a deep pull of strength, coughing from the burning sensation in my throat.

"Yeah baby!" They said in unison.

"Yo, Player!" D-Love spoke out. "What was you so into that you had to be frontin' on the celly last night?" He downed his liquor, "UUHH! This shit here is strong!"

"Yo' D, chill out with de questions man!" I said, as I closed my eyes and passed the blunt to Rick.

"Aight Player, but if I know you, you probably was out doin' that freak from de club," he said with a little envy in his voice.

I opened my eyes and stared at him and said, "And I know you gon' let me..."

"Oh...so, it's like dat?" D-Love commented.

"D! Shut the fuck up!" Paul screamed on 'um.

"Suck my....!" D grabbed at his crouch. I wanted to laugh but couldn't. My head was banging and I was in desperate need of rest.

"Let me find out you had a threesome with, what's that freak name you left wit' after her girl walked out? You ain't shit nigga?" He laughed.

"I see you not trying to let a brotha get some rest, so I'm gon' say this…"

D-Love cut me off saying, "Hold up, now. I just wanted to know how you gon' have a threesome without cha' boy! That's all."

This fool *is* high!

"Now why would I do that?" I raised my head to look at him. "Even if that was the case, you and I both know you couldn't handle one of them, let alone two, wit'cho impotent ass!"

"Impotent theze bitch!"

Everyone was on the floor laughing! I just laid my head back and dozed off. All that other shit going on didn't faze me! I had too much on my mind to be incited by his humor.

Here it is going on eight months since a brotha has seen home. All this traveling from state to state was tiring! I was worn out, performing the same shit over and over again! I'm telling you, if it wasn't for the chronic and a few pretty bitches in every state, I don't know what I would do! Detroit was the only city I didn't have some designated pussy set up in. Thanks to that chick, Summer, I've got a nominee. I ain't gon' lie, sex is like a drug to me! I just wanna get higher and higher. I simply can't live without it! I'm kinda feelin' Summer tho'. She makes me laugh with that pretty ass smile of hers looking like the chick from LL's video, 'Luv U Betta.' If things were different I might be talking bout lockin' it down, but it's impossible. That will never happen. I have too many ho'z to even consider monogamy. To keep it real, they make me laugh too. I guess being a dog is part of my genetic structure. I crave attention, from a princess to a scandalous freak. It keeps things interesting. So far I got every state covered, and with Summer added to the plate, she's now part of my Player's List. Humph. My girl.

*****

SUMMER

The phone rang, but I decided not to answer it this time. I was sure it was only Grams. She's still disappointed with me for not attending Miss "IT's" party. Canceling my date with Ol' Boy was a dead issue.

I quickly jumped in the shower because I had places to be and niggas to see. Monique had left several messages on my answering service for the last few days. She's probably trying to curse me out for leaving her the other night at the club. She worked my nerves real bad; I couldn't deal with her at that moment.

I finished up my shower, and dried off in front of the bathroom mirror. My body was still dripping wet, so I added some body oil to my bronze skin, rubbing my hands across my firm breasts and behind. "Flawless!!" I said, admiring myself. I made exotic faces and bust some sexy moves to Lil Kim's new CD. I had it blasting through my apartment.

70

I had something freaky tossed to the side to put on; a piece by *Eve,* from her new clothing line, "Fetish." I decided I'd cover some avenues with my unblemished body snuggled against my outfit. I was about to hit the streets! *DANGEROUS!*

I tidied up a little before I rolled out. Ol'Boy left such a strong scent throughout my space. I was really feelin' him. He had worked that game of his, and now I own him in more ways than one…

My answering service was calling my name; blinking off the chain with over ten messages on it.

"Hello, Ms. Lewis? This is Doctor Tice calling again. I've been trying to reach you for quite some time now. I would greatly appreciate it if you would return my calls. Thank you."

Hearing his voice brought back the reality of my situation. I just wanted to stop him from calling all together! It should have been obvious to him that I wasn't trying to come in to hear how many months I had left to live. "Just leave me the hell alone!" Here comes the stress all over again! I dropped my purse to the floor and sat down on my couch, staring at the ceiling. My mind was going non-stop. *I'm dying… Please God, let me… never mind.* What's the use of prayer when my judgment is already set? I refuse to sit here and cry over spilled milk. I stood to my feet, inhaled deeply, and walked out of my space. I decided to let the chips fall where they may.

On my way to the elevator, I could hear my neighbors going at it again. This is the norm for them. The worst part of it all was. …They were both dikes! I pressed the button, waiting patiently.

"COME 'ERE!" One of the chicks screamed to the other.

There's no way in the hell I would put up with some broad beatin on my ass. That shit is crazy! I shook my head in disgust as their voices echoed through the hallway. I try not to get involved in domestic disputes. No matter how some of these women get treated out here, they're always running right back to them fools; been there done that.

The elevator finally opened, I stepped in, drop 21 floors, and I'm off to start my day. I made it to my truck, and sat there, thinking about the Wonder Woman days. *Treasure sure looked crazy in her costume, thinking she had powers*! I couldn't help but to laugh thinking about it. We had such short memories. ...Good memories though. Now that's all lost...

*****

OL'BOY

"Yo!" D said answering my celly.

"Hi," the voice said seductively. "Is Ol'Boy around?"

"Naw. Who dis?"

"Monique, we met in Detroit a couple of days ago. He knows me."

"Too much information Baby, but I'll let'um know you called, aight?"

"You sound so familiar. Did we meet?"

"Yo, I'm not that nigga. I'll tell Ol'Boy you called (CLICK)."

That's the type of groupie shit I be talking about! All that, "You sound so familiar," bull was just some game to get next to the man that knows the man! If they can't get the man, go for his boy. If that don't work, holla at his body guard. No luck there, try a look-a-like, the limo driver, security or anything that would get their groupie ass in the door. D wasn't down for dat. He'll check'um in a heartbeat!

I just met this chick and she's already callin'! I knew she was just another headache, but yet and still I failed by givin' her my hitter. Grimy broad at that! If Summer knew I kicked it with Monique, God forbid! Unlike most situations like this, bitches don't care. That was part of being a celebrity, everybody wanna fuck us, be seen with us, and steal our style!

I was in the back of my suite chillin' with this fine chick I hit up every time I'm in Indiana on tour. She knew how to take care of a brotha swell!

"SSSmmmm...Babyyy...harder..."

The only thing I could hear between moans was that pussy poppin' while wrapped around my dick. I was trying to knock the bottom out of dat shit! I had her legs on my shoulders, fallin' deep into her loose walls!

"You...Like...That...Girl?" Sweat was pouring from my head.

"YES! GET CHO PUSSY!" She dug her fingernails in my flesh, pissing me the fuck off, but I kept at it! I wasn't gon' let that stop me!

"THIS! IS! MY! PUSSY!"

I was trying to crack her skull up against the headboard the shit was so good! This is exactly what a brotha need after havin' sex for days at a time. I'm not gone lie! I can fuck until my dick is sore! I'm a horny nigga, yo! Ma, be carrying on a whole conversation while I'm hittin' it too. If I wasn't fully aware that I had a big dick, I would probably be feeling a little insecure.

I got my nut, and it was time to get rid of the bitch. I don't play that stickin' around mess. *Get cho shit and get the fuck out,* is how I roll. I try not to be rude to most of 'em. ...You know, the ones that pay to have daddy in their presence. That's right! Some of these chicks be payin' ya' boy. It ain't just the females that be hookin' for the dough. Celebs be getting they swerve on too! OOH YEAH! I ain't by my damn self neither, trust me.

I let my Indiana freak chill next to me a little longer than anticipated. I fed her every lie she wanted to hear because these ho'z simply can't handle the truth. I tried that truth trip one time and it ended up costing me two cars, three cribs, and some mo' shit.

In another hour or so I have to get my black ass up and prepare for a show! I'm gon' lay in this bed and let Baby-Girl rub me down, and then she's got to go!

THIRTEEN

DENIAL

*****
TREASURE

"All rise," the Bailiff announced.

I rushed to try and organize my paper work so I could get out of here. Standing to my feet as Judge Levitt entered the courtroom, I dropped some papers to the floor.

Can my day get any worse?

Before the Judge had a short recess, I was finishing up a trial on one of my cases with a fifteen-year-old male. This young child was charged with several counts of grand theft. His mother was on drugs and there's no father in the home. I can only imagine what he's going through. It's sad to say, but without his addiction to drugs, fighting for his freedom would have been a waste of time. He ended up receiving 365 days in a rehabilitation center.

I glanced at the clock over the Judge's head. I had another appointment to get to at the office.

Only thirty minutes to get there.

The rush hour traffic down here was going to be hard to get around. I snatched my things up and quietly made my way to the exit to face another delay....Darryl Mitchell.

"Treasure, I would like for you to meet a client and a very good friend of mine. Ferrell Holmes, Treasure Lewis. Treasure Lewis, Ferrell Holmes." Darryl could tell I wasn't in the mood to be courteous, but I had to be professional. I politely spoke, barely shook his hand, and gave the gentleman little eye contact.

"Beautiful," he complimented, holding my hand in the most discreet way.

It forced me to pay closer attention to what was standing before me. If I wasn't mistaken, I would say I was staring right into the eyes of Mekhi Phifer. But, in reality, this guy was just another one of Darryl's drug dealing clients. *What a waste.*

"Nice meeting you, Mr. Holmes." I ignored his compliment.

"Please, call me Ferrell," he insisted.

"OK, Ferrell. Will you excuse me? I have to go. I'm late for one of my appointments."

I waved them both off, trying to lose myself in the crowd, heading for the elevator. When I looked into his eyes, I just wanted to escape from whatever those feelings were I was having, but, Darryl was persistent.

"TREASURE, hold up!" Darryl took my arm.

"Yes, Mr. Mitchell." I exhaled, as I pressed the elevator door button multiple times. I was nervous.

Like that would make it open any faster.

"Listen. What are your plans looking like later?"

"I'm busy, especially if you're trying to play matchmaker. I know you Darryl Mitchell. I also know that grin on your face. There's definitely something behind it." He instantly wiped the smirk off his face. "Don't even try it," I said placing one hand on my hip, holding my briefcase in the other.

Before he could continue, the elevator door opened and I stepped in between the crowd to avoid anymore of his dating game routine. The last thing I saw was his face following the door as it closed.

I began staring at the ceiling in the elevator. There were people all around me. I felt smothered, like they were holding me back from getting to my destination. Spoke too soon...

"You need help with that?" Ferrell asked, reappearing out of nowhere as I stepped off the elevator.

Before I responded, I looked around to see if Darryl was somewhere hiding. He plays entirely too much.

How'd he reach the lobby before me?

"No thank you. I can handle it." I said sliding by him. He followed.

"Please, can I just have a few words with you, Ms. Lewis."

"I really don't have any time to spare, Mr. Holmes, Ferrell, whatever. I'm really late for an appointment." I tried to be cordial, but he made me a little uneasy.

"Oh, you remembered my name." he said surprised.

"As much as I would love to chat, I have to go. ...Maybe some other time."

He tried to say something, but like before, I didn't give him a chance. I flew out the revolving door, leaving him to fight with the crowd.

Treasure, did you see the smile on that guy?

My mind was taking over. I had to check myself. I didn't want to have these thoughts, these feelings. It's not like me to be like this.

What is wrong with me?

I jumped in my car, paid for my parking, and rode off into hectic traffic. I truly wasn't ready to face these slow driving people. I'm almost anal about being on time; I'm usually at least ten to fifteen minutes early to any function.

I made it to the office a few minutes before the scheduled appointment. That was one good thing about working in downtown Detroit, my office was only a few miles away from the courthouse.

I turned the car off, reached behind my seat, and grabbed my jacket. I stepped out into a puddle of water. "When are these people going to fix these darned potholes?" I blurted out. I shook the water off my shoe and made my way to the front.

"Oh my God," I muttered, catching sight of what seemed to be Mr. Holmes.

I swear, if there are three of him, I'll die right here on the spot; thinking about my first encounter with the triplets.

I couldn't help but laugh at the sight of him... again! The fact that he was stalking an attorney was even funnier, as he must've had some nerve.

"I just have one question for you." I stood at the bottom of the steps staring up at him amazed. "How did you beat me here?"

"I walked," he said smiling.

"Oh, so you're trying to be funny. Now, all jokes aside. You had to know all that I went through to get here. ...And you walked?" I brushed past him placing my electronic card in the door.

"All that I went through to catch up with you deserves a chance at having dinner. So, what's up?"

"I already have plans."

"And after that?"

"NO," I said sternly.

"I'm not accepting no for an answer," he snapped back.

I stood in the doorway, shaking my head at him.

Don't lower your standards Treasure...keep it moving.

"Alright then, I won't give you an answer," I retorted.

"My girl." He winked.

"Listen, I have a client waiting."

"Okay. Maybe we can pick back up on this another time. That is, if you don't mind."

I have to give it to him, he is persistent!

"You just won't give up, will you?" I shook my head kind of amused at his persistence.

"Dinner?" He started again.

"NO," I shouted.

"I thought you said you wouldn't give me an answer."

"Goodbye, Mr. Holmes."

"I like hello better, Ms. Lewis."

He walked off as smooth as a cape in the wind. His loosely fitted suit jacket enhanced his well structured physique as he walked up Jefferson Avenue, leaving a scent of his cologne clinging in the air. I made my way inside thinking; *I am checking him out a little too much.* I'm sure I looked like a confused woman, the way I was staring at him.

How did he know my place of business? Darryl, of course.

My mind was so preoccupied that I didn't notice that my bootleg secretary was nowhere around. The closer I moved toward my office, the easier it was for me to convince myself that I was hearing noises. Someone was moaning. I followed the voices to the break room, opened the door, and what did I see?

"What is going on here?" I couldn't believe my eyes. Renee was engaging in a sexual act with my client!

"MS. LEWIS!" She jumped up off his lap, fixing her clothing. "It's not what it looks like. I was helping Mr..."

She doesn't even know his name.

I threw my client a fixated glare, "Mr. Davis, not only is your appointment cancelled, but I will no longer be handling your case. And while you're on your way out, take Ms. Promiscuous with you."

That was the straw that broke the camel's back. Giving her the boot came easy. I had given her every opportunity to prove she could present herself in a professional manner. She's just another wasted seed in our society.

FOURTEEN

THE LAST MINUTE

*****

SUMMER

My line beeped while I was on the phone with my little Caucasian friend, Autumn. With her wanna-be-black ass! She my dawg and all, but she can get on my damn nerves! I was practically begging her to go to Miami with me this weekend.

"Summer, I'm going to ask you to answer the other line and tell whoever that is to stop interfering with our convo." Autumn was becoming irritated with the constant clicking noise in between our words. I tried to ignore it, but whoever it was kept hanging up and calling right back.

"Hold on!" I clicked over and disguised my voice to conceal myself from the unknown. "W-H-O-L-L-O?"

"Hello, this is Doctor Tice calling. Is Ms. Lewis in?"

Damn! I hope he doesn't recognize my voice!

"No sir, she's not in at the moment," I continued, distorting my voice.

"Do you know when she will be available for me to speak with her?" He asked in a desperate tone. "I've made several attempts."

"I'm sorry Sir. Summer is out of town on an emergency. Someone in her family passed away. As a matter of fact, she probably won't be back anytime soon, but I will give her your message. I'm just here house-sitting for her." I nervously waited on his response.

"She already has my information. I'll just try to track her down some other time. Thank You."

Didn't I just tell this fool I won't be back anytime soon? And what does he mean, "Track me down"? I wish he would stop calling me!

Autumn was impatiently waiting for me on the other end. I hated to leave her on hold for too long, she gets a serious attitude. I clicked over...

"Summer! I don't believe you, leaving me on hold like that! I should've hung up!"

"What the fuck ever! That was my Grams and I know you gon' let me talk to her!"

I would've said anything to shut her up. Autumn whines too much, and it could sometimes be irritating, but right now she's the closest thing to me since I lost my girl. That's how we met, through Vette. I'm not the one to allow too many in my space, but Autumn knew Vette, so I made an exception.

Picking back up on our convo, her smart ass said, "You lucky it was Grams ho." Then she shifted the conversation to some bullshit about a shirt. "What in the world is this on my shirt?"

Here we go. ...Miss "Prissy" and her spot on her thousand-dollar blouse. I don't know why she sweats the small stuff. She got mad gear throughout her *exclusive* walk-in closet that *still* had tags on them.

"You need to cut all that out! I'm not trying to hear about no damn spot on your shirt! Are you rollin' to Miami or not?" She was aggravating me.

"Summer, this is serious. I cannot get this spot out of my blouse! I paid over fifteen hundred for this top," she pouted. "I don't believe this."

"Look, white girl! Are you..."

"Ho, you better tone it down! I see you must have forgotten about me and my friend that plays in the NBA. You were supposed to be hanging out with me, remember?" I could still hear her fidgeting around with her blouse. "I can't believe you made other plans."

"You're right Autumn, I did forget. Look at it this way, I would rather hang out with my "Celeb Boo"...let me rephrase that…Single Celeb…than to be messing around with a *married* pro-ball player. I've warned you, Autumn. When wifey finds out about you, it's going to be trouuuuuuble, trouuuuuuble…" I crooned.

"Woo…I'm scared. I'm gon' do me BOO! And I know you don't think that Mr. Rapper don't have peoplez. You gettin' played too, Ma!"

"Shut-up." She was right. I knew I wasn't his only, but none of that would matter in the end, *'because I'm taking him with me…*

"Damn, who am I gon' take now? Messin' round with you, I could've been on the phone asking someone else," I said.

"What about Jade?"

"Oh! I can't believe I forgot to tell you what happened to her."

I thought back to the conversation I had with China, who would always have something juicy to tell me about anyone but herself. China was good at holding secrets when it came to her own drama.

"Check this out. Jade ran up in Strictly Sports Wear on 7 Mile and caught her dude in there splurging with the next of kin! They were kissing and some more shit up in that joint!"

"Who bitch?" She was all in. Autumn was messy.

"Jade's Mother…"

"You L-Y-I-N'…"

"No, I'm not. "Apparently Jade's mother is the bomb for her age and all. …I do remember Jade telling me how her man used to be chillin' at her Mom's crib a lot. She thought it was all innocent. Dude was takin' Moms places and everything! Got'z ta be more careful!"

"What happened when she caught them? Don't tell me that bitch didn't kirk out Summer."

"The usual routine. You know how Jade is about dude. Her ass stood there and cried. "WHYYYY! How could you two!" I mimicked Jade's whinning. We were cracking up! "Come on now, Autumn. You know Jade's been going through this drama with this fool for years. How old is their son, lil Marsean? Two? Three? The busta didn't even try to explain. He got that much control over her, but her peeps apologized and then turned around in the same sentence and said how much she loved him. All of them need to be on the '*Oh Drama!*' show."

"Mother or not, I would of smacked dat ho," Autumn said.

"Jade loves that nigga too hard. And the problem is that he knows this. That's why he treats her the way he does! She needs to stop contradicting herself! When she threatens to leave him, she needs to run and don't look back! Let that fool feel the realness. Maybe then he'll have more respect for both her and their child. If you put up with niggas' shit, they become comfortable. Fuck that!"

"Mmm. I still say it couldn't have been me. Now, what about China and Monique?"

"I'm really not trying to take Monique. That slut? I can't deal with her, but you know what? Now that I think about it, I could use some ho'z on this mission. Ol'Boy road dawgs would be pleased to have those freaks." We agreed. Before I hung up from Autumn, I promised to call and give her the hotel number once I made it to Miami.

FIFTEEN

A FIGMENT OF MY IMAGINATION

*****

TREASURE

"Treasure, Sweety. How are you?" Mrs. Jackson appeared with some briefs to break the uneasy silence. I don't know what I would do without her. Mrs. Jackson was one of the best legal secretaries ever.

"Better..." I relaxed behind my desk, kicking off my shoes to make it more comfortable.

"You want to talk about it?" She could see the exhaustion in my face.

"Not really."

"Okay, Sweety. Call me if you need me."

"Would a nice loud scream be better?" I forced a smile.

She nodded and pulled my door closed. I really respected her for putting up with all of us. She's like the mother of the firm. She would work overtime to make sure we all had it together. I felt like we were placing too much on her. That's why I hired "Ms. Promiscuous"; dismissing the fact that Mrs. Jackson had insisted that she didn't need any assistance. I'll listen to her for sure the next time.

I sat around for most of the evening doing paper work and going over cases. I had to rebuild my reputation from all the damage I had caused in the past. It's amazing how things came back to haunt you.

Why can't I get this Ferrell guy out of my head?

He looked like someone my sister would date; only he seemed to have a little more class than the bums I've seen her bring to Grams'.

I have to admit, he did look handsome in his suit today. His brown sugar tone complimented his young tender touch of class, but there was an underlying problem gnawing at me. I remember Darryl talking about this Ferrell character a few months ago. He mentioned that he was a retired drug dealer that had cleaned himself up and did positive things with the riches he had gained. That doesn't make it right. He still stole homes, lives and dreams. Knowing all of this and trying to convince myself otherwise, didn't change the uncomfortable feelings I was having right now.

I think I figured it out, I thought, trying to rationalize with denial. *Ferrell, my feelings...It's all just a figment of my imagination, that's all. ...It's not real.*

At last my day was over and as nighttime fell, I was left with nothing to do but go home to my spacious condo alone. I should have been used to that routine. I stepped through my door, dropped my keys on the shelf, my briefcase on the floor, and stripped down to my naked body. I was ready to feel some steam. Turning the shower on full blast, I stepped in to release some of the day's tension. As I rubbed my body with the soapy scent of some perfumed body wash, I fell into a deep daze. I could feel a man's hands wrapped around my waist pulling me into him. I felt his hardness sliding in between the line of my buttocks. His sizeable flesh glided up and down finding its way to my untouched womb. I lifted my foot upon the side of the tub allowing water to massage my pearl. In my daze I imagined his finger brushing against me bringing a pleasurable feeling I've longed for. ...He appeared. A clear picture of him, the man from earlier...Ferrell.

My phone began to ring; I didn't want to answer it. I had to experience the unknown, the unfamiliar. ...It was like the ring tone in my phone became louder and forced me back to reality...*Damn.*

"Hello?" I answered irritably.

"Treasure Lewis!" I had to catch the voice.

"Who is...Darryl?" I stepped out of the shower.

Perfect timing, Darryl Mitchell....

"Listen, I called Martin and Keith, inquiring about the assistance they need on that high profile case in Maryland. Did you still want to participate on that? It's going to pay off real big girlfriend."

"Not interested. I have some other things going on right now, Darryl. Plus, I don't feel like I've had enough legal experience to be a part of something like this."

"I don't want to hear nothing about experience. I realize that you've lost a few high profile cases Treasure, but here's your chance to shine Love."

If only he knew the truth behind those cases.

"Why, thanks Darryl. You helped me to make a quick decision. ...No."

"Is that your final answer?"

"Look, Regis," I teased, giggling.

I knew how much he loved that *Who Wants to Be a Millionaire* show. I threw on my robe, cleaned my tub out, and then made my way to the kitchen to make hot cocoa, while Darryl rattled off as usual.

"I keep telling you Treasure. You need to take on bigger challenges. You have what it takes!"

"Darryl, I'm not ready for all that. Now, let's talk about the set up move you pulled today with Mr. Holmes. You were real funny, sending him to my office like that. I thought your joke was very intriguing," I said resting on my sofa, enjoying the warmth from the cocoa. I licked the whip cream off my top lip.

Mmm.

"What?" He acted surprised. "What are you talking about Treasure? I played no role in that today."

"No, Darryl. I'm not mad at you, okay? You can stop the games."

"Listen Treasure, I have done many things and played many jokes, but this one I did not participate in, I swear."

"Humm. That's interesting. I wonder how he knew…"

"Come on now. It's not like you're not listed in the phone book. Wow, he must have really wanted you bad, girlfriend. You think he's one of those types who can smell a virgin? … Oops!"

"DARRYL!" I whined, almost spilling my drink. I placed it on the table, standing to my feet.

How'd he know I was a virgin.

"I'm sorry Chile, I didn't mean…"

"Yes you did!"

"Look, its okay, but it has to be hard to not have had any Peter for this long," he said chuckling.

"You remember this MISS!" I shouted.

"Miss? Was that pay back? HEY, there's no secret to my game," Darryl said.

"Whatever! I don't think anyone in our firm knows you're gay, Darryl. You hide it very well, you know."

"You're right, I do. You know society doesn't respect gay people. And I'm an attorney too! Oooh, girl! I tell you one thing. …I'm not alone. You remember what I told you about this secret life. …You would be surprised how many men and women have desires and hidden affairs with the same sex. Since that new novel was released exposing closet homos, it's *really* going to be drama. Watch what I tell you, girlfriend."

He just revealed my secret. Has Jacqueline been talking to him?

I walked to my room, laying across my bed, finishing up our conversation. It was very interesting. I guess it wasn't hard for him or anyone for that matter to notice my celibacy. It's obvious that I'm a bore without a man. Darryl had been gay all his life. I had no idea until we became close friends and he confided in me. I was really shocked. He was very attractive and I never detected anything feminine about him. Either way, I really love his silly behind. He lifted my spirits when I was down. I hear women say how gay men make really good friends, and so far that has proven to be true. Darryl is hilarious!

He explained how serious Ferrell is when it comes to protecting his investments. Ferrell hired Darryl as his attorney to oversee all his legal assets. I was curious to know, by them being business associates, whether it was possible that Ferrell had any gay tendencies. Darryl reassured me that Ferrell didn't have a gay bone in his body.

Nevertheless, Ferrell's reputation was once built on the drugs that he distributed. His lifestyle and all that he owned stemmed from drug money. Even though Darryl said Ferrell is no longer a dope dealer, I couldn't get past the fact that he once was.

SIXTEEN

HANGIN' WITH THE ENEMY
*****
SUMMER

I decided to give this Monique and China thing a shot. I was desperate. I might as well accommodate his friends too. I don't really get down with taking chicks that are just as pretty as me on trips like this anyway. Besides, with the short time I have to work with, I had to settle.

Here I go calling Monique back. I've been dodging her since the night we went to the club. I hate calling her crib. For one, she talks too loud and two, she doesn't know when to shut up! When I dialed her number, she didn't allow it to get one full ring in before she answered.

"HELLO!" She was out of breath.

"Monique, can the phone get a full ring?"

"Summer! What's up Boo! I've been trying to reach you for the last couple of days!" Only half deaf people talk as loud as her. I had to hold the phone away from my ear.

"Monie! Can you please turn the volume down? You're talking too loud!" I released a sigh. "Look, I called to see if you wanted to go out of town with…"

"HELL YEAH! I'M WIT IT!" She didn't even give me time to finish. This is what I'm talking about. *Are you making the right choice, Summer? Think this through... please.*

"Monie? What you over there smoke'n on? You too hyped, Boo."

"Summer, now you know I keep the trees over here Baby Girl. But, yo, I'm ready to do whatever. I'm bored, and Kenny ain't acting right. Let's do this."

Who the hell is Kenny?

88

"Summer, you know you don't have to ask me twice."

"Ask you twice? I didn't even ask you once, yet!" I fell back on my bed, staring at the ceiling. *Why me? Why now?*

"You don't understand Boo. I'm just ready to get out of Detroit and breathe new air. I'm tired of the same faces. Where are we going?"

"Oh, now you want to know where? Girl, you're special. Miami, baby. Ol'Boy invited me down for a video shoot. You know I'm hyped, right? But, check this out," I cut the convo short. "I have to go. I need to have us out of here before Friday. So peep this, I'll hit you back with the reservation people on the three-way so you can give them your information, okay?"

"You don't want me to give it to you now?"

"Didn't I just tell you I would call you back and let you do it? Hold on Monie while I call the man that drives the yellow bus to come pick yo' ass up!" She started laughing.

"Okay, okay, Summer," she said giggling ignorantly. "You crazy girl! The yellow bus? … As long as the driver got a big dick, I'll ride!" She was the only one laughing.

"Bye Monie!" I got ready to hang up.

"Summer! I wanted to ask you. …What happened with you and Ol'Boy the other night? How did things go?"

"We can talk about that later, Monie. I've got to handle this business before we don't go anywhere, but I will say this. …The dick was lovely!"

There was a sudden moment of silence. I was damn near about to hang up on her, actin' all funny. Damn, I hope China had someone else in mind, because I'm not really feelin' this bitch right about now. Her ass is strange. She ain't been the same since I fucked her dude a couple months ago. Sometimes I feel she knows somethin', and try'n to sneak me on the low. It's all good. I'll just keep the bitch in my peripheral, just in case she tries to pull somethin' grimey while we're on our trip.

I laid back on my plush king size bed while I called China; I was just getting ready to hang up when some thug answered.

"Yeah!"

"Wha'sup, is China there?"

"Who dis?"

"Summer."

The guy, that answered, held the mouthpiece so I could barely hear what was going on. If I wasn't mistaken, I could have sworn he threw the phone at her.

"Hello?" China's tone was raspy.

"What's up Boo-Boo?" I said.

"Nothing, girl. You aight?" She said clearing her throat.

"Naw, are you aight and who was that answering your phone?"

"Hold on, Summer." I could tell she walked into another room. Dude, that answered the phone, sounded familiar. I couldn't place the voice, but whoever he was, he's got her on lock.

"Hello," she said in a lower tone.

"China what's up with you? Why you sound like that?"

"Summer, I can't get into that with you right now. We'll kick it later. What's up anyway, this ain't like you, callin' me, what'z really going on?"

"You want to hit the sky with your girl this weekend?"

"Hell yeah! Where we goin'?"

"MIAMI, BABY!"

"You know I do. Let me find out that rapper, auuhhh, what's his name…"

"Yeah, yeah, yeah, that's him. You don't have to broadcast my business over there with yo' peoplez, Love."

"I got' chu. I think Bru-Brian! I think Brian's gone, girl," she stammered.

"Who the hell is Bru-Brian?"

"Naw," she said, laughing. "His name is Brian, and you don't know him."

"China, don't let me find out you was about to say that busta ass nigga Bruce. Jade will kill yo' ass about her baby daddy!" I said laughing. I knew that anything was possible when it came to their Trio.

"What the fuck ever, Summer. Now, what..." My line beeped in the middle of her sentence.

"Hold on, let me get this...." I clicked over. "Hello?" I again changed my voice up. I could never be too careful these days.

"Summer, did you talk to the reservation people yet?" I wanted to jump through the phone and tag Miss Impatient right in her throat! I can't believe her. She didn't even give me a half an hour to call her back!

"Monique! Did you hear me when I said *I* would call *YOU!*"

"My bad. I just didn't want to risk missing yo' call. I was about to step out and go get my nails done. You want me to hold on?"

"Yeah, while I load my gun. I'm on my way over there to shoot yo' dumb ass!"

"You are so stuupid," she said, giggling.

"15 minutes! That's when *I'll* call *YOU* back!" I clicked back over to China. "China, yeah that was Monique. Please tell me you have someone we can invite other than her," I begged.

"Monique? Now Summer you know I don't care for Monique. The only time she's in my space is when I'm hanging with you. And I can't think of no one in this short amount of time."

"Well, Monique it is. We just have to make do."

"On the real, I don't care right about now. I just need to get away. How long will we be gone?"

"A week."

"Bet."

After I made all the reservations I glanced over on the night stand and noticed how Chuck, this baller I had met a couple of nights ago, left his two-way pager. I didn't notice it at first, but what irritated me was when I picked it up; he had turned it off. It's all good though.

Spread my love around Chuck! I'm not trying to fall in love baby! I just want to give you what you came for. ... Yeah, that's right, the booty. Beautiful, sweet, raw, dangerous, and disguised!

Valencia R. Williams

SEVENTEEN

TOO MUCH INFORMATION

*****

TREASURE

Today was going to be different. I decided to change up a little and wear this designer outfit Jeraldine purchased for my last birthday. I never planned to wear it; it was too revealing, but now I felt sexy. Plus the outfit was perfect with the shoes that my Aunt Kim had given me; I liked the way they accentuated my nicely toned legs.

I have always been insecure about my body. I remember looking in the mirror at myself growing up; I was pale and had no shape, compared to Summer. I always envied her well-formed physique. She was built like our Mom. Unfortunately, I took on my Dad's frame.

There was something about this particular outfit that changed my whole appearance, and my outlook along with it. Today, I felt like a new woman.

"Hello ladies," I said smiling as I walked past everyone toward my office.

Mouths dropped, and all conversations ceased. I tried to act like I didn't notice all the attention, but I couldn't hide the nervousness.

"What's the occasion?" Jacqueline said walking closely behind me.

"Just the mood I'm in today Sweetie, that's all." I placed my laptop on my desk.

"You sure all of this is not for the gentleman that called here for you not too long ago?" She folded her arms, looking at me like I owed her an explanation.

"What gentleman?" I asked, knowing the answer even before she spoke.

"Ferrell Holmes, a man with a desperate sound in his voice."

"Oh, him? He's nobody," I waved it off, "just one of Darryl's clients. He needs help on something, that's all." I fingered through stacks of papers on my desk, acting as if there was something important I was looking for.

"MmmHmm. Here's his number," she said slapping it on my desk. "Call him. Like I said, he sounded desperate."

"Excuse me, you two." Jeraldine joined our casual meeting. "I see you wore the outfit, huh?" I looked up to smile at her as she entered my office.

"Yes, you like?" I modeled.

"Nice." Jeraldine nodded approvingly.

"Too revealing?" I asked Jacqueline as she turned to walk out.

"What's wrong with you?" Jeraldine asked Jaqueline before she could leave.

"Mind your own business," she snapped.

"That girl has issues." Jeraldine said, ignoring her sister's attitude.

"I know." I agreed.

"So, what's the occasion?" Jeraldine smiled, taking a seat on the opposite side of me.

"None, I just felt like a change. You know how that is."

"Uhhh...Yeah, right! Now, the truth....Who is he?"

"Can't I try something a little different without all of you thinking it's for someone other than me?" I giggled.

"No." Jeraldine folded her arms giving me a serious look.

That was one thing about the three of us. We all knew each other too well. I knew it would come to this. Wearing clothes like this is like dying my hair pink. Maybe it was a little too flamboyant for the office.

"How about we talk later?" Jeraldine continued. "Hopefully by then you'll give a sista more details on your secret admirer. I have to meet a client in another twenty minutes, but I will put you up on a little drama that happened a couple of days ago. Guess who got busted?" She was talking in a low tone. I stared at her without saying a word, waiting for the answer. "Jacqueline. Mom found out about her and her lesbian lover, Jordan." She snickered.

"Stop playing," I whispered.

"Not this time. I told Jacqueline to just tell Mom. It was only a matter of time before she popped up and saw something wasn't right with the roommate situation."

"What did your Mom say?" I was curious.

I knew Jacqueline was hiding her relationship from their mother, but like Jeraldine said, it was only a matter of time. They were becoming too comfortable and careless with their lifestyle. It wasn't my place to say anything to Jacqueline about it. She wasn't the type to take anyone's advice anyway.

"We'll talk later." She winked.

I knew something was bothering Jacqueline. I had been blind about her attitude. I thought it was about us.

Let me go talk to her.

I knocked on her door, entering her aggressive space. She had paintings of beautiful women all over her walls. Her taste was hard, but nice. She can really turn a room into something interesting.

"Is something wrong, Sis?" I walked over to her. She was sitting, staring out the window, with her fingers intertwined under her chin in deep thought.

"No, not really, just a few problems at home."

"Like what? You want to talk about it?"

"Maybe some other time, I have work to do."

"Okay, I'll come back later."

"Wait, wait. I'm sorry Love...please, stay." She turned toward me.

Jacqueline was still gorgeous. She wore nothing but the finest. Her pants suits were all tailored and cut to fit her dominant frame. They gave her the persona she wanted to project; a no nonsense attitude. They were like her signature. It was her way of demanding respect. And she got it.

"Tell me about your new friend. I have a few minutes to spare," she said with a wicked smile.

"You keep asking about a friend. ...Why?"

"You know how I am. I have always been over protective of you, as well as my other sisters. I'm just curious."

She is so full of it.

She folded her hands behind the head of her seat, sitting comfortably, staring at me.

"Stop looking at me like that Jackie."

"Why?"

"It makes me uncomfortable," I said.

"So?" She shrugged her shoulders, dropping her hands to her lap.

"So? Something's wrong with you today. I should be questioning you."

"Oh, really?"

"Yes, really," I replied.

"Well. ...Run it," she snapped.

"What's happening at home? You mentioned problems there."

"You're changing the subject, Treasure. You still haven't answered my question." She never changed her expression. She's always so serious.

"Later. I have a phone conference in a couple of minutes." As I turned to walk away, I heard her stand to her feet.

"Can a sister get some love?"

"Sure." I walked over to hug her. There was something about the way she held me...something different...something I was scared to question.

"Later," she responded, releasing me from her hold.

I went to my office, closed the door, and stood against it for a few seconds.

I hope this secret about us doesn't blow up into something I can't handle. This could truly be damaging to our business relationship.

I finally was able to organize all the chaos on my desk. I had completely forgotten about Mr. Holmes' telephone number that Jacqueline had put on my desk, until it reappeared. There was a part of me that wanted to return his call, but the other side of me, that stubborn side wouldn't allow it.

*****

Just about everyone was gone for the day except for Mrs. Jackson. It was after 5:30, and I'd just about had my office organized when she paged me.

"Yes, Mrs. Jackson."

"I have a gentleman here by the name of Ferrell Holmes asking for you. He doesn't have an appointment," she said nervously.

"Thank you Mrs. Jackson. Let him know that I will be with him shortly."

I clicked her off before she could say another word. I know how paranoid she could be when it came to strangers walking in after hours, especially when she knows there are no appointments scheduled. I freshened up and made my way out into the lobby to again confront the most attractive man I had ever seen in my life. I felt naked the way he stared at me. It was almost like he could read my mind.

"Hello, Mr. Holmes." I smiled, reaching out my hand to him. Mrs. Jackson had this puzzled expression on her face.

"How are you Ms. Lewis?" He held my hand in the gentlest way. The way he scanned my body made me a little uncomfortable but not enough to run again. "You look stunning," he said, smiling. His smile gave me a sense of security.

It was time to say goodbye to Mrs. Jackson.

"Treasure, would you like for me to hang around to help out with anything?"

She was standing beside me now, staring at Mr. Holmes like he had stolen something. He didn't seem to be uncomfortable at all, but I was.

"No thank you Mrs. Jackson. I think I can handle it from here. You can leave."

"Are you sure Sweetie? I don't mind working over."

I grabbed her coat and bag off the desk, placed it in her hands and eye-gestured her away. "Thank you, but I can handle it from here Mrs. Jackson. See you tomorrow." I opened the door for her as she slowly walked out, and then pushed it closed.

I didn't expect for things to happen the way they did, once I turned to face him, I had very little breathing room. Now I was really nervous.

"You are going with me?" He said. The deepness of his voice sent chills up my spine. He was so close I could feel his warm breath on me.

"Going with you where?" I slid from in front of him.

"Whoah, whoah, where you going?" He took my wrist, pulling me back in front of him.

What am I doing? This man is everything I once despised. I need to re-evaluate myself before I do something that I might later regret.

"I'm not leaving this place without you on my arm."

I found myself making very little effort to remove myself from in front of him. "You expect me to leave with you right now?" I replied.

"Look at you." He took hold of my hands. "You look like a Superstar, Girl. We're going somewhere, you hear me?"

"Uh, Uh, I don't just up and leave with strangers. I don't know you like that. Not to mention, you know nothing about me. So slow it up a little, will you?" I moved toward the chaise that sat in front of the bay window.

"What if I told you I know more about you than you give a brotha credit for? Will I at least have the chance to eat with you by my side tonight? I'm hungry, Baby." He stood there looking handsome, strong, and slightly bow-legged in his casual suit.

"I guess you need to be making your way to eat alone because you know nothing about me other than my name."

Then out of the blue he said, "Treasure Renay Lewis, born here in Detroit, Michigan to Gloria Lewis and Malcom Young. You temporarily resided on the eastside, before you ended up with your grandmother, Margie Lewis and her daughter; your Aunt, Kim Lewis. You attended the University of Michigan, successfully graduated, and then furthered your education at U of M Law School, receiving your Law degree there. You have a sister, Summer Devyne Lewis," he cleared his throat. "A touchy subject, so I'll move on."

He was blowing my mind! I interrupted him. I couldn't take any more. "H-How do you know all of that? Who? Where?" I was confused. My mouth was dry from hanging wide open.

"Now can we eat?" He grinned.

"Don't ignore me."

"I promise, I'll reveal my sources over dinner. Then I'll share a little background with you, about me."

Now this is going to be interesting...

I said silently, taking my position, "Better now than later, let's see... your name is Ferrell Laron Holmes, born in North Carolina to Silvia and Rodney Holmes. You're 28 and rotten to the core. Your family relocated to Detroit, and now resides in Farmington Hills. You enjoyed a rather privileged life. You have a sister, Tyeisha Holmes, 26, and a baby brother, Rodney Jr., who just turned 16. You have a son, Marquis Holmes, birthed by a beautiful woman named Keyonna Bryant, drama queen, oh and uh, are you still hungry, Baby?"

He looked astonished. We stood there laughing at each other, caught up in each other's eyes. That's when I felt things getting a little serious. I don't know what type of powers he had, but I was mesmirized. Seconds later we were kissing softly, slowly meeting each other's every motion.

This is not a dream... this is not a dream.

My mind was floating on a cloud that only appeared once every decade. It's been that long since I kissed a man like that. To be honest, I had never kissed anyone so passionately in my life.

He's so sweet, my mind chanted. *Ohh Sshh... What's he doing to me now?*

He was unbuttoning my blouse. I needed to stop him, but not yet though, not yet. I like the way that feels. He was kissing my neck. I could feel his tongue slithering like a snake down the middle of my chest.

Oh my, not my, sshhitt. ...not my breast My back was against the wall; there was nowhere to run.

"You have nice breasts," he complemented, cupping them both in his hands, massaging them gently.

I didn't respond. I just kept my eyes closed. I wanted him inside me.

No, this is moving too fast!

"I can't do this," I said as I slightly pushed him away.

"Relax," he whispered.

I could feel myself becoming weaker by the moment. His hands dropped down to the sides of my hips, pulling my skirt a few inches above. I gently bit his bottom lip. I wanted him just as badly as he wanted me. I moved my legs apart, rotating my hips; pacing myself. He had my approval. His fingers slid up in between my thighs; entering the untouched. I shivered with anticipation. It was an easy slide; I was so wet. His hand was covered in my richness. I was really feeling this until I heard the sound of his zipper. That was when reality kicked in.

"Ferrell," I exhaled, pushing him away, covering my face, ashamed. "I'm sorry, I just can't do this." What surprised me was how he handled the situation. His behavior was something I wasn't used to.

He straightened himself, placed his arms around me and said, "Look at me." He pulled my hands away from my face. "Don't you ever apologize for something so precious that belongs to you. This is your body, your gem baby. You make the decisions, not me or any one else. Cherish your precious gift. I want you bad Treasure, I do, but I respect you. I'm not your average nigga that takes advantage when I hear the word, 'no'. As you can see here, my boy *was* ready for some action," he said revealing his bulge in his slacks. "But he can wait baby and so can I. We have a lifetime. Now, can a brotha get some grub?"

My life was about to change...

EIGHTEEN

EAST COAST/ WEST COAST

*****
SUMMER

If murder were legal, these chicken-heads would be dead within minutes. I can't believe I got myself caught up like this. That's what I get for scheduling a last minute trip. Now look at me, on the plane, with President and CEO of Dumb, Inc. arguing like they don't have any damned sense!

"I don't care what neither one of y'all say, Mary J. Blige's first CD was 411," Monique argued.

"Who gives a fuck? Would ya'll shut up!" I retorted.

"Listen, I'm trying to finish my drink and chill. It's bad enough I'm scared of flying, and having to listen to Monique's mouth, is making it even worst," China said.

"Excuse me ladies. Could you all please keep the noise down?" The stewardess politely asked.

Oh God...

"I apologize. My associates here had a little too much to drink," I said.

"Whatever, I'm sober with a bad headache. Do you have something for a headache Miss?" Monique asked the woman.

"Sure." The stewardess was very considerate in spite of her ignorance. "I'll get something for you."

"Thanks. OH! Excuse me. Will there be a movie playing in this section?"

"Yes. It will be showing in about another thirty minutes or so."

"What's playing?" Monique continued to annoy the woman.

"*Billy Bob & Son.*"

"Awww hell naw! Can we get some *Soul Plane* up in this piece! Don't no black people wanna see no Billy whatever the fuck," Monique snapped.

"Monie. Shut... I'm sorry Miss. You have to excuse her," I said elbowing Monique in her arm. She shot me an evil stare, but I ignored her. The stewardess walked away nodding her head in disgust. I had my mind made up, when we landed, I was jumping in a cab and rollin' out with Ol'Boy.

After a bumpy plane ride, we landed and jumped into a waiting limo. We headed to the Marriot where our room was already reserved and paid for. The room was so humongous that we were all able to have our own spacious solitude. China and Monique acted like they had never been in something so expensive and beautiful.

I can't believe I came on a trip like this with two broke ho'z !

"Ya'll wanna choke?" China said pouring the contents of some weed on the table from a small sandwich bag. The smell was potent.

I grabbed a small glass, tossed in a few ice chips, and sipped on some Grey Goose and cranberry. This room had a fabulous bar set up, a full kitchen with all the accessories, and some tight furniture.

I might just have to take some of this with me. I can use some new shit at my crib.

"Light that shit up!" I sat down on the lounger sofa. The elegant chair was positioned in front of the French doors that overlooked the scenic Miami Beach area.

"Move over," Monique said, patting my legs.

"You better go over there and sit with yo' dawg!"

"Don't play." China peeked up at me as her tongue snaked the paper to seal the blunt.

"Y'all ho'z aint shit." Monique swayed over to the empty chair.

"Girl, bye," I said waving her off.

"Oh yeah, I wanna hit that. That smells like some Ganja! My boy, Tank, used to cop that shit off the Ave," Monique said with her eyes fixated on the blunt.

"Monique, cop this." China rubbed her love.

"I knew it! China, you wanna eat my pussy don't cha?" Monique looked at China waiting on her response. I could see the rage and embarrassment in China's eyes.

"Aw, hell naw! I'm about to whip this bitch ass. Summer, hold this!" China passed me the blunt, and then dashed for Monique. Monique ran into the bathroom, locking the door behind her.

"You not gon' stay in there forever ho!"

"China wanna eat my pussy...China wanna eat my pussy..." Monique crooned through the closed door.

"BOOM! BOOM! BOOM!" China was banging against the furnished wood angrily.

"I'm about to light this up y'all two." That was all I remembered before I was knocked out...

I woke up with the loud ringing of the hotel's phone, "Hello."

"Hi Pretty. How was your flight?" I rose up so fast from the sound of his voice, I felt dizzy. I forgot to wrap my hair and it was all over my head.

Damn...

"Nice. Where are you?" I looked around the empty room for China and Monique. They were nowhere in sight.

"I'm close...but not that close."

"Please not another unexpected visit from you," I teased.

"How I wish. Are you coming with me?"

"I hope so," I seductively responded, picturing a good ass nut.

"Then rise up off that lounger chair and meet me at the bar downstairs."

"How did you know where I was laying?"

"Look to the side of you." I followed his demand, and there sat a tropical bouquet complimented with a small box of Godiva Chocolates.

"OHH...you sent me these?"

"Better. I brought them to you personally. I was playing in that pussy the whole time I was there. You were sleeping so peacefully, I didn't want to wake you. I can still smell you."

"You're a freak. Why didn't you wake me?" I blushed.

"You seemed tired. Plus, I enjoy the feeling of a woman's warmth when she's relaxed." He hung up.

I was so out done about his unknown presence, and the gifts! He made me feel really special. I eased my fingers down in between my thighs and felt my honey. I was so wet. I could feel that someone had made himself at home in my sweetness. I didn't waste any time pulling myself together. I felt a little queasy, but I still managed to look fabulous. I was just about ready to make my exit when Monique appeared.

"Going somewhere without your girl?" Monique said, while leaning against the wall.

"Girl, you scared me. I should be back shortly. Ol'Boy just called. He wants me to meet him downstairs."

"Mmmm." She folded her arms, staring away.

"Where's China?" I asked.

"You ask me about that trick one more time," Monique snapped.

"Damn, don't get ill with me."

"I'm just saying. I can't stand that ho. And look at you, about to leave me with the bitch."

"Not my problem. Ya'll both agreed to come."

"It's all good. I'm gon' find me something to do. I'll probably see ya'll out there later," Monique said, disappointed.

"See who, out where?" I hesitated, turning to her.

"You and yo' peoplez. I'll be at the bar in a few minutes. Just gotta get my shit together, that's all."

"Do you, Boo? Because trust and believe; you won't run into me tonight. I have plans that do not include you. See ya."

She must be crazy to think I would have her ass tagging along with me. Don't work like that girly. I don't do threesomes.

I glanced one more time in the mirror, mumbling to myself, *"Bitch you fine as shit."* I noticed Monique behind me, stoppin' at the doorway.

I hate that bitch. Monique pushed the door up.

I made my way off the elevator and was attacked by jealous eyes.

Here go me. I know I'm a dime piece!

The stares were envious. I had a few sistas compliment me on my attire, while the others just hated.

This one chicken-head was staring me up and down, so I stared back!

I made my way to the bar to look for Ol'Boy. He was surrounded by all kinds of women. I could tell he was used to all the attention. He acted like it was nothing to him. I just stood back watching him with his fine ass! He looked good.

Well, what do we have here?

"One of the chicks that was staring at me hard was making her way over towards Ol'Boy. Now it's time to make my presence known. I strutted over to him, admiring his smile. He winked caressing my waist as I sat down beside him.

Move Ho'z.

The chick looked surprised. She knew by the way he treated me; I wasn't just another one of his groupies.

Meet Jane Black! Anyone that seen the movie *Meet Joe Black* would understand that comment. "Could you ladies excuse us please?"

They stared at me with an evil glare.

"Ya heard my girl. It's been real ladies." They trampled off like a stampede of horses.

"What took you so long?"

"Babysitting," I uttered.

"Sounds like you have a big responsibility."

"You have no idea." I smiled.

"Got something for you, Beautiful." His eyes lit up.

"And what exactly is that s*omething?*" I rested my chin on my closed hand.

"Summer, Summer, Summer. You are a pretty muthafucka." He teased me with the fingers that he had played in my love with ealier.

"You are so nasty." I released this rehearsed laughter.

"I can't get over the scent you wearin'." His two fingers rested under his nose, after pulling them from his mouth.

"Does it taste as good as it smells?" I enticingly asked.

"Like brown sugar." He responded seductively.

"Well, you ready?" I asked.

"I don't know. You tell me." He pulled my hand and placed it on his hardness. "All that from just looking at you."

Damn! There's that smile again. I'm fallen already, willing to give him whatever he wanted, when he wanted it. He took my hand as we stood to leave the bar. We were approaching the exit when he slid his tongue in my mouth, tasting my juice that was stored for him only. I had no idea that when our lips parted, Monique would be standing in front of us.

"You two make a nice couple," she said sarcastically.

"You finally made it, huh?" I tried to be humble.

She irked me, but I decided to be nice in front of my friend. It seemed that Monique went out of her way just to come down to the bar. I would say that she was trying to out do me, but *for what reason?*

"Ay, Beautiful, meet me at the limo," he said releasing my hand and walked off.

People again surrounded my Celebrity Boo immediately, trying to get an autograph or anything. He brushed them off as he made his way through the lobby.

"I can't believe you pulled that nigga, Summer." Monique watched Ol'Boy leave.

"It was easy," I said smirking.

"I bet it was."

The way she watched Ol'Boy made me a bit uncomfortable, but I was sure it was only because he was a star. Monique was a devoted groupie.

"You have a good time Boo," she said, walking on into the bar.

"You know I will."

I left whatever feelings I had toward her reactions in the lobby. I was going to have a good time with Ol'Boy. I'll deal with Monique's behavior another time.

Before I could get inside the limo and get comfortable, Ol'Boy was all over a sista. From the seat, to the floor he had me wide open. I wasn't wearing panties. That did something to his sex drive. Within seconds, the only thing I could feel was raw meat slamming up against my love.

"UHHSSS! UHHSS!" I moaned out in ecstasy.

I liked it rough, just the way he was giving it to me. He was lost inside of me, running his nine inches deep down into my canal, puncturing my hole like a stubborn nail being hammered. I was prying my nails into his flawless skin and biting down on his shoulder. He was swinging my petite frame all over the place. I let him have his way.

Why not, might as well enjoy our fate.

He was pounding, beating my shit up. It felt like he was punching a sand bag. I knew I would feel this in the morning, but right now the pain was tolerable. Drenched in his sweat, breathing hard, laying against his chest, we finally reached the finish line.

"I bet the chauffer got his," I said.

"That fool gets his damn near ev'ryday baby. He's my chauffer, I ain't gon' let 'um go hungry." He smacked me on my naked ass. "Sit up. I gotz' ta show you something."

"Could that something possibly be what you were talking about earlier?"

"Maybe." He reached behind the console, pulling out this beautifully wrapped box.

Oh shit, I know I'm in the house now. Bitch! You did dat!

"For you." He passed me the surprise.

I almost broke down. Not because of the considerate thought, but because of my motive. He was a good guy, not deserving this at all. Then again, I feel I didn't deserve this either.

Too late for sympathy.

"Thank You!" I took the box, trying to guess what was in it; it was a square foot, maybe some lingerie. I was slowly tearing the paper from it.

"Girl, rip that shit off of there!" He laughed.

"OOOOO…These are nice!" I held up several expensive pieces to wear for him only. He made that clear. "What make you think you will see each piece on me?"

"You're not going nowhere girl. No one ever leaves me." He brushed his finger across my stimulated nipple.

"Oh, you're that secure, huh?"

"Do I have a reason not to be?"

If only he could read my thoughts…"No, of course not."

NINETEEN

WHAT GOES AROUND COMES AROUND

*****

SUMMER

I made it in around six in the morning. I thought China and Monique were asleep. I know they didn't hear me come in; I was extremely quiet. I made my way to my room and jumped into the shower with the sweet thoughts of Ol'Boy still fresh in mind.

Why did my life have to be this fucked up? Why me? Here it is, I finally found the man for me, someone I want to be with, but I have to die.

I was just getting ready to lie down when my space was invaded by the one and only, Monique.

"Summer, can I holla at you?"

"Monique, can it please wait 'til after I catch some Z's. A sista tired, Love."

"Too much dick?" She stared with an arched look in her eyebrow, waiting for my response.

"I guess you can say that." She slammed the door, storming off with a serious attitude. I'm too tired to check her now. I'm gon' get her though…later.

*****

I woke up to find the suite empty. No China. No Monique. *Good.*

I wasn't feeling Monie's attiude right now. I assumed they went shopping or something, but they wouldn't, not together; that was

110

too much bonding for them. They probably went their separate ways, I'm sure. Ol'Boy invited all of us to his VIP gathering tonight. It's the opening of his new hit. All kinds of celebrities would be there. I forgot to mention that to Monique, but hell, she had such an attitude, I was thinking about going without her.

Damn, here these ho'z come wit' their loud asses.

"Could you believe that nigga had the audacity to try to holla after that shit?" China said to Monique, walking through the door with shopping bags from different stores.

I was in the middle of choosing an outfit to rock tonight. I snatched up a few new pieces before I left the city. Miami got some hot shit, but they could never fuck wit' the 'D' when it came to gear.

"Where ya'll been?" I asked, walking out of my room.

"That's tight Summer, where you wearing that to?" Monique asked, walking over checking out my flavor.

"To Ol'Boy's VIP party. He invited all of us. Y'all need to be getting ready."

Monique strutted away. I thought about bringing up that situation from earlier, but I left it alone. I already knew it was jealousy.

We all looked fierce when we finally got our shit together. It was gonna be like Destiny's Child making a grand entrance up in that place! We quickly headed out; Ol'Boy had the Maybach waiting for us. ...A very exotic and expensive ride, I might say. Monique and China were feelin' so special; they were throwing the diva attitude in every direction.

"I'm gon' ask ya'll to not act so damn pressed tonight and don't fuckin' embarrass me!" I said.

"I can't help it! Look over there! I know that's not who I think it is." China noticed a few West Coast players as we pulled in the lot.

The place was fabulous. I couldn't begin to name all the familiar faces. It was celeb haven. Cats that were supposed to be beefin' in the Biz were chilling together. To think all that drama was only for ratings. I ain't mad at'um.

The girlz and I looked deadly! That was how we did it in the 'D'. Stepping in the spot, people thought we came straight off the set to party.

Yeah, all eyes on us.

We all felt lovely, parlayin' in baller heaven. Ol'Boy met us at the front, taking my hand, pulling me to the floor to get our groove on.

"Show me what you workin' wit Gorgeous." He smiled.

"You know I have to show you off."

We danced damn near the whole night away. I was really enjoying myself 'til my muscles started tensing up. That's when I had to take a seat.

This HIV ain't no joke. There was a time when I could go all night.

Ol'Boy socialized with his so-called "enemies," while I pulled up a chair and kicked it with China and her new acquaintance.

"You aight, Boo?" China asked.

"Tired."

"You? Tired?"

"Girl, I don't know what's wrong with me," I lied.

"Chill, Boo. You want something to drink?"

"I'm tight."

"I'm gon' ask you again. And believe me, once you see what I see. ...a drink will be in your best interest."

"Wha'chu see...?" I followed the direction China was looking in. "What the fuck is she doin'!"

Monique was all over Ol'Boy on the dance floor. The way she was freakin' him told me somethin' wasn't right. Monique was plottin' on what I had from jump. That shit aint goin' down. They say paybacks a bitch, and I may have fucked her dude, but revenge will not take place up in this joint!

I jumped up, ready to crack some head!

I was surprised at China stopping me. "Summer! Hold up!" She pulled my arm. "You are a sista with too much class. This is not you, Baby Girl. I know you couldn't possibly think that nigga want Monique's funky ass! Don't stoop to her level. Girl...No dude ever got this reaction out of you. I don't care who he is!"

Damn, I'm trippin'!

China was right. It's definitely out of my character to react, but when I get the bitch back to the hotel. ... fuck any conversation or explanation! I'm tappin' that ass!

I tried to relax, carrying on casual conversation with some other famous player that was standing around. I wasn't feelin' him for real. I was only doing it to prove a point. But it didn't get me anywhere.

When I glanced back over in Ol'Boy's direction, he was nowhere in sight. I lost it! Not because I didn't see him, but Monique was ghost too! I searched the whole joint like the DEA. Gone. They had left the premises! You know a bitch was HOT and ready to die! I snatched up China and we were out! No explanations!

Where's the whip?!

The driver was no where in sight. We had to hitch a ride back to the hotel. I couldn't believe Ol'Boy did me like this! Heated, was no way to describe the anger.

As soon as I got in my room, I paged him over 10 times and waited for his call as long as I could. China tried to calm me, but I wasn't trying to hear shit! I threw on some beat me down gear and asked China to ride or die. She, of course, chose to ride. We searched every motel and hotel down the strip. I wasn't givin' up! Damn waiting for morning to come! I kept running into dead ends, almost giving up a few times. I had one more hotel to check out, and what do you know. ...There sat his limo with the driver knocked out inside. I peeped inside. No Monique. No Ol'Boy.

China and I made our way inside the exclusive hotel. I was thankful that the nighttime clerk was some horny looking, dork.

This should be easy.

I told China to lay low while I worked this fool.

"Hi Sir, how are you?" I tightened my stomach, lifting my chest.

I brushed my tongue across my lips to make things even more interesting. China disappeared inside the bar adjacent to the desk, where I stood.

"I'm fine Miss. How can I help you?" He stared heavily at my bust. I could tell sex had skipped past him all his life.

"My flight just got in. I'm tired and in need of a massage. Do you all offer massages here?" I rubbed my neck, rolling my head in a circular motion. I could feel his eyes all over me.

"I'm sure I could accommodate you in that department," he said sinisterly.

"Good. I'm meeting Robert Taylor with Unit Selections record label. We have a video shoot early in the morning and I'm drop dead tired." He looked as if he wasn't following my story.

"I'm not familiar with that reservation, but I'll check."

"The room is already reserved Sir. Mr. Taylor should be here. It's under Robert Taylor for security purposes. He's a celebrity, of course, you know him."

"I'll check for you." He didn't seem pressed. I tried to redirect his attention to me.

"I'm running a little late myself. If you could give me a key, I can prepare myself for that massage, okay?" I winked.

"Sounds like a good idea. Give me a moment to look up that information."

He turned back, pulling something up on the screen of the computer. I held up my finger to China, smiling.

"Oh, here it is, Miss. The gentleman is staying here with us until morning. He just checked in last night," Stupid said, turning and facing me. "Shall I call and inform Mr. Taylor of your presence?"

Hell naw, you ugly muthafucka!

This fool didn't realize how desperate I was. I needed to catch them fucking! That's concrete enough for me to whup ass tonight!

"No, he's probably asleep. He was supposed to pick me up from the airport hours ago!"

"I see." He pushed his glasses back. I wanted to laugh at him so bad. He looked crazy as hell! "What time will you come down for your massage? I have oils and some other things that will make your body feel real good. Look at these hands. My ex-girlfriend used to love what I could do with these."

Eww... His nails were dirty! Only for the beat down could I stand the sight of him this long.

"The sooner you give me a key, the sooner I can get back down here."

"Oh, I'm sorry. I almost forgot. Here you are." He scanned the plastic card, passed it over to me, and I was out! I could feel him watching me all the way to the elevator. I didn't care at that point.

China came up and played her role like she was trying to catch a ride up to a room neither one of us truly had.

"I can't believe I'm doing this China," I said in a peep tone.

"I can't believe you got the key that easy!" China looked at me. She was definitely impressed.

"There ain't nothin' I can't get. You know how I roll. Ya girl got skillz."

"You did that Boo." China agreed.

"I know. Its gon' be all good, because after this, Monique gon' wish she had of stayed in the 'D'. Humph, messing with my steelo. She knows I don't play that!"

"As long as I can get a few licks in," China engaged.

"I got you."

The elevator door opened. My heart fluttered as we made our way off and down the quiet hallway. "Room 112." I read the key number out loud, and then we continued making our way down the hall.

"109, 110, 111, 1...12."

TWENTY

ROOM 122

*****

SUMMER

"Girl, I feel sick," I said.

"Kick the freakin door in! I got cho back, Boo!"

"Shhhh. Chill out. I want you to stay right here while I check it out."

"Are you crazy? I came to see the drama, not to be a look-out!"

"Ho! You gon' get yours. I need you to guard the entrance!"

"Bitch! I ain't the bodyguard! I came for some gangsta shit!"

I just stared at her. China knew what my eyes read...

Chill ho!

"Just hurry up. My damn feet hurt!" She said, aggravated.

I slid the key in, quietly pushing the door open.

These fools didn't even put the chain on!

I crept inside the dark hotel room, feeling my heart beating faster! This is a first for me, catching a dude in the mix. ...and with Monique! There will be nothing to discuss. I followed the moans to a room where the light streamed through the cracked door. At first I paused, scared of what I was about to face. I could hear Ol'Boy enjoying her. He was never that into me. Not to mention having the lights on. I know I'm prettier than that bitch! The only thing that stood between me and them was a few steps.

"UUUUHHHHHH SSSS!! GIMME DAT ASS! YEAH SSS! YEAH!"

116

I couldn't take it. I took a deep breath before I slowly eased the door open, and to my surprise....no Monique in sight. I was struck. Shocked! Ol'Boy was so into what he was doing; neither he nor his friend noticed me standing in the doorway. I covered my mouth, backing out slowly. I wanted to rewind the whole scene and do some editing. I didn't want to believe or accept what I saw. ...Ol'Boy and another popular cat in bed together. TWO THUGS! SUPPOSEDLY ENEMIES, AT THAT! HELL NAW! All that bullshit they be talkin' in them magazines, and they fuckin! Damn that East Coast-West Coast bullshit!

I turned around slowly, still hearing their moans of pleasure and pain. They were so into each other, they didn't even notice me! The way Ol'Boy was runnin' up in dude's ass, it was hard to understand how either one of them could enjoy women.

I pulled closed the hotel door, grabbed China, and rolled out. I wasn't feelin' no questions, and I damn sho wasn't giving up no answers! I just made a bee-line to the elevator!

"Summer, what the hell is wrong with you! You look like you seen a ghost."

I swallowed the lump that was in my throat and said, "A ghost would look good right about now, China." I held my hand up at her. "Please. Don't talk to me right now." I couldn't talk no more. I felt nauseated.

We took a cab back to our room. China stared at me the whole ride over. I didn't care. My mind was still back at that hotel! I'd be a fool to tell anyone about this.

Ol'Boy had too much game. He showed no signs of that side of him. He was smooth, rough, and aggressive. He was a rapper! People looked up to him! To find out, after all this, he's a butt-banger was enough trauma for a lifetime. Just think, if I wouldn't have gotten out of there when I did, they probably would have had China and I killed. The secret would die with me.

I can't explain how relieved I was to see Monique on the sofa lounger knocked out, drunk. China had her answer when we made it in. She knew at that point, whoever was in that room with Ol'Boy, it wasn't Monique.

If Monique is here, who was that in the room with Ol'Boy? China asked herself.

The only thing I desired at that point was to hit the sky.

On the plane, I was silent the whole way. I had nothin' to talk about! My thoughts were getting the best of me. I was thinkin' on Ol'Boy's every move, the way he talked, dressed, the way he looked at me, the way he fucked me. What did I overlook? Where were the signs? He was so damn smooth. ...

Damn, you just never know which way the wind will blow...

TWENTY-ONE

THE PHONE RANG

*****

TREASURE

It was a romantic, rainy day as I watched Ferrell sleep quietly. Not in a million years would I have ever imagined being in bed with a man like this.

The things we run from...will be the first things we run to.

Raindrops fell against my windowpane, followed by roaring sounds of thunder. He was sleeping so peacefully. I hated to wake him.

We had been together for months. He took me by surprise, hanging around as long as he did. Maybe it was because he had not yet reached the ultimate goal, my virginity. He doesn't pressure me at all. Sometimes I feel like there's someone else but, he reassured me there wasn't. Then again, where would he find the time? Between his schedule and mine, I find it virtually impossible. Why am I worrying? It's too soon for this kind of concern. Who am I fooling! I have every reason to be concerned. Here is a man who's wealthy, young and attractive. The women are all over him and he knows so many people. Everywhere we go someone's calling out his name. I am falling deeply for him. I am about to get my groove on.

At first I thought he was kind of offended when I told him I wanted him to get tested for HIV before we engaged in anything sexual, but he did agree. Although, I can't stress enough, the importance of having it done, I can't help but wonder if a part of that request was about buying time. We both went to get tested. I

119

had no concerns about myself, but you can never be too careful. I was happy to find out that he wasn't another statistic.

I don't know what to say to him right now.

I felt like a fool staring at him, saying nothing. His breathing was so deep and smooth. I was nervous.

"Ferrell," I whispered.

"Yeah baby?" One eye eased open.

"I'm…I'm ready."

How did that sound? Did it sound stupid?

"Ready for what?" He yawned.

"You know." I was becoming uncomfortable.

"No, I don't. Enlighten me."

No he didn't have the nerve to elevate his head on the pillow, placing me on the spot like this. He knew what I was talking about. He was just trying to watch me unfold, slowly. I could tell he was enjoying himself.

"Forget it," I pouted.

He reached for me, and I grabbed my pillow and hit him with it. He was laughing, trying to bring humor into the situation. I was too embarrassed to respond. I pulled the comforter over my head to hide the shame. You don't do this kind of thing to a virgin! He gently got on top of me tugging at the blanket.

"Leave me alone!" I stuck my tongue out at him.

"Aww, come here Beautiful. I'm sorry." He made me a playful sad face.

I couldn't help noticing the protruding muscles in his arms and chest. Even with the subdued light from the clouds reflecting through the window, he was my king. He was tickling me, trying to rekindle my desires. I was ready to give in to the experience. …until the phone rang.

"TREASURE! Oh God, I'm glad I caught you!" I attempted to push Ferrell off me. He moved aside, allowing me to sit up.

"What is it Aunt Kim?"

"It's your Grams, Treasure! She had a stroke!"

"Grams had a stroke?" My heart dropped. I felt nauseous. I could barely get the words out.

"What's wrong baby?" Ferrell asked out of concern.

I was on my feet by then. He stepped off the bed, walking over to me, placing his hand around my waist. I lost it, dropping the phone to the floor.

"My Grams! I don't know Ferrell!"

He grabbed me, holding me as I cried on his shoulder, and somehow managed to pick the phone up from the floor without letting me go.

"Hello," he spoke into the phone.

"Who the hell is this?" The last voice Aunt Kim expected to hear was a man.

"I'm a good friend of Treasure's. She's extremely upset right now. Can you please tell me what's going on, so I can know what I may be able to do to help her?"

"I'm sorry. You have to excuse my behavior."

"There's no need to apologize, I understand. Please, tell me what's going on."

"M-My Mother...Tr-Treasure's grandmother..." Aunt Kim's words were staggering. "She's in intensive care. She had a stroke," she said, hysterically. "We're at Henry Ford Hospital. Please bring my niece...please."

With Ferrell's warm patience and assistance, I was able to get myself together. We made our way out the door and headed toward the hospital. He treated the situation like it was his own. I couldn't get the vision out of my head of Grams having a sheet pulled over her lifeless body. I felt like we wouldn't get there in time.

"I wonder if your Aunt contacted your sister."

"I don't know Ferrell, I really can't think about her right now. It's too much."

He brushed the tears from my eyes, and then caressed my shoulder and said, "It's going to be okay baby."

"Thank you for being here with me."

"You don't have to thank me. Everything's going to be okay. Stop worrying."

Pulling into the hospital made me feel even more apprehensive. The unknown was getting the best of me. Before Ferrell could park, I was opening the door to get out.

"Let me out here," I said.

He slowed down, stopping in front of the emergency room doors. I jumped out, leaving the door of his truck open. I had one objective, and that was to see my Grams alive.

"Treasure! Oh, come here niece!" Aunt Kim ran over to me, placing her arms around me. I could feel her heart pounding against mine.

"I want to see Grams! Where is she Kim?" I was hysterical, trying to get out of her hold.

"Oh Treasure, that old woman had me so scared. I thought we lost her. The doctor came out right after I called you." Her eyes wandered between Ferrell, who had just walked up, and me. "He said her condition is stable now. We can't go in to see her yet, but she's okay, she's going to be fine." She reassured me, brushing her fingers through my hair, and then embracing me even tighter. I can't put into words the stress that was lifted off my chest at that moment.

"Thank you, Lord," I sighed.

"Treasure!" It was Storm and Jamon, my cousins.

"Hey, guys!" I hadn't seen them in a while.

He's standing at 6'3 now, an aspiring pro basketball player, with hair down his back; and Storm, well, I couldn't believe how much she looked like Summer.

"Girl, if you and Summer don't look like twins," I said to her.

"Everybody tells me that. Treasure, I was watching a movie called, *Breaking All The Rules* last night, and I finally figured out who you remind me of." Storm smiled with her colorful braces.

"And who might that be, little Summer?"

"Gabrielle Union; doesn't she y'all?" Everyone nodded, agreeing with her. My mind was still on Grams. I wanted to see her.

"Jamon, look at you. So, what have you been up to?"

"Well you know, I'm still hoopin', I got to stay on top of my game."

"He thinks he's a player." Storm giggled.

"Shut up." Jamon snapped.

"Don't start you two!" Kim retorted.

"Let me introduce you all to a very good friend of mine. Ferrell, these are my cousins, Storm and Jamon. And this is my Aunt Kim."

Aunt Kim looked embarrassed, thinking about the way she had begun their conversation earlier, "I am so sorry, Ferr-"

"Hey, you don't owe me any apologies, really." He made her feel at ease. Ferrell always had a way with people.

"Where's Tony?" I intercepted.

"He went to see if he could locate that sister of yours."

"Huh, good luck." I waved off that endeavor. "Summer is always missing in action. It's no telling what she's into at this very moment. Family is always last with her."

"I'm so mad at that girl! Do you know she had her number changed? She didn't even bother to call and give us the new one." Aunt Kim was obviously as upset with her as I was.

Summer being inconsiderate was making me angrier by the second. Grams almost died on us. Not only was she nowhere to be found, she had her number changed and didn't even bother to notify Grams.

We all drifted off into our own thoughts for a second, then Aunt Kim said, "So, Ferrell, how did you and my niece meet?"

"In passing." The deepness in his voice set off an instant arousal that I can't explain. "You truly have a wonderful niece. I was totally enchanted with her from the moment we met." He winked at me, making me feel every word he'd just said.

"Well, you two look good together. It's a pleasure meeting you. Sorry it couldn't have been under different circumstances." Aunt Kim smiled.

"It's a pleasure meeting you as well. I've heard so much about you and your mother. She's in my prayers," Ferrell consoled.

"Thank you. You don't know how much that means to me."

As, Tony walked in, Ferrell walked over toward a table filled with magazines and began to finger through them.

"Treasure! How are you? Why is it always these occasions that we all see each other?"

"Hey Tony, I'm good, I can't complain. How are you?" I could feel Aunt Kim staring at the both of us.

"Tired. That sister of yours got me running all over the place trying to find her. As you can see, I had no luck." He glanced over at Ferrell, as he was approaching us.

"Tony, I would like to introduce..."

"Ferrell! Son! How are you?" Tony already knew him.

"I'm fine Tony, man. What about you? How've you been? Haven't seen you around in a while man." They held hands casually. Aunt Kim and I looked at each other, wondering how they knew one another.

"One day at a time Son. One day at a time. How'z your father?" Tony asked hesitantly.

"Hey, why don't you give him a call? The number's still the same, man. I'm sure he would be surprised to hear from you."

"Yeahhhh, why don't I do that," he said, uneasily.

I was picking up on an uncomfortable vibe.

TWENTY-TWO

AT LAST

*****

TREASURE

I was finally able to see Grams. She was still beautiful behind all the plastic tubes and IV's. It hurt me to see her this way. She smiled and tried to mumble a few words. I was just happy that she made it through.

After making sure Grams was comfortable, I left and scanned the area to look for Miss *Missing in Action*. I had no luck. I flew by her job on Grand River Avenue. The name on the building read; *Tax Smart*. Her disgruntled supervisor was more than happy to give me the low-down on her so-called-job.

"Hi, Sir, my name is Treasure Lewis. I spoke with you earlier about my sister, Summer."

"How can I help you, Ms. Lewis?"

"I understand she works for you."

He invited me inside his office to explain why he was upset with my sister. It seems that she has been exaggerating about her position with the company.

"Summer is a maintenance worker. She has different people calling here for a Summer Lewis that works as a regional director. Not true. And as soon as she returns, I'm giving her her walking papers."

"Sir, I can understand why you would be upset with her, but maybe if you could just talk to Summer, let her know that this is not acceptable, and at least give my sister a final warning. I know she really needs this job."

"I don't know Ms. Lewis, I'll think about it," he replied.

"That's all I can ask. Here's my card. I really need to get in touch with Summer about family matters. If you could contact me when she gets back, I would really appreciate it. I have no other way to reach her."

"Alright, Ms. Lewis. I'll keep her around at least until I know that you've made contact. After that, we'll see."

"Thank you so much, Sir." I extended my hand, as I stood to leave.

He took my hand and squeezed it. "No problem. I know how it is when it comes to family."

I just may have saved your job Summer. You owe me.

*****

"Long day, huh?" Ferrell turned to me as I walked through the library of my condo.

"Like you wouldn't believe," I said sighing.

"Come here," he seductively pleaded.

I slowly walked toward him. He licked his lips so passionately. I was ready for the experience of a lifetime. Here we are, finally. He pulled me to the floor, gently lying on top of me, kissing me all over. The warmth of his breath against my neck had my body tingling. He slid my right breast from the cup of my bra, then the left one. He gently took them into his mouth. OOOO...SSSSS...I love the feeling. My body craves for this attention. I've waited so long...

Ssssuhhh.

"Ferrell...my shirt...you're tearing..."

He slid his tongue into my mouth. I accepted him. His moisture filled my mouth with tasteful pleasure. My skirt lifted, my bikini slithered down my thighs. He threw them to the side. I'm into him. He's into me. Deeply. His long fingers worked their way up my thighs. He's inside...

Uuhhhhsss uh!

He goes deeper, his fingers were lost in my firmness. I'm nervous. He unzips. My body trembles.

"Stop."

"I won't hurt you," he whispers.

His voice gave me comfort. I feel a little more secure. I pulled him into me.

"That's right. My girl." He becomes wild. He's filled with magic tricks. He made our clothes disappear in between kisses. A smooth operator. Here he goes...

"AUUUHHH!" I screamed!

"Its okay, Baby." He continues to move in slowly. "I'll be gentle. Trust me, I love you," he comforted.

"It hurts Ferrell." Tears trickled down my face, but he continued. I didn't think the pain would ever end...

A FEW MOMENTS LATER...

"YES! YES! MORE FERRELL! MORE!" I was pulling my hair out it was so good.

I was on my fourth orgasm and he still hadn't had one. He had a lot of discipline. Now it's his turn. His mouth dropped, his eyes squinted, and I watched him prepare for that feeling he had given me multiple times. I'm staring up at him, watching his muscles protrude, his rhythm sped up...it's about to go down...

"AUHHHHH! YEAH! SHIT!" He moaned out loudly. His sweat dropped into my eyes causing me to blink. I didn't want to miss this. I wanted to see his every expression as he enjoyed something I held on to for years. He was breathing harshly.

"You okay baby?" I asked.

"Mmm Hum..." He kissed my forehead, rolled over and began to snore.

Is this supposed to happen afterwards?

127

TWENTY-THREE

200 KILOS

*****

TREASURE

It's going on 4 o'clock in the morning and I can't sleep. I'm still up! He should be the one staring at the ceiling, not me! I'm jealous. And the problem with all of this was; he left me hanging.

I wanted to know how he knew Tony! Curiosity was getting the best of me.

"Ferrell." I shook him.

"Yeah Baby." He turned over pulling me into him.

"How did you and Tony meet?"

"Who?"

"Tony. How do you know him?"

"Can't this wait 'til morning? You wore a brotha out Baby Girl." He smiled.

"That will be too long. I can't sleep." He pulled the pillow on top of his head.

"Oh, so it's like that, Mr. Holmes. Okay. I'll just read a book. I have a good one here. I've been wanting to read it anyway; a new one by Donald Trump, *How to Get Rich*. Or better yet, I'll just read a couple of my Oprah Magazines. Yes, that's what I'll do. I guess I can turn this light on and read OUT LOUD for a couple of hours." I reached over on his side and turned the light on. I was going to irritate him until he gave me what I wanted.

"Okay, okay. Turn that bright ass light out first."

"You're cursing at me?"

128

"I met Tony through my dad." He ignored my arrogance. "They were alright until Tony betrayed his trust." He placed the pillow behind his back, sitting upright, and exhaled a long sigh. "My dad used to move some heavy weight. Tony had been around our family for years. He was like family. My dad wasn't the type to allow many people in his space, but he trusted Tony, and of course Tony had some special privileges. Well, the story unfolds like this. …Tony got caught up on a federal charge in relation to something personal he had going on with one of his side deals. He was facing 50 to life, easy. You know my man Tony didn't hesitate to turn state evidence on my dad to get himself off. He was one of only a few that knew my dad had 200 kilos to be shipped to the states. Meanwhile, Dad had purchased a home next door to one he parlayed at with the honies."

"Hummm…like father like son." I snuck that in.

"Yeah, okay. Anyhow, this new crib he purchased was going to be used only for that big shipment of drugs on the low. But that particular morning, dad had decided to keep a kilo at his old spot to snort on with a couple of chicks he was entertaining."

I had my back against my pillow, sitting up, arms folded, staring at him intensely. My interest in this story was far more than he could ever imagine.

"Tony didn't know about the new crib, but he did know about them kilos that were due to touch ground. Dad didn't see it coming, it happened so fast. The Feds came barging in, and to their disappointment, they only retrieved the one brick. The other 199 were stored next door. So dad got 7 ½ years for the one Ki, and yo' boy got immunity. Do you know after all that, we're not mad at him? When dad first found out he wanted to kill him, but as he did his time, he realized it wasn't worth it. No one's worth blood on your hands when it comes to this. When you get to that level of violence, you should give it up. The game is no more. All you've worked for is now at risk. It's a do-or-die game that no one ever wins."

I wasn't expecting to hear all of this. I knew all the time there was something about Tony. I just couldn't place my finger on it. Oh well, that's Aunt Kim's problem now. I wouldn't doubt it if she knew the score already.

TWENTY-FOUR

I'M NOT FEELIN' THIS

*****

SUMMER

As soon as I returned from Miami, I paged Autumn. It was unusual that she didn't call me right back, but after I opened my phone bill, I remembered my number had been changed. I re-paged her, placing in my new number and there she was kirkin' out. Now that's the Autumn I know. I wasn't braced for her slick tongue, but it was better than listening to Monique and China's mouth. I was so happy to be rid of them. We said our goodbyes and I was out. I didn't hesitate filling Autumn in on what happened with Ol'Boy. Of course, the joke was on me, but it was all-good. I can laugh now that I'm away from the situation. The shit wasn't funny when I was there.

I mentioned to Autumn I wanted to do something different. Next thing I know I was at the Palace...

"WOO! WOO! WOO! GO B-BALLERS!!" I shouted through the loud roaring crowd.

Autumn and I sat in the VIP section, watching the NBA finals. I don't do the basketball thang too much, but I was bored, depressed with nothing else to do. So here I sat at the Palace, fakin' the funk, knowing damn well I could care less for either team.

On the other hand, I really didn't mind hanging out. I would do just about anything to try to forget about Ol'Boy.

"Are you enjoying yourself Ho!" Autumn said taking her seat. She'd been jumping up and down all night. Her ass is too hyped for me.

"No bitch!" I rolled my eyes.

"It's all good. Before the night is over, one of these ball players will become your *prisoner*." She jumped back up out of her seat, yelling for her fling.

For once, this ho had a point.

Let me see... which one of you millionaires wanna die?

TWENTY-FIVE

MISTAKEN IDENTITY

*****

SUMMER

The game was almost over, Thank God. I didn't know how much more of it I could take. Autumn was all over me. Hyped! I felt like Eddie Murphy in "Coming to America." I didn't know what the hell was going on. My mind had drifted off elsewhere. Let's see...where was I? Mmmm... I remember now.

"Autumn? Who is dude right there? Number 44?" I inquired.

This cat got to be at least 7'5. He was very aggressive on the court. I had to have him...tonight.

"Uh-uh, he's married. Pick another one."

"Ho, I know you're not talking about married! Check the one you wit!"

"My friend is unhappy, thank you!" She smiled deceitfully.

"Don't hate on me Autumn! Now hook a sista up!"

"You don't want him Summer! Trust me, he ain't no good."

"None of them are. You know how these ballplayers are. They marry white Paris Hilton chicks like you, and fuck sistas on the side. Then, soon as one of them groupies set them up, they wanna holla, "That bitch is lying on me!" I'm not in this for the fame or the money. I just want some head for the night. Keep my mind off shit, you know?"

"Whatever, Summer. You act like I don't know you. And stop calling me white."

"Ohhh, are we still suffering from identity crisis? I'm sorry. I know you wish you were a fine black bitch like me. My bad."

"Fuck you Love." She rolled her baby blue eyes at me. Autumn knows I don't feed her attitude. I just simply ignore her ass.

"I guess that means you're not going to hook a sista up. It's all good. What up with dude sitting behind the coach?" I noticed this fine cat whispering back and forth in the coach's ear. "He looks good from a distance."

"Who?! Over there?" She looked surprised.

Let me find out she's really hatin'!

"Yeah Bitch! Right freakin' there! Don't piss me off Autumn!"

"OH, MY GOD!" She laughed. "You best trust and believe! I'm gon' hook you two up!" She was laughing so hard, I missed the joke.

"What's so funny Autumn? I don't get it. What did I miss?"

"That *HE* you're pointing' at is a *SHE*!" She continued to laugh.

"Oh, you got jokes. Stale ones, I see." I was calm.

There was no way she was going to make me feel any worse than what I already was. She's not going to steal my joy. I'm holler'n at dude. I don't give a damn what she say.

"Okay, okay!" She was winding down. "Let me be serious."

The game was coming to a close. Our home team had whupped the other team by six points. I could care less. Win or lose, I was ready to go. I had enough of watching these women drool over these stankin' NBA players. They're not all that! I was even surprised to see some female actresses sittin' in the VIP floor seats without their hubbys.

Interesting.

"You trippin' Autumn and you're pissing me off!"

"Damn, you asked me to hook you up and I'm trying to tell you that the one you want is a chick! She's a WNBA star, but she love pussy, Summer. That I do know." Autumn smirked. I could tell by the glow in her eyes, she wasn't lying.

"Oh no, you playing right Autumn? Please tell me that ain't no woman. Tell me the truth!"

I was beggin' for this not to be a chick! I mean, I was looking at all the male features on this dude. ...I mean chick. Hell, I don't know what I mean. From the dreds to the masculin' tie. ...This here was a man! A dude!

"Play time is over and so is the game. She'll be at the after-party tonight. You can get your groove on there, Love." Autumn stood up to go see her friend.

"Hold up hooker! Don't play with my intelligence! You know I don't do the woman thang. I don't care how much that bitch look like a dude! I don't get down wit' dat shit Autumn."

"I hear you. Let's go. I need to see my friend before he leaves. The after party is jus' 15 minutes from here."

"I can't stand you!" I blurted off some steam.

"WHAT-E-VERRR!" Listen to her sounding like the annoying white girl she is.

"WHAT-E-VERRR!" I mimicked, following her to the back where several very tall men stood, drenched in sweat and ready to par-lay!

Women were all over the place, fighting for a single touch or even a sniff of their dirty draws, anything to be next to a Star. They just don't know what some of these men are about. But I do.

*****

We finally made it to the after party, so Autumn and I slid in the powder room to freshen up.

"OUCH! I broke my damn nail!" Autumn screamed out. She was trying to fasten her Christian Dior buckle.

There were so many famous people in the house, I felt like a star my damn self.

"If you slow your roll, you wouldn't be breaking nails and shit! Now, come on dammit! I'm ready to get my drink on and mingle with the big dawgs!"

"ALL RIGHT! ALL RIGHT! Rushing me."

Autumn lit a joint on our way over here, so I'm high as hell too! Tonight's the night to bust me a nut soo deep, everything going on in my life won't exist.

"Excuse you!" Some broad yelled out as Autumn rudely pushed her way through the over-crowded room to get to the bar.

The music was sounding so good.

"Truth Hurts," That's my song!

She was setting the scene off with her fly lyrics and smooth grove. She picked the perfect name for her demo. The truth does hurt. That's why I ain't trying to find out.

I was following my short friend, enjoying my surroundings.

"There go my baby, Summer," she said with excitement.

She was doing all she could to get his attention. I was surprised he saw her, as crowded as it was. Autumn and I were ants compared to these giants. While she was makin' her way over to him, I was lookin' around for his wifey.

Autumn better watch herself.

He signaled for her to come his way. As we got closer, I was able to see what she was workin' with.

Damn, Autumn. He was all that.

"How you ladies doing?" His deep voice extended my nipples.

I gave him eye contact, letting him know Autumn and I ain't all that tight. We can do the damn thang!

"Hi baby." Autumn smiled, jumping in his arms.

He comfortably took hold of her, kissing her freely without concern of anyone else. I guess that's the way they do things here.

"I would like for you to meet a really good friend of mine, Summer." She turned to me. I just gave him a seductive nod.

136

As the three of us were casually talking, my mind continued to twirl.

Look at those big ass fingers and feet on bruh! I bet he got a big dick.

I looked around and admired his friends. They all looked fabulous, but it was something about him that was catching to the eye. I know it's the fact that Autumn has got him. Sneakin' and freakin' is my motto. *Watch it Autumn!* I can picture riding his nine inches or, let me see there...10...

Heyyy, Autumn's my dog, but I gotz to keep it real with self. That never meant anything to me in the past. ...ain't no need to start now.

Someone suddenly walked up behind me, making me feel uncomfortable.

"What's up 6'9?! Ladies?" The big chick spoke, appearing out of the darkness.

Autumn's friend hugged the dude-lookin' broad in a brotherly love hold.

This is not happnin' to me, I thought, staring in the eyes of the *SHE-HE.*

I wanted to pass out. Too close for comfort.

"You aight, Beautiful?" It took me a moment to respond to him, I mean her!

Shit!

"I'm tight. You just threw me off," I arrogantly replied.

"Mmm. Hey Autumn, you been aight?" The big chick asked.

It was like they were long lost friends. I peeped Autumn staring back and forth between us as they were kickin it. She thinks she's slick. We gon' fight tonight if she try to play with my intelligence.

"I've been fine, Madeena. Let me introduce you to my girl. Summer, Madeena. Madeena, Summer." She secretly bumped my arm.

I wasn't going to say a damn thang! I just wanted to enjoy myself without any gay distractions.

"Nice to meet you," I said with discomfort.

"The feeling's mutual. Yo 6'9, check this out. I'm gon' get up with you later. I got peoplez here tonight. I'll holla." Madeena gave 6'9 a high-five. "Autumn, Summer." She winked and walked off into the crowd.

My heart was racing. I was nervous. I don't know why. I guess 'cause I never stood that close to a woman that looked so much like a man! I pictured her with a pussy and liked to fell out! This shit here is crazy!

"What are you thinking Summer?" Autumn asked.

"About whuppin your ass. You better be glad you didn't front on me with that big bitch."

"Girl, please. Let me say this, and then I'm going to chill with my Boo." 6'9 was kicking it with some other players while Autumn and I talked.

"You need to get a grip Summer. Woman or no woman, the bitch got mad loot and is ready to pay! I know how she rolls. She doesn't mess around. And you a virgin too! She loves women that never got down before. It's called a challenge."

Right then I knew Autumn had mentioned me to this broad before.

"How I *wish* I was still a true virgin. I probably wouldn't be in the shit I'm in now. Givin' up the booty, and for what! A death sentence," I said.

"What?"

I can't believe I just said that in front of her.

"What's that suppose to mean?" Autumn stared at me waiting for an explanation.

"Nothing, just thinkin' about Ol'Boy and some more shit."

"Oh. Anyway, like I was saying..."

"Look Autumn." I held my hand up in her face.

She was not going to convince me to sleep with no broad. That was a dead issue.

"Get your hand out my face, Summer! You're going to listen to me!" She moved my hand.

moved, but I could read her mind, I felt the vibes of disappointment that clouded the room. Excuses and broken commitments were all she knew when it came to me. For the first time in my life, I realized she was right. I just wanted to say what I had to, and leave.

"Grams." I sat on the side of her. She continued to stare out the window. "I'm sorry..."

She hates when I say that.

"I don't know what to say. I've let you down so much, disappointed you. Please." I began to cry, something I hadn't done in a while. I've always felt like crying was for the weak. "All I ever wanted was for you to love me," I continued. "That's all Grams..." The tears were uncontrollable. "Was that asking for too much from you? Did you ever wonder why I continued to make mistakes? I just wanted *love*. I can't do this alone, Grams." I wiped my eyes, stood up and walked over toward the other side of her bed. I wanted her to look at me.

She was hooked up to all kind of machines, taking me back to that sad day when Mom died. With all of this going on around me. ...I knew in my heart, I'd one day endure that same pain of slowly dying.

"Grams," I sniffled, not looking at her. I could feel her staring at me, I knew she was disgusted. She has every reason to be, "soon, you will be free from all the stress. Free from me." I walked out, crying, emotionally distraught.

Autumn was waiting close by. She followed, giving me some room. She didn't smother me with hugs and questions. We quickly got on the elevator, leaving a place that I wish I'd never stepped foot in. Grams was all I ever had. I wanted nothing but to make her proud. I had failed.

The elevator opened. As Autumn and I stepped out, I thought I would be able to put this place this behind me, to move on with my hidden agendas, and what do you know. ...Another problem.

"MS. LEWIS! MS. LEWIS!"

Out of all places, of all the people, how could I run into him, Dr. Tice?

"Oh shit! Let's go Autumn!" I pulled her arm racing for the exit.

"What in the hell is going on?" Autumn asked, snatching her arm from my hold.

I wanted to leave her, but I knew that I would later regret it. So I stopped, cursing in my head.

Autumn is so freakin nosey! I can't let her know what's going on. She would never come around me again; after the way she abandoned her friend who died of sickle-cell. Our relationship would never be the same. That's how it is when you're suffering from a disease like the one I knew I had. Everybody that once loved you would eventually forsake you.

"Ms. Lewis!" He was breathing harshly. "Are you avoiding me?" Dr. Tice asked, kneeling over to catch his breath. He was basically running, trying to get my attention.

"I'm sorry. Autumn...Dr. Tice. Dr. Tice, my girlfriend, Autumn." I introduced them.

I was so nervous. I had to think fast.

"Nice meeting you Doctor. Summer, can I have a word with you?" Autumn asked as she pulled me over to the side. "What's going on?"

"I can't go into details right now, but I will say this. He's been stalking me ever since I let him examine me."

"Oh."

She went for it, Thank God.

I told her to wait in the car, and then I made my way back over to face my fear, to hear the truth...

"Have you received any of my messages?" He asked in bewilderment.

"I haven't had time to return any calls lately. Been busy." I was barely listening to him.

I knew what to expect already. He was used to relaying bad news. I was standing there before him, trying to prepare myself for disappointment.

"Busy. Mmm, Interesting." He gazed in my eyes like he didn't believe a word I was saying. At this point I didn't give a damn what he believed. I didn't owe him an explanation anyway!

"Could you please get straight to the point? I have some business to attend to." The anticipation had me antsy, becoming irritated by the moment. The more he procrastinated, the more nauseous I felt.

"The point is, Ms. Summer Lewis. I've been trying to reach you to get a dinner date since the first time I called you. But I guess…"

Did this man just say he wanted a dinner date?
"Excuse me?"
I know he didn't just say what I thought he said.

"A date, if I must repeat myself. I was going to invite you over to my home for dinner. That's why I've been calling so much."

I feel so stupid.

"Is that a problem?" He continued, "Apparently, I'm not good enough. …Or, maybe I'm not young enough?"

"Let me get this straight. YOU wanted to take ME, on a date…for dinner?"

"That's correct, if you don't mind having dinner with a white man." He winked.

"I don't believe this."

After talking to Michael, I had these crazy feelings going on. First, I couldn't figure out what a man like him could possibly want with me. And second, why didn't he just leave me a message saying that he wanted to holla? Does he know what I've been through? Oh my God! This is crazy! I've been on the run for months, paranoid about that HIV shit and now I find out all this been about a date! I need a blunt and a few X's. I'm about to get high!

TWENTY-SEVEN

MY BABY'S DADDY

*****

TREASURE

"Grams, how are you feeling?" I asked, entering her room after Justin and I returned from the cafeteria.

"I feel fine, Sweetheart," she said, trying to hide the tears that were filtering from her eyes.

"No, you're not Grams. Where did Summer go?"
Grams shrugged her shoulders, turned and stared out the window, deep in thought.

Summer did it again.

"Justin, are you going to be here awhile?"

"Yeah, I'll hang around. You do what you have to do. I'll hold down the fort," he said followed by a quaint smile.

"Thanks. I appreciate that." I kissed Grams on the forehead, picked my purse and cell phone up off the stand, and raced out.

I wanted to catch Summer. Something was definitely wrong with her. I had to know. Summer's going to talk to me! I don't care what it takes!

When I finally made it down to the lobby, she was nowhere in sight. I tried valet, which is one of her favorite spots. That girl loves valet parking. If Churches Chicken had valet parking, she would use it with her high-maintenance self.

She escapes me again.

She didn't leave us any numbers to contact her, and she looked a mess. It appeared to me like she hadn't slept in weeks.

Between the hospital, the courtroom, and my sisters' behavior, a nervous breakdown was inevitable.

My cell phone went off. I glanced at the screen to see the number. "Hi, baby." I excitedly answered my phone, smiling ear to ear.

"What's up Gorgeous? What's my future wife doing?"

A look of surprise came over my face. "I'm at the hospital, standing out front, on my way back inside. Why? What's up?"

"Standing out front, for what?"

"Nothing, it's nothing. What's going on with you?"

"How's Grams?"

"She's doing well, thanks for asking."

"You hungry, baby?"

"Ummm, yeah, I guess I could take a bite out of you right about now," I teased, thinking about the love we made earlier.

"Sounds good, but let's save me for dessert, and head out to eat. It's around 2:15. Can you meet me at my office?"

"Yeah, I guess that could be arranged. I only had the usual, a cup of tea and a donut in the cafeteria here."

"Well, I'll see you when you get here."

"Okay, I'm on my way." I ended the call and turned back around to head out the revolving doors.

Ferrell has been a tension reliever ever since I've been with him. I feel so secure now that he's around. At first I was so concerned about my image and reputation that I questioned everything about him, like how was I going to introduce him to Grams and my friends. Now I've made up my mind to love him for him, and not to concern myself with anything other than that. It's time to stop trying to meet others' expectations. Ferrell has been by my side since our first encounter. I shared things with him that I found hard to discuss with some of my closest friends.

I had the pleasure of meeting his beautiful parents and younger brother, Rodney Jr., whom is exceptionally talented. Rodney Jr. loves to sing. I mentioned to Ferrell that he needs to invest in his brother's talent. I was shocked at his response.

He bluntly said, "Oh no, not my brother! Singing's for fags!"

I couldn't help but to look at him like he was crazy. I told Rodney Jr. that if I come across someone involved in the industry, I would plug him in. That boy can sing, no better yet, he can sang...

Ferrell's Mom welcomed me with open arms. It made me feel really good to have her support. It was like she was relieved to see her son with someone like me. She made me feel warm, like the mother I wish I had. His father was nonchalant. I could tell that he was a very private person. After what he'd been through, I don't blame him.

Last but not least, *THE BAD SEED*...his sister, Tyeisha! She's corrupt, disrespectful, stuck up, and spoiled rotten! She has caused me nothing but trouble since the day I first met her. No wonder he took so long to introduce us. He was so hesitant when I brought up the idea of meeting her. Now I know why. I wish I'd kept my mouth closed. That girl has been nothing, but cold to me. Reminds me of someone I love very much. Ferrell spoils Tyiesha. He purchased her a hair salon, a luxury vehicle, *and* continues to give her money! No wonder she acts like she does. I tried being nice to her because of him and his family, but no matter how hard I tried, it didn't make things between us any better. For example, I would call the shop looking for Ferrell when he wasn't at his home or other office, and she would answer the phone and say, "He's not here!" Then rudely slam the phone down in my ear. Every time I step foot in that shop with Ferrell she rolls her eyes at me and doesn't speak. I have just had it up to here with that girl! My tolerance level has just about run thin. This type of behavior never pays off in the end.

When I finally met up with Ferrell at his office, he mentioned he had to swing by the hair salon. I had it made up in my mind that I would wait in the truck. Well, Ferrell felt differently. He wanted me to come inside with him. *I thought he told me he was hungry.* He failed to mention he had other obligations along the way. I should have been used to this by now.

146

It was always a stop here and a stop there, never a direct route to anywhere. There have been plenty of times when we have not made it to our destination because "something came up."

As soon as I stepped foot through the door, the drama began. I wanted to turn around and walk out, but he took my hand and proceeded to the back of the salon. Along the way, he made a pit stop at the receptionist booth, which is near his sisters' hair station. He released my hand to tend to whatever it was he had to handle at the desk. I couldn't help but to notice how Tyeisha was leaning down, whispering in her clients' ear. They were chuckling, while at the same time staring at me. Out of common courtesy, I spoke. "How are you ladies doing?" They both rolled their eyes and turned the other way. Personally, I was fed up with Tyeisha's crap! I wanted to smack those curling irons out of her hand onto her client's lap, but that's not my style.

So instead, I followed Ferrell to the back, trying to hide my aggravation. Once inside the office, he asked if something was wrong. I felt no need to trouble him with his sisters' pettiness, so I lied and said I was thinking about Summer. It works everytime. Ferrell was fully aware of my relationship with Summer, and my feelings about it. He tried to comfort me with a small peck on the lips, followed by a brush of his nose up against mine. Before he could pull away, Tyeisha rudely walked through the door.

"Don't do that shit up in here! Go to a hotel, or better yet..." She looked me up and down. "A motel," she said smirking.

"You better turn around and leave the same way you came in Tye! I ain't feelin' you right now girl!" Ferrell retorted, pointing at the door.

"Negro please, this is my place of business too. Don't be trying to show off in front of *ONE* of yo' ho'z. I ain't the one!"

Did this little girl just call me a whore? She's lucky Ferrell stepped up.

"Don't disrespect my girl Tyeisha!" He chastised her only inches from her face.

147

I thought he was about to smack her. I sat down on the opposite side of his desk, out of the way, and turned my head toward the computer screen while they argued back and forth.

"Bye Tye! Out! Get the fuck out!" He pushed her out the door, slammed it, and then turned to me.

"I'm sorry baby," he apologized, sitting down in his chair looking fine as ever, even when he was upset.

"Oh no baby, you don't have to apologize. I know she's just trying to protect her big brother," I responded, reaching over his desk, tracing his lips with my index finger. "Ouch!" I snatched my finger away from him, as he playfully bit down on it.

"You know what Treasure?"

"What is it handsome?"

"I'm always trying to look out for my sisters' young, stupid ass. This salon; her expensive clothes; jewelry; cars; and all kind of shit that she asks for, she gets. Yet, she's always coming to me for something more, it never fails. She's not my damn woman. If she was, her ass would be in a chained box somewhere at the bottom of a river."

"I would supply the box." I tried to add humor to diminish some of the tension the two of them had left in the air. In a way I was serious. That girl will bring out the worse in a person.

"You think I'm play'n! Sometimes I want to snap her neck! I'm sick of her high-maintenance ass!"

"Baby, baby, shh...calm down. It's okay. Handle your business so we can go eat." By then I was standing behind him, massaging his shoulders, trying to relax him.

The craziest thing about all of this was that I was kind of turned on by the way he defended me. That was true love to me.

Tyeisha paged him on the intercom, informing him of a call on line one. I walked back around the desk, admiring pictures of him and some celebrities hanging up on his wall.

"Yeah?" He answered. I could tell in his voice that he was still irritated. Without saying two words to the caller, he instantly slammed the phone down on the receiver and said, "Let's go!"

He quickly shut down his system. Everything was happening so fast. I was becoming a little uncomfortable. I noticed on the way out of the salon Ferrell gave Tyeisha this distracted glare. She wasn't fazed at all. She stared back, sticking her tongue out at him, like a two-year-old child. I assumed she had pulled something. Sure enough I was right. We were up out of there so fast that I barely had time to catch my breath.

When we made it to his truck, he told me that his baby's mama, Keyonna, started tripping on the phone, so he hung up on her. He felt that Tyeisha had paged her, informing her of our presence. Tyeisha and his baby's mama are close, and they both love drama, so he wanted to leave as soon as possible before Keyonna came.

This is too much.

TWENTY-EIGHT

HERE COMES THE DRAMA

*****

TREASURE

As we headed off to our destination, a car began to tailgate us. The only thing I could see was what seemed to be a young woman driving. She was ranting and raving, trying to get our attention. Then I noticed the tip of a baby's forehead appearing over the dashboard of the vehicle. I assumed this woman was the "Baby Mama." The way she was driving was suicidal. The child only had his car seat, hopefully properly restrained with a seat belt, protecting him from her recklessness. This was unbelievable. The psycho driver of the vehicle behind us *was* his baby's mama! We hadn't made it a mile from the hair salon before this enraged woman was riding our bumper. No matter how much he tried to avoid her, dodging through traffic, she was right on his tail.

What did I get myself into?

Unfortunately we ended up having to stop at an intersection because of the red light. I'm sure if cars weren't in front, forcing Ferrell to stop, he would have easily run the stoplight to avoid her.

"Fuck man!" He screamed out, banging his fist on the dashboard. He was scaring me. "I'm telling you Treasure, if I pull over it's not gon' be nice. Look how she got my son in the middle of this shit!"

At least he showed some concern for the child.

"What's wrong with her?" I asked while staring back and forth through the rear view window.

The way she was pointing at me, I could tell she was ready to do something crazy. She was able to weave through traffic and end up on the side of us, where she was sitting in an uneven lane in the middle of 6 Mile at Greenfield. I was convinced she had some serious issues.

While he didn't once turn his head to look at her, I, of course, couldn't help but to.

How could she allow their child to be exposed to this kind of behavior?

She was yelling and screaming, trying to get Ferrell's attention. He was still ignoring her, waiting on the light to change, becoming angrier by the second. She was out of control! I could hear her cursing, see her crying. She even had the nerve to call me out my name, challenging me to step out. I ignored her.

This is beneath me.

The light finally changed and he sped off, with this crazy, madwoman still racing closely behind. He grew tired of the situation, so he pulled into a nearby restaurants' parking lot, placed his truck in park, jumped out, and raced towards her car. As mad as he was, I didn't know what his intentions were. I was concerned more about the child, because I knew he could handle her. I wanted to grab the baby, but the problem was between them. I tried to stare away, tried to relax, telling myself that he had everything under control.

Who am I kidding?

I had to see what was going on. The only thing I could see was Ferrell and her yelling back and forth.

Cars were slowing down as they entered the parking lot. He had his finger pointing in her face as if he were holding a gun. She pushed his hand out of her face and then made a dash toward me. Without hesitating, he grabbed her arm, trying to force her back into her car. I was praying that they didn't start fighting! I should have prayed a little harder. Keyonna tried to swing on him while he was trying to force her into the car! Luckily, he ducked before her nails pierced his face.

Now why did she do that?

That just made his temper flare even more. He grabbed her with both his hands by her blouse, tearing it! I wanted to yell

151

out to him, but I couldn't. I could clearly hear the baby crying. It was a terrible sight. I was becoming angry and impatient!

She screamed out, "GET YOUR FUCKIN' HANDS OFF ME AND TAKE YOUR SON!! TAKE'UM!"

Ferrell angrily trampled around to the passenger side of her car, yanking the door open, darn near pulling it off the hinges. He then unfastened the baby from his car seat, and grabbed him from the vehicle. The child was kicking and screaming, reaching out for Keyonna. Ferrell ignored his child's reaction, restraining him under his arm like a package, and brought him to the truck. Keyonna drove off, leaving the scene that she had caused.

"I hate that Bitch!" He spat.

I can't believe her! How could she leave her son like that?

No man is worth a child's sanity! No man! After what my parents put Summer and me through, I could never put a child through this. What about the children? They're so innocent. Yet these stupid females don't care.

"I'm sorry, Baby," Ferrell said, apologizing to me while trying to place his upset child in a seat belt in the back. Ferrell was sweating profusely.

"That's okay." I grabbed some napkins out of the glove box to absorb the sweat on his forehead.

The baby was traumatized. He was crying and screaming at the top of his lungs.

"Shhh…okay man, okay." Ferrell was trying to calm the child.

I could tell he had not been spending much time with his son. Due to the way the child was acting, I knew Ferrell was a stranger to him.

Ferrell closed the back door and jumped back in the driver's seat, pulling off. I could tell he didn't want to talk about what had just taken place. He was embarrassed about the situation. The baby was still screaming.

"Ohh, he's so cute." I had to raise my voice above the sound of the baby's crying.

"I'm sorry about this, Treasure. I didn't expect you to meet my son under these circumstances," he said as I wiped the sweat from his forehead.

"That's okay, it wasn't your fault. Things happen. I'm sure he's going to be okay. Don't worry. It's all going to work out." I didn't believe a word I was saying. The way this child was screaming. ...This is going to be a challenge.

"That's my Boy! Yes it is! That's Daddy's Man!!" Ferrell tried to drive and slightly look back at the child, using baby talk. "That's my heart," he said, turning his attention to me. "I just can't deal with his mother. She can't accept the fact that I don't want her. Damn! What the fuck am I supposed to do now? I don't know shit about taking care of no baby! I don't even know how to change a diaper!"

"Let me see, Baby. Maybe I can try to calm him down." I unfastened my seat belt, turning around in my seat. "Hi man! Shh...it's okay Marquis, do you want some candy?" He just looked away, continuing to cry.

He was becoming very exhausted and congested from crying hard for so long. I had no experience with this kind of thing. I felt that if I didn't do something fast, he would cry himself sick. So I took him out of his seat belt, pulled off some of the extra clothing he was wearing, and held him up against my chest. I rubbed his back, trying to rock him to sleep, or at least calm him down. I noticed Ferrell staring back and forth between the road and me. Ferrell placed his hand over mine, as we together rubbed Marquis's back in a circular motion. At first Marquis was trying to break away from me. I was very patient, because I knew I was a stranger to him. After rocking him for about 10 minutes, he became quiet. I grabbed a piece of tissue from my purse, and gently wiped his eyes and nose. He started whining a little and pushed my hand away. He didn't want me messing with his nose, so I went along with him, trying to appease him. It was pretty clean anyway, because most of his mucus and tears were already on my $300 blouse. It was worth it.

Marquis finally dozed off to sleep in my arms. Ferrell and I were relieved. I could see how much he appreciated me from the expression on his face when he said, "Thank you." It made me feel good. The love and warmth I felt from both of them was wonderful. I slowly turned the child around, trying not to wake him, so I could hold him in a more comfortable position. I stared at him noticing he had this cute little nose like his dad, and just about everything else like his mom.

Keyonna was beyond beautiful. That was one thing I could say about Ferrell, he has an eye for beauty. I have to admit; I was a little jealous. She reminds me of the actress Lisa Ray. I'm curious to know what happened between them. Why did he leave? I'm nowhere near as beautiful as she is. I have not yet brought myself to ask him why they separated, nor has he volunteered the information. I don't want to seem like I'm pressed or insecure. I'm sure he still has feelings for her though, but for all that it's worth, I trust him. I will allow his actions to speak for him. He says he would never go back, that chapter is history. And you know what? I believe him. As jazzy as this woman is, I believe him.

TWENTY-NINE

WHAT'S YOUR'S IS MINE AND WHAT'S MINE IS MINE

*****

SUMMER

Pulling up to Dr. Tice's home in the burbs was like hitting the jackpot!

You did it this time girl! This man is rich!!!

The first thing I saw was a wrought iron fence graced with the initials, MT. It was electronically monitored, so I pushed the button on the intercom box and waited patiently for a response.

"Tice, how can I help you?"

"Hi, Summer here to see..."

Before anything else was said, the gate began to open. I entered, driving up a half mile driveway, bordered with neatly groomed hedges. The greenery hid the house for most of the drive up. Finally, the roof started to emerge, California style.

A dream house. Just like I've always imagined for me and him, I thought, planning ahead. His place was like something out of the Architectural Digest.

I'm about to work this cat.

I stepped out of my ride, looking fly as ever, and walked toward the front door. I don't know why I was feeling nervous. I guess I should be after what my paranoid ass been through. I went and got myself re-tested; I was scared as hell, but a bitch lucked up *again*!

The door swung open before I could even raise my finger to the bell. There before me stood this handsome, well-dressed white man. His smile made my body shiver.

He has to be mixed with something.

This was our first encounter since our run in at the hospital.

"Summer, please come in," he said scanning me from head to toe as he stepped aside.

"Mmmm...a man with class." I looked around, admiring his space.

"I learned from the best."

He followed me. I could feel him watching my hips sway as I proceeded to walk down the cathedral hallway. I followed the aroma of something that smelled good.

"Let me find out you're the one to blame for the scrumptious aroma seeping through the air." I turned around and smiled.

The way he was lookin' at me, I knew I had him. He was all in. My body was draped in expensive shit, stuff you don't see on *nobody* but me. It went perfect for the occasion and highlighted every one of my curves. I was dressed in all black complimented with some $2000.00 strap up designer sandals, laced up my legs to my Beyonce thighs. I truly don't think he can handle this, but I got something special for that ass.

"I can cook while you're playing!" He joked.

I liked his sense of humor and I was feelin' what he was freakin', the boy got taste himself. He was dressed casually in a linen designer shirt, linen shorts, and matching crock sandals.

Hmmn ...I like.

"Do you like fettuccine?"

"I like just about anything right now, baby. Sister-Girl is starvin'!" G-H-E-T-T-O, I couldn't believe the way I just said that.

"Good, I figured you would like just about A-N-Y-T-H-I-N-G." He stared deeply at me, moving in closer.

Oh yeah, this is going to be interesting.

156

"Come on, follow me." He took my hand, leading the way.

Once we made it to the kitchen, I was impressed watching him do his thang. I offered my assistance, but he refused, saying he wanted to be my slave. I laughed, and leaned against the corners of the loop entrance. I was happy he decided to do it alone.

I was never the cooking type. ...I'll never forget this one time I was trying to do the cooking thang for some baller around the way; frontin', trying to lock a nigga down. ...Doing his nails, giving him pedicures, massages, cooking easy shit like fried chicken, fish... Anyway, Dude wanted a sandwich. I pulled out all kinds of meat for a simple ham sandwich. It was crazy! Before I knew it, I had slapped two end pieces of bread up against some ham, salami, and bologna; threw it on a plate, dry as hell, and gave it to his ass. He just looked at me like, *"What-da-fuck-is-this?"* I didn't care. Hell, he ate it! That was the extent of my cooking...

I grew tired of standing around watching him play Master Chef and I ventured off to explore his home without him. I reached a room that had a wall length aquarium with beautiful tropical fish in it.

Finding Nemo.

I loved that movie. I was the biggest kid when it comes to that kind of stuff. Standing in this room made me feel like I was in the bottom of a tropical ocean. Staring into the beauty, my mind drifted off. I didn't even hear him sneak up behind me.

"Sweetheart, let's eat..." I turned to him and we just stood there and gazed at each other.

"Thank you for inviting me over, Michael." I smiled.

"Anytime."

While we ate in silence, I would glance up at him from time to time, silently saying to myself...

Grams, I made it! I finally found someone in my life that you would approve of! Treasure has always been the one to set a perfect example...now it's my time to shine.

The meal was over and my plate was clean.

"Did you enjoy your meal?" He leaned back in his chair.

"It was the BOMB!"

He looked confused. "The Bomb? That's good, I hope? I mean I wouldn't want you to explode. Not on our first date, that is."

I couldn't hold back my laughter. Although he was joking, I could tell he was truly lost.

"No," I said, still laughing. "No, Michael..." I had to place my finger up, pleading for a second to calm down. "The Bomb, means your cooking was excellent. Well done, Boo."

He let out a chuckle. "The bomb, humph, interesting."

"You get it, the bomb? Good? Never-mind." I waved it off.

"Mm-hmmm."

"I can see I'm going to have to put you up on some thangs," I said, giggling.

"Please do." He took the napkin from his lap and placed it on the table.

I noticed paintings of some young beautiful sistas on his wall. He wasn't lying when he said he loved him some black pussy!

"Who are those women in the paintings?" I observed them all individually.

"Oh, just some women from my past," he responded nonchalantly.

"You must be a collector."

"Something like that. They were all very special to me in their own unique way. As you can tell, I favor women of your culture."

He looked disturbed as he made his last comment. They must have used him like I plan to. He didn't elaborate.

"Is there something wrong?" I asked.

"No, not at all Gorgeous. I think I just ate a little too much, that's all. Feels like I'm about to explode." He winked.

"Cute. Listen, if you don't mind, I have something personal I would like to ask."

"Go ahead."

"Have you ever been married? Or if not, presently involved, maybe?"

"Well, let me see, how I can put this." He pondered.

"To the point," I bluntly stated.

"Am I involved with someone right now? The answer to that is, no. I have been married once. As a matter of fact she's still very much a part of my life. Does that surprise you?"

"No."

I was pissed, but it's all-good. I am still going to work him. Married, single, or whatever. ...This here is business. Love doesn't have anything to do with this. Word.

"Angela's her name," he continued.

"Oh, so are you still in love with her?"

"Deeply. She took a part of me with her when she died."

Died? ...Did he just say she died?

I cleared my throat. "How did she die? I mean, oh my God, I'm so sorry Michael."

"Don't apologize. I hate sympathy." He threw his napkin on the table and stood up. "Let's go for a swim."

He exhaled, looking up at the ceiling. I could tell I made him uncomfortable with my line of questioning, but I wanted to know who he was sharing the dough with. Now that it's been verified that I was in this alone, it's on.

"I didn't bring a suit."

"Don't worry, follow me." He reached for me.

I stood and took his hand, allowing him to lead me to this room filled with clothing. ...Beautiful, expensive clothing with the tags still dangling from them!

Good, because I wasn't placing my pussy in no other woman's bikini.

I was lookin' at Burberry, Louis Vutton, Gucci, and St. John. ...Every designer you could think of hung from these walk through closets!

"Whatever you desire, Darling. Enjoy."

"The only time you wear Burberry to swim..." I crooned one of *Jay-Z's* songs while checking out the wear. He just stared at me smiling.

"Meet me at the pool." He turned toward the doorway.

"Where is that?"

"You'll find your way." He closed the door behind him, leaving me in designer heaven! I glanced at the tags as I browsed.

Expensive. I'm feelin' this shit already

I tried on a few pieces, and then made my way out the room. ...I was greeted with rose petals that led me to the pool and Jacuzzi area. He relaxed, resting his head on a leatherhead piece with a Corona in his hand, and his eyes closed. I loved what I saw. His body looked good! ...Chest toned up, an even complexion, lips pink and juicy...for a white man.

"Still awake?" I whispered in his ear.

"Mm-hum..." He slowly opened his eyes. His eyelashes were so long and thick.

He has the potential to get this right now!

"Join me," he insisted.

"My pleasure." I slid my toe in first, trying to feel my way. "Hot..."

"I know. You can handle it. Come on." He assisted me in, pulling me close to him.

The water was damn near scalding, but I got used to it pretty quick. He relaxed me.

"Feels better?"

"Mmm-Hum." I snuggled under him. He kissed my forehead as he held me close.

"Did those women on your wall receive this kind of attention?"

"Make love to me." He ignored my question.

"Right here...right now? Stop playing."

After everything my sub-conscious was saying', I wasn't sure at that point if I wanted to go through with this. He was moving too fast.

"Can I at least get my drink on first?"

"I want you. I've been waiting on this for months. Satisfy me, please..."

He never once looked away as he spoke every desperate word. He wanted this good shit bad! That's how men are about my juice. Look at him... haven't even tasted it and acting like he's gotta have it! If I do this with a sober mind, he's not going to be any good afterwards.

I allowed him to guide me where he wanted me. On top...

I can come so well when I'm in the driver's seat.

He slid my bikini to the side, and I took him on the ride of his life. Before it was over, he pulled me into him, releasing his all inside of me. What took me by surprise was what he said once it was over...

"Summer," he said exhaling.

"Yes."

"You the bomb..."

Got'um.

THIRTY

WHERE'S MARQUIS?

*****

TREASURE

"Hello Treasure, Mrs. Jackson. How are you ladies doing this afternoon?" Jeraldine greeted us as she walked into the office, picking the mail up from her tray.

"Hey Sassy!" I teased.

"Hi sweetheart, did you see the file I prepared for you on the Albritton case?" Ms. Jackson asked.

"Yes, I have it right here. Thank you."

"Treasure, can I speak with you for a moment, please?"

"Sure love, what's up?"

"Jacqueline and my fiancé are about to drive me up a wall! I'm sick of them both!" She pressed her hand against her forehead in frustration.

"Hold on, Jeraldine…Mrs. Jackson, can you please place my files in my tray when you're done? I'll grab them on my way out?"

"Sure Sweetheart, I'll take care of that for you right away."

"Thank you so much Mrs. Jackson. I don't know what I would do without you."

"Anytime, Sweetheart."

Words can't express my gratitude for having Mrs. Jackson in my life right now. Marquis has been at my place for the last few weeks and all the minor disruptions have wrecked havoc on my routine. Thanks to Mrs. Jackson's staying on top of things at the office, I've been able to maintain.

"I'm so sorry, Jeraldine. What has you stressing so hard on this pretty, hot summer day?"

"Well...." She signaled for me to follow her into my office for some privacy.

We both knew that Mrs. Jackson was a nosey something. Once we were inside, Jeraldine pushed the door shut and took a seat behind my desk. I knew this had to be serious the way she plopped down in the chair laying her head back. I was becoming worried, but before I could say anything, she continued.

"Treasure, Jacqueline's been beating on her Lover."

"Jordan?" I couldn't hide my surprise. I removed some files out of a chair and sat across from her.

"Yeah." She placed her elbows on the desk, and rubbed her temples.

Even though I was a bit shocked at Jeraldine's news, I guess I shouldn't have been surprised. Jacqueline has always been aggressive. Her tolerance level is zero. The girl definitely has issues. I can go back to our college days when we used to play Monopoly. One night, after I had won every game we played, she got so upset that she threw the whole game out the dorm window.

Oh and how can I forget the court stunt she pulled on Judge Martin? Her client was found guilty and received a 20-year sentence. Jacqueline lost it! She let the judge and the court know that the verdict and the sentence were a total outrage and a miscarriage of justice. The judge warned her that if she said one more word, she would hold her in contempt. Well of course, that was like an open invitation for Jacqueline. The judge charged her with contempt and ordered an immediate apology to the court. Jacqueline refused and sat in a jail cell for three days before she finally decided to apologize. The most hilarious part of it all was her clients' reaction while she was throwing her little tantrum in court. He was trying to calm her down, and *he* was the one smacked with time! It was funny then, but now this type of aggression is being displayed in her personal life and there's no one, like the judge, to mediate and set boundaries. This was serious.

"How long has this been going on, Jeraldine?"

"You probably won't believe this but..."

"Yes I would. Anything's possible when it comes to Jacqueline."

"I know, right," she said, shaking her head. "My sister has been abusing Jordan for a while now. As a matter-of-fact, one of their lover's quarrels broke out right here in her office. And guess who tried to break it up? Me. That's the last time I'll ever come between them. Can you believe Jordan actually defended my sister...and this is *after* I had just pulled Jacqueline off her behind! They're crazy! That's all I know."

"You know, in situations like this, the only thing you can hope for is that they both seek some counseling. They are obviously dealing with some serious issues."

"That's a dead issue, Treasure. Jacqueline is not going to see a shrink. If I even brought the idea up to her, she would freak out!" She laughed. "She might even try kicking my ass. I'm trying to tell you, the girl is nuts!"

"Let's just hope something happens that will encourage them both to seek help."

"And I know just what that something is," Jeraldine interjected.

"I'm listening."

"Jordan needs to beat that ass!" We laughed.

"Besides that, right now I am too hungry to evaluate the situation any further. How about you ride with me to Grams for dinner? I'm telling you, we are about to have a soul feast up in there, sista love."

"Hey, you don't have to convince me. I am there!" She walked over to her office across the hall while I called Ferrell to make arrangements.

"Hello?" He answered.

"Hi, Baby. Where are you?"

"I'm on my way to the salon for a minute. Is dinner still on tonight?"

"That's why I'm calling. Do you want me to pick up Marquis on my way to Grams?"

"Sounds good, I have to get up here and see my sister. She claims she has something important to discuss with me. It's about money, I'm sho'. Other than that, yo' BOY is ready to grub!"

"Okay, I'll meet you there," I said, laughing.

"All right wifey."

"You and this wifey thing," I said.

"You don't like it when I call you my wifey?"

"Only if my ring is at least five karats," I giggled.

"WOO-WEE, FIVE KARATS! Humph, I guess I can dig that up from one of my spots."

"Cute, Rel. I love you and we'll see you later."

"All right, Baby. Hold up!"

"Yes, Mr. Holmes?"

"Did I hear you say five karats for the ring?"

"I might be willing to negotiate four if the loving is right tonight."

"How bout' I was thinking more like seven, without the loving."

"Ohhh...that's sweet. I love you."

"I know."

How does he know?

He kills me with his confidence and secure attitude, but that's one of the many things I love about him.

Jeraldine and I left the office. Picking Marquis up was our next stop. I brought him a change of clothing to the daycare, and we made our way to Grams' place. Marquis has really adapted to his new environment. The daycare took some time, but he came around. I think he grew attached to the pretty little girls in his class. They're always all over him when he leaves. I remember the very first day he started. I couldn't get him to stay. Now I can't get him to leave! I told Ferrell that Marquis was going to be a player just like him...

*****

FERRELL

"Hi, Ferrell."

"What up Kelly." I spoke and kept it movin'.

I try not to carry on too much conversation up in here. I keep it short and sweet, with these females. They be sweatin' a brotha hard, every chance they get. All of them wanna give me some. I can't get down like that. Business and pleasure just doesn't mix up in this joint. I learned my lesson well!

Keyonna was a prime example. She used to work out of my office. She had it goin' on too, with the long hair, nice body, fat ass, and tight walls! I'm not gon' lie! Every time I saw her, I had to stick her. I couldn't resist 'pimptation'! I just *had* too run up inside her. Now look where it got me!

This salon is a gold mine. The clientele is off the chain! I bought it for my sister, but I wasn't crazy to turn over all the ownership rights! She doesn't know a damn thang about payin' no bills! So on the real; she's really just an employee with her name on the front of the building.

I know one thang. I got to hurry up and handle my business before one of these Drama Queens up in here calls my baby mama! These ho'z love drama. If Keyonna knew I was up in this joint, she would run up in here quick!

"Rel?" My sister called out to me, following me to the back. "Did you call Mama? She wanted you to bring Marquis over before he went home."

"Push the door closed." I sat down at my computer. I was working with very little time. "Tye, I haven't had the chance to make that move yet, Baby."

"Listen, Rel." She sat on the corner of my desk.

"That's what chairs are for, find you one," I snapped. I wasn't in the mood for her. I know she wants money. That's all she ever wants.

"You know what," she said sarcastically, taking a seat.

"Get to the point. I gotta go."

166

"See, this is what I'm talkin' about. What I am trying to tell you is personal. You so caught up in that damn computer. You can really make it hard for a sista to tell you somethin'."

"That's only because yo' smart ass take so long to tell me!"

"Fuck it! I'm pregnant." She stood up and walked toward the door, massaging her shoulders.

"If you don't get cho' skinny ass out of here and terminate that muthafucka, I will!" I snapped. I wanted to whup her ass! "I can't believe you didn't use protection with that punk ass nigga. How?!"

I took the closest thing I could find and threw it at her. She ducked, threw me an evil stare and walked out. I cursed at her.

I'm not even gon' trip off this shit right now! I got'z to keep it movin.

Concentrate on what's most important, Treasure. She's been really good to a brotha lately, helpin' a nigga out with his Shorty. I like that.

There was a tap at my door, just as I was closing out a file on the computer. I didn't even respond. I knew it was Tye trying to come back with something else. I had no time for her.

"Where's Marquis?"

This is not happening to me right now.

"You might as well turn yo' ass right back around and shut my muthafuckin' door, Keyonna! You must have forgotten about that stunt you pulled! Our son is in good hands, Baby Girl. Hit me up later. I gotta go." I stood, throwing papers in a drawer, ignoring the presence of my baby's mama. I knew one of them messy ho'z was gon' call her. I wouldn't doubt it if she had a lookout on the payroll.

"Ferrell, please baby. Just give me a moment."

There goes that seductive tone she uses on me when she's about to lay some pussy down. She was making her way toward me. I tried not to make eye contact. I don't know what it is about them eyes of hers, but it usually gets me in bed with her every time. I had to get out of her presence before I ended up stickin' my dick in her.

"I'm not trying to hear all of that right now Keyonna." She was standing in front of me.

I couldn't avoid how good she was lookin' and smellin'. She was wearing that shimmering lip-gloss that I loved seeing wrapped around the head of my flesh.

OOOOhhhh...Boyyy. Here we go...

"Please...please." She begged in a seductive whisper.

"What is it girl? I told you, I gotta go." I released a deep sigh. "Now, hurry up."

I tried to be strong, act as if the feeling wasn't taking over. I towered over her, as she licked her lips and slid her arms around my waist. I couldn't resist. She has too much control over me. Always did.

"You got panties on under here?" I slid my hand inside her easy access pants.

She probably purposely wore 'em to entice me.

"Sss, mmm... You know I don't."

She lifted her knee up on my desk, allowing her hairy fat lips to smother my two fingers whole. It was wet and warm, and my flesh was hard and ready. Within a few seconds, I had her touch'n them toes. She took all my anger and frustrations that I had balled up inside me since our last encounter. I hate this bitch! But a part of me loves her too. She confuses me sometimes.

I continued to push my way inside her. I was trying to break her thighs in two. Before I was about to cum, it occurred to me that she was good at settin' a brotha up. I pulled out. She wasn't gon' have a brotha' hemmed up with another Shorty. After I got mines, I made her get herself together and put her out. I lost respect for her. The only thing we have in common is my son.

I noticed the time...

Damn, I gotta get out of here!

I ran out to my truck, grabbed a pair of Ralph Lauren boxers that I had purchased the other day, and ran back inside to wash up. I cleaned up as much evidence as I could, just in case

Treasure happened to come by. I smelled my hands, making sure I didn't leave any scent of pussy on them, and made my way out the door.

Tyeisha was staring at me with this expression on her face. I'm willin' to bet she was the one who called Keyonna! She loves drama. That's why they get along so well. Even after the mess that went down with her and my peeps, them ho'z still get along. I wish Tye would stop trippin' on Treasure. I be peepin' that shit she does to my girl. She acts like someone's taking her place. I got mad love for Tye's spoiled ass. No woman can come in between me and her. She's silly as hell, though. Tye know I've never been serious about women in my life. I didn't know what serious meant 'til I met Treasure. Spending all this quality time with one broad, uh uh...that was *not* my thang. I got ho'z in different area codes! Even with Keyonna, there were still women around like Camille, Icyss, Chilli, Shantanique and Antoinette. They all had something unique goin' on. I had to cut 'um loose though, move on. I preferred married women. That way, when I get mines, they can go home to their husbands, leaving me with no headaches. That changed too. Too much of this had 'um trying to get a divorce.

Back to what just happened with the baby mama, this is gonna cost a brotha, I know. I'm not gon' sweat it though, 'because if Treasure hears about this, it's all about who she'll believe... Humph, that nigga himself... that's right. . .

Ya'Boy.... Relly!

THIRTY-ONE

WHY YA'LL LOOKIN' AT MY MAN LIKE THAT?

*****

SUMMER

"Sweetheart, you look beautiful as usual," Michael complimented me, as I relaxed in the passenger seat of his new 2004 Bentley.

"So do you, baby," I said to him

This was one of the happiest days of my life! Grams finally get to meet the Doctor. I finally got my shit together. I've been chillin' with Michael for a minute now. I was anxious for Grams to meet him so I broke down and called to check up on her after the hospital incident. I was surprised she forgave me after walking out the way I did. Grams could tell I was in high spirits. When she invited me over for this dinner, I instantly took her up on it. It was a grand opportunity for me to show off my new rich playmate.

"I can't wait for us to get back home so we can make love, Summer. I promise, it's going to be a night you will never forget. I want this to be a little different."

Different like what? You gon' let me use a dildo?

"Mmm, I can't wait." I stared off into space, thinking about these new designer outfits and handbags I just purchased, only half paying him any attention.

"I know you get tired of me saying this to you but..."

"I know. I remind you of Angela with my hair like this, right?" I turned to him.

My hair was in a style I saw in one of the local hair books. I can only do so much with this thick shit. I'm thinking about cutting it. ...But, then again, I don't want to change the Angela image I'm portraying.

Michael brushed his fingers across my left cheek and said, "Humph, yeah. It's like every time I look at you, I see her. Your resemblance... I don't know. It's strange."

No, you're strange.

I see what I'm going to have to do now. He just confirmed it. I need to accept the fact that it's the dead bitch he sees when he looks at me.

I bet she could get anything out of him. Okay Mike. I'll be Angela...

I got it all planned out. As long as I resemble Angela, I can spend up as much loot as his pockets can hold. Oh yeah! I'm down with that.

When I say all eyes were on us when we pulled up in front of Grams, believe that. There were several people outside, all having a good time.

Whose Rover is that? It looks familiar. I know I've seen it in the hood a couple of times.

N-E-ways, my cousin Storm ran over to the car, yelling my name when she noticed it was me. I was loving all the stares. It confirmed the fact that I'm still important. Michael stepped out and walked around to open my door for me. He gave Storm a strange stare at first, and then spoke. Probably because she looks so much like me. He's going to have to get it together. Tony, Aunt Kim's husband, came walking over from the yard. He introduced himself before giving me the chance, so while he and Michael sparked up a conversation about Michael's car; I made my way inside with Storm. I headed toward the family room, noticing the cutest little baby-boy in the arms of one of Treasure's triplet friends. I could never tell them apart, so I tried to avoid too much conversation. Somehow, without being too noticeable, I was trying to get her to tell me which one she was.

"Hi. That's a pretty baby." I sat beside her.

"Thanks. His name is Marquis. Say hi, Summer," she said to the child, lifting his hand in the air to wave at me. "So, how have you been, Summer?"

Damn! Now I have to ask her name!

"I'm well. What about yourself, uhh…"

"Jeraldine," she confirmed.

"So Jeraldine, is this your son?"

She looked at me like I was crazy and said, "Girl no! I don't have the patience, nor the time for kids right now. This is one of your sister's headaches."

"*My* sister?" I pointed to myself. She had to of been mistaken.

"Yes, your sister. You didn't know Treasure's a Stepmom now?"

"Whatever. That girl doesn't know anything about taking care of no baby." We laughed and shared a few more words, and then I made my way over to my Grams.

I can't believe Treasure's taking care of some dude's baby. She done lost her mind. I can't wait to see who this cat is. I would know immediately whether he's just using her as a baby-sitter, a piece of pussy, or both. Storm was the snitch of the family. She doesn't miss a thing. If I want to know anybody's business on the low-low, I can get it all from her. She did mention Treasure having some young dude in her life. I can't see her taste in men being nothing I would look at twice. So when storm described how he looked, I had to see for myself.

While I was sitting there chatting with Grams, Michael walked in with Tony, and the whole room got quiet. They must have forgotten who Summer was. I will kirk out in a heartbeat! Family or no family!

I looked around at the silence and boldly asked, "Is there a problem!"

They all just went back to doing their thing. Michael was dressed to kill! I knew it wasn't his attire. These haters were just tripping because he's white. It was all-good though, because none of them are stealing my joy. Eventually, they gave him his respect.

...When they learned he was a doctor. Then they were all in his face trying to get an appointment. I can't stand fake bitches!

"Come here baby, I want you to meet my Grams. Grams this is Dr. Michael Tice. Michael, this is my Grandmother, Margie Lewis," I said it loud enough for the haters to hear.

"It's a pleasure to finally meet you. Summer speaks highly of you. Summer, are you sure this is your *Grandmother?* She looks a little too young," he said, smiling at her. She was just soaking it all up too. He made her day, with that tired line that all men use.

"Well, you just stop, Michael. I try to keep myself in shape, but this one right here and her sister are the ones I blame for all this gray hair." I noticed she let her dye grow out, but she still looked like a redbone Indian.

"Gray hair? I've learned that gray hair signifies beauty and wisdom. And I must admit you are truly blessed with the both of them."

Oh, that's it. She's probably ready to bust a nut now.

"So you're a doctor?"

"Yes, I am. My practice is OB/GYN."

"How interesting," she said, smiling at me like, *'GO GIRL.'* This is what I've been striving toward for years. ...Her approval.

While Grams and Michael rambled on, I casually scanned the room to see if I saw Treasure. I'm too stubborn to ask. We aren't like that anyway.

Who is dude on the celly?

I've got to get a little closer so I can get his attention. That's one thing about being a pretty bitch. It's easy to grab men's attention, no matter what they're doing, *and even the gay ones,*

"Humph." I had to laugh to that thought.

As I made my way closer to him, I noticed Aunt Kim and Treasure a few feet away. I didn't want to mingle, so I made my way over to the kitchen area. I kept looking back at the guy, thinking real hard trying to remember where I knew him from. He looked very familiar, and I couldn't place his face for the life of me. If he wasn't in the same room as Aunt Kim and Treasure, I could easily grab his attention. I'll try later.

Later never came for me and the guy on the celly. He ended up being the one Treasure was with. I couldn't believe it. I had to laugh up under my breath as I tried to picture my boring sister with a thug. The shit was fuckin' hilarious! As we were all sitting at the table eating, my mind clicked to where I knew him from. He use to kick it with this broad I knew named Camille. We knew some of the same ballers in the hood. I never met this dude personally, but I remember her taking me up to some salon on the West Side to drop off her check to him. The dude is a male prostitute! All his ho'z pay! Camille was bringing home at least five grand a month. He would get the whole check! He was runnin' her shit. I stopped fucking with the dumb bitch after she tried to kill herself, over this fool. I thought that alone was whack! But I heard he has it going on in the hood! And his baby mama is crazy! I can't believe Treasure! It's all adding up now. Treasure is an attorney, best known as, an asset. She's so stupid. He's going to have her on the blink too, watch. I just hope when that day comes, she won't be as lucky to survive like Camille...

Drop dead bitch!

My peeps were all over Michael. I could see the envy that was floating in the air. I noticed how Ms. Matlock (Treasure) and her assistant (Jeraldine) kept staring at my man.

Why ya'll lookin' at my man like that, DAMN!

They kind of made me uncomfortable, but I played it off. The Doctor was all over me, while the drug dealer rudely talked on his cell phone all night. So I can kind of see why she was staring.

Don't be 'J' Treasure.

At one time I had to snap Michael out of whatever trance he was caught up in. He was staring at me so hard, like I was a ghost. Everybody noticed, I'm sure. That could have been ONE of the reasons he caught stares. It's all good, because none of them wouldn't have ever expected me to get someone like him. I'm sure it was a revelation to the majority, which was all a part of my plan…

*****

When Michael and I got back to his place, I was exhausted. I truly wasn't in the mood for sex, but I couldn't help but notice his attitude when I said I was tired. He became upset and left the bedroom. I knew I had to be careful when it came to this. It was all about protecting my investment. So I got my tired ass up, pulled off everything but my g-strings, and made my way down the hall. He was lying on the chaise in a guest room, reading. I walked over to him, took the book from his hand and seduced him; throwing him in a trance that blew his mind. I threw this sweet honey on him so good; I knew from that point the spending was unlimited.

THIRTY-TWO

TAKEN FOR GRANTED
TREASURE/FERRELL

***** *

TREASURE

I was still craving for Ferrell after we returned from the dinner at Grams, but he seemed to be extremely tired and drained. He turned over and his snoring kicked in almost as soon as he hit the bed. I felt deprived.

He mentioned that Keyonna had called his dad yesterday, making arrangements with him to get their son.
Oh, so now she wants to be a mother?
Hummm…that's a surprise. I thought she was becoming comfortable with the freedom of being without her son. He said that he would make some arrangements for her to see Marquis. From what he explained, she seemed to have calmed down. That's good. Maybe we can all try to be adults for the child's sake. I'm not planning on going anywhere, anytime soon.
Keyonna, you might as well get used to me Sweetheart.
Well, let me get my sexually deprived behind out of here. Some of us have to work for a living. Unlike some of us women that are used to their men taking care of them. I love my independence, because I refuse to go though life having to put up with a man's mess; chasing him up and down the road for that dollar. Oh no.

*****

FERRELL

"Hey baby, I picked my Shorty up from day care. I'm heading towards my Mom's. I made arrangements for Keyonna to pick him up there. You know I'm trying to avoid seeing her in anyway possible. Plus, Mom wants to see my little man too. Love you... see you sometime this afternoon." I pressed the end button on my cell, patting it against my chin.

I love that girl. This relationship thing is truly different for me. I've transformed from a stick-and-move nigga, to a half-way-settled-down brotha.

"DADDY!" Marquis called out to me, looking so innocent in his car seat.

I hate to give him back to Keyonna, I really do, but I'll make some kind of arrangement to pick him up on weekends.

"Let daddy hear you say TREASURE... Come on man, say it." I reached around, pulling at his new gymmies that Treasure bought him the other day. He had finally stopped whining, playing with some toys that hung from his seat.

"Trrea-sure," he said, laughing.

I dropped my son off with my Mom, and he had a fit when I tried to leave. Kind of made me feel good, to see him want his Poppy. This was only his second time visiting my peeps, given the circumstances. My parents don't care for Keyonna at all. My Mom hasn't felt her since she pulled that stunt that damn near had me locked up!

One day I rolled up on Keyonna driving some dude's truck! That was her way of pissing me off over something we had it out about earlier that day. She accused me of doin' her cousin Rebecca. I told her to push on with all that! That just pissed her off even more. I was too tired to argue, so I headed over to my peeps to shoot some pool with my Pops. The last thing I would have expected was for her to disrespect my Moms. Keyonna had a history of drinking excessively, especially when she's trippin' off some bullshit! This day in particular was the day that any respect I

177

may have had for her, was lost. She drove up on my peeps' grass in dude's truck; talking cash money shit to my Moms, but Moms was just as crazy as Keyonna! By the time I made it outside, Keyonna had Mom in a choke hold! I lost it! I beat her so bad, I blinked out. Every inch of anger was taken out on her. My Dad tried to pull me off of her before the police came. Mission *not* accomplished...

By the time I regained consciousness, I was in a cell waiting on a bond hearing. I was facing 10 years hard time for assault with intent to do bodily harm. *TEN YEARS!* The court didn't consider the fact that she was on our property! Or that she was committing an assault against my moms. They just seen a paid brotha like myself in front of them, and tried to jam me. I was hit! I knew I was going down. The judge was a chick too! Oooh boy... That left me no choice other than to holla at Keyonna. I went by her crib and fucked the shit out of her a week straight until them charges were dropped. After she dropped them, I dissed her! I hadn't seen her until she chased Treasure and me down with my son. Now she's back in my life with more drama.

My mother never trusted Keyonna after that. She always felt Keyonna was out for my change. Mom was to the point of being over protective of me and my wealth. It's all good though, that's my Moms.

THIRTY-THREE

OPEN

*****

TREASURE

"B...L...A...U...H.... Oh God! What is wrong with me?" I was throwing up and coughing. "BLAUH!"

I had to excuse myself while court was in session. My co-counselor on the case, Reggie Chandler, took over for me.

I'm sick... *What could I have possibly eaten to make me feel this way?*

"Oohh..." I held my stomach, forcing myself to my feet. "I have to get out of here." I was trying to catch my breath. I was still trying to figure out what caused this.

I had a bagel, mmm, and some yogurt...

I haven't eaten any lunch yet. I'll just make my way to the lobby and grab something that will hopefully soothe my upset stomach. I feel so dizzy. Maybe I need to lie down for a couple of hours. That's what I'll do. If I'm not feeling better by then, I'll try to make my way to the doctor.

"Treasure, are you okay? You look a mess girl."

"Why thank you, Jeraldine, that makes me feel much better." She walked beside me as I made my way to the elevator, stepping on.

Thank God for Reggie.

"Let me carry that." Jeraldine grabbed my brief case and laptop.

"Thank You." I struggled with the words, I was feeling so ill.

"I know you're not up to this, but I recovered a little information on your boy, Dr. Tice." She pressed the lobby button.

"You're right, I'm not up to hearing this. I'm not in any position to handle bad news."

"Oh, it's nothing like that, not yet anyway. Mr. Tice, so far has a clean record, but I still have some more research to do. I have a friend at the DPD working on it. You can never be too careful."

"I really believe it was just me, Jeraldine...Ohh..." I groaned in discomfort, but continued in spite of it, "You think I...I might be a little jealous, Jeraldine?" I can't believe I admitted that to myself out loud.

"Come on Treasure. This is about your sisters' welfare. What is going on with you? You need me to drive you home?" Jeraldine massaged the small of my back.

"No, I'll be all right. Like I was saying, Summer made a good choice. I think I was acting a little jealous." The elevator doors opened and we walked off.

"All that may be true. But the fact still remains, you and I could both see that he looked crazy!"

I forced a chuckle. Jeraldine watches too much *"Murder She Wrote."*

She walked me to my car and I was so relieved to be finally sitting in the driver's seat. I felt like I wanted to pass out. I promised my worried friend that I would call her later. She could be almost as bad as Grams at times. I decided to go to Ferrell's. His place was closer. Plus I could've used a little tender loving care. I was sure it would make me feel better.

"The customer you've called is either out of the area or is not available at this time. Please try your call again later," the recorded operator voice spoke. I tried his office. No response. So I left a message with his secretary, informing him that I could be reached at his place. Hopefully he will retrieve my message and meet me there soon.

THIRTY-FOUR

CURTAINS

*****

A couple of hours after Keyonna picked up Marquis, she called and left Ferrell a message, urgently demanding him to come see about their son, claiming that he had a high temperature. Her voice was in shambles. Ferrell had just retrieved all his messages from his voice mail. A fever alone wouldn't have warranted his immediate attention, but the tone in her voice did. It sounded serious, like something was really wrong with Marquis. Ferrell, who had been on his way to meet Treasure, immediately made a U-turn to go see about his son.

During the weeks Ferrell had Marquis, he'd grown attached to him. He would lose it if something were to happen to his son. Ferrell was racing through traffic with his mind only on one thing. ...His seed. It never occurred to him for one moment that Keyonna would use their child to get to him. He whipped up in her driveway and jumped out the Rover, rushing to see about his son. Entering her space with his set of keys, he headed toward Marquis' room.

"KEYONNA!" He called out as he raced up the steps of the luxurious space they once shared.

"I'm in here Ferrell." She came out of her bedroom, following behind him as he walked into Marquis' room.

"Is my son in here?"

Ferrell, breathing hard, pushed the door open, only to see that Marquis was resting peacefully. He quietly eased up to him in his circular oak cradle. He couldn't help but to rub his fingers through Marquis' rich, curly mane that he inherited from him. Keyonna stood at the entrance in her designer robe, purposely allowing her nicely firm breast to show.

181

"I gave him something to bring his fever down. He's been out ever since."

"Is that right?" His tone was suspicious. "This lil' nigga looks fine to me. I can't tell if anything was *ever* bothering him. You made it sound like it was something serious on my answering service. You playin' games with me girl?" Ferrell shot her an annoyed stare.

"Baby, he was...if you could've only been here an hour ago. He was screaming and crying. He wouldn't let me put him down! What have ya'll done to my baby?" She tried to flip the script.

"Keyonna, don't go there. And lower your voice before you wake him up."

"Listen Rel. I don't want to argue with you. I just needed you to be here. I was scared. I didn't know what to do," she whined. She was putting up a good front. Ferrell was beginning to let his guard down.

"Close your robe up, titties all hanging out and shit." He walked toward her. "Let's take this conversation to the bedroom. I don't want to disturb my son." They both headed into the spacious room to talk.

"Where you get this?"

He noticed a new bedroom suit that graced the room. He didn't want to admit to himself that he was feeling a little jealous, thinking that it was possible some other cat was looking out for his baby's mama.

"You know I had to get my hustle on. You haven't been around."

"Whatever, Keyonna. I've got business to take care of. If my son gets sick, take him to the hospital and hit me up. I'll meet you there." He started to exit the room.

Keyonna wasn't having that. She had something up, and now that she had achieved one goal, getting him there, she has to set the other one in motion.

"Ferrell, wait." She walked up to him, pulling his arm.

"I don't have time Keyonna." He exhaled. He knew what would happen if he chose to stay any longer.

"Just hear me out baby, please. Come here, talk to me," she said seductively, pulling him back toward the bed.

Without an attempt to break away, he followed her lead. She smiled and stared at him seductively. He returned the stare.

Boy, you better get up out here, it's a set up!

"You set me up didn't you? Don't lie to me." He grabbed her neck, staring heavily into her eyes.

Keyonna wouldn't tell him the truth, even if her life depended on it. They've been through this process many times before. Keyonna will stick to her lie to the bitter end, and so will he.

"No..." She held on to his wrist.

Ferrell's grip became tighter. He shoved Keyonna back on the bed, not releasing her neck, his mind filled with a mix of jealous rage and all the vindictive things she's done in the past.

"Ferr..." She was choking. "Ferrell st...op!" She squealed.

He continued to hold on, as he detached his rhinestone buckle that read, "Relly", and pulled out his hard flesh.

"Is this what yo freaky ass called me over here for? Huh?" He loosened his grip some. "Move your leg!" He demanded, pulling her robe open exposing her flawless body.

Her bush was trimmed neatly like he loved it. He hungered for her, unwilling to admit it to himself. Keyonna loved it rough. She wouldn't have it any other way. She continued to play this no-stop-you're-hurting-me role to intensify his sexual aggressiveness. Treasure was temporarily forgotten. The only thing on his mind was busting a nut. He grabbed Keyonna's left leg, clutching it over his shoulder, plunging his hard flesh inside of her. She moaned in pleasure, pulling him deeper, digging her nails in his skin saying to herself, *Yeah...sssmmm...this belongs to you baby daddy. I'm going to make sure your bitch knows who Mommy is.* The bed continued to rock. Ferrell released his grip around her neck, wrapping his arm around her waist. He was falling deeply inside her ocean with hard long strokes. You could hear splashing sounds as he collided against her walls. The finger marks he left on her neck symbolized the frustration he had, thinking about having to deal with her for the rest of his life.

"Who you been giving this pussy to?" His sweat fell to her eyelids.

"No...no...nobody Ferrell. I've been a good girl." She lied. Keyonna gets her hustle on, no doubt. The fellas be all over her. Getting her bills paid has never been a problem. She has a list of men waiting to pay each one.

Ferrell pulled out, easing down to taste the honey that poured from her love. He devoured her, making Keyonna go crazy, easily giving her multiple orgasms. And he wonders why she's psycho... Pulling her fat hairy lips apart, it was time to finish where he'd left off. He thought about coming inside of her, the feeling was so good, but he knew the sensation was not worth the risk. That's exactly what she wanted, to prove to Treasure and any other chick, that daddy never left her side. Their bodies entangled. Ferrell restrained her hands above her head, tearing down the walls of her fountain of love. He didn't care how he handled her jewel. All respect was lost. Straight taggin' it like it was his last.

"Bring yo' face here!" He pulled her towards his flesh, releasing his warmth.

"Mmmmmm..." She accepted him. "I like that."

She enjoyed every moment of it, draping her tongue wherever cum fell. Once he reached his goal, he turned over and fell into a deep sleep within minutes.

Yes! The moment Keyonna's been waiting for. She knew his routine after sex...Comotose. Her plan was falling into play. Wiping her face, she reached for his cell phone from the nightstand. Scanning through it, she found Treasure's cell phone number. *Ohhh, yes,* she said silently. Pressing the send button, it was on and poppin! *Bitch, I'm going to show you whose running this!*

*****

Treasure was lying across the bed, waiting on Ferrell to come in and hold her. She had fallen off to sleep when her phone rang, waking her up. Treasure glanced over at the clock.

Four twenty? I've been sleep that long? She picked up the phone to see who the caller was.

"Ferrell?" she answered, still not feeling any better from earlier.

There were a few seconds of silence, giving Keyonna enough time to finish the setup. Keyonna laid the phone back on the nightstand, leaving Treasure on hold. Treasure was still calling out Ferrell's name. Then Keyonna shook him to wake him up.

"What?!" Ferrell snapped.

"I thought you said you had something to do. You've been sleep over an hour now," Keyonna confirmed loudly. She had to make it sound good for Treasure.

"Damn! How...? Never mind. Pass me my jeans off the floor." He sat up. Never once did he look at his phone... Keyonna tossed him his Girbuad Jeans and made her way in to the bathroom.

"I just have one question."

"I ain't in the mood to answer shit! Give me a warm rag so I can wash up."

That's right, Baby Daddy, keep talking, she smirked, thinking to herself.

"Why you lookin' at me like that?" She made her way over toward him with a steaming hot rag.

"I guess because I love you. Why you make love to me knowing damn well you going back to that new bitch. What's her name again, Treasure? I don't want that ho around my son, Ferrell!"

"Keyonna, I'm not going to feed into that shit you just said. Check it, from now on...when I want to see my son, I'll make arrangements. I'm not fucking with you no more."

"You'll come back. You always do." She secretly glanced over at the phone to see if it was still on. *Yup, the bitch is still listening!* She thought.

"I don't want your ass! You know what Keyonna! You love drama and I don't have time for your shit!" He said as he wiped her juice from his flesh, slid his boxers and jeans back on, and stood to his feet.

"Oh, 4-real 4-real? I got'chu player! Hold up, before you go, I need a few dollars to buy my little man some gear." He looked at her, lying across the bed. That's when he realized that she was not worth the risk of losing Treasure. He pulled a couple of C-Notes out of his pocket, tossing it on the bed.

"You fucked me real good Ferrell," she said, playing with her nipples. "But I like the way we did it in the back of the salon the other day. You know I like that kind of shit. Was my baby with that bitch while you had me bent over on your desk ramming your flesh up in me?" She asked sarcastically.

He ignored her. He knew it wouldn't have been worth going there. He nodded his head, and picked up his cell phone to leave. He glanced at it, feeling a vibe that something wasn't right, but he just shook it off, stopping in Marquis' room on his way out.

"Daddy love you man." He kneeled down, kissed Marquis on the forehead, and headed out to meet up with Treasure, still unaware of the setup.

Treasure had heard all she needed to hear. She was tormented, confused, not knowing what to do next. Her first reaction was to destroy his place, but she was too weak. She forced herself up out of the bed, snatching up her things, making her way out of his home.

"YOU BASTARD!!! I LOVED YOU! I GAVE YOU A PART OF ME! HOW COULD YOU HURT ME LIKE THIS!!!?" Treasure was yelling, beating her fist against the dashboard.

She pulled out of the driveway, almost hitting a teenager on his bike. In her mind, she knew she couldn't forgive him after this. It was over and there was nothing he could say or do to change that!

*****

"Ms. Lewis? How are you? Are you feeling any better?" The doctor asked, re-entering the examination room.

"Not really." Treasure responded.

Her eyes were swollen and red from all the tears she had cried on her way over to the hospital.

"Ms. Lewis, I don't know how to say this..." The doctor dropped his head to the floor.

The only thing she could think of after what she had been through was that Ferrell had given her something that penicillin couldn't cure.

"Tell me what? Please, I need to know."

"It's nothing terminal Ms. Lewis, if that's your concern. But it is something that could bind you and your partner together for the next eighteen years." Treasure knew what was next, and she wasn't ready to hear it.

"I'm pregnant?" She looked surprised.

"With triplets!"

"WHAT!"

The doctor laughed. "Just kidding."

The doctor noticed she was upset when she came into his office. He just was trying to add a little humor to the situation.

"Please. Don't scare me like that," she said, holding her chest. "You almost gave me a heart attack. So, I'm not pregnant?"

"Oh yes, you're definitely pregnant, but it's a little too early to determine how many you've been blessed with."

Treasure couldn't believe what she was hearing. Just when she thought it was over, the drama begins...

THIRTY-FIVE

THOUGHTLESS LOVE

*****

"Black," Tyeisha spoke nervously. "I told my brother I was pregnant." She knows her brother despises her man, and vice versa. Tyeisha set herself up for one of Black's callous comments.

"Oh yeah, well, did you tell him I don't want the muthafucka?" He said with no remorse, placing 20 G'z she had just given him in a safe. He simply has no respect for her.

"Why do you treat me like this? I give you everything, Black!"

"TYE, Shut the fuck up! I'm not beat for all that whining right now!" He blew her off, walking away to the bedroom, separating himself from her by slamming the door.

She just stood her pitiful ass in the middle of their living room floor, pouting. The girl was so used to having her way, not ever knowing what the word NO meant. Now she's having a hard time. Black doesn't cater to Tyeisha's needs like her brother, Ferrell. She's only good for the money, some head, and that ass.

Black's not as wealthy as the big bro', but he does have a little sumthin'-sumthin', thanks to Ferrell. Tyeisha has been lying to her brother, taking large loans, and passing it straight down to that pimp-juice nigga, Black. Whispering in her ear every lie she wants to hear, she's completely unaware that Black's been using damn near every dime to keep his drugs floating through the hood. He laid one of his famous lies on her, "Baby, you know I been trying to get my record label off the ground. Show daddy some love." In her eyes, he's one of the most honest guys she'd ever messed with.

"Tye!" He yelled from the bedroom.

"Yeah...wha'sup baby," she responded, wiping the tears away on the sleeve of her robe.

She walked to the door and eased it opened. Black laid naked across his custom made waterbed that she'd paid for. Tyeisha hoped that he would respect their space, meaning, "I don't want any other bitches in my shit!" She wasn't aware that her dawg, her best friend, the one she shared her bedroom secrets with, Fatima, was creeping with Black every chance she got. She was smooth with it, waiting for Tyeisha to have wall-to-wall clients, then slither her snake ass around the way to see Black. The dick gotz to be lovely, because Fatima was far too familiar with the fact that Black wasn't the one holding the dough. Tyeisha would never suspect her; they hung too tight for Fatima to find the time.

"Come here girl," Black demanded, stroking his flesh in one hand, while the other was propped under his head.

Tiesha knew what Black wanted, and she was always willing to satisfy him. *Foolish love.* She dropped her robe to the floor and like a Panther she exotically crawled toward him taking his flesh in her mouth, leaving him with nothing but P-L-E-A-S-U-R-E...

THIRTY-SIX

PENALTY

*****

Ferrell had no respect for someone like Black. They've exchanged words on several occasions, mainly Ferrell leading in the argument. With all that, it didn't change the way Black treated Tyeisha.

Ferrell couldn't control who his sister slept with; he knew she was a ho. Ever since she had sex with his boy El, shit hasn't been the same. Ferrell looks at Tyeisha in a totally different way now...

It was some straight Super fly shit how Ferrell caught Tyeisha and El. El was loyal when it came to business, but with Ferrell being one of Detroit's largest distributors during this time; he had to be careful with the company he kept. Ferrell was the man behind the scenes. No one knew who or where that good dope on the streets was coming from. In order for someone to deal with him, they had to undergo an extensive process. Since he was investing a lot of his time into El, he decided that he needed to have him checked out before they did any further business together. Ferrell purchased El a new Hummer for his birthday, providing the perfect opportunity to have him checked out.

Before handing over the truck, Ferrell had it plushed out with all the fabulous things like; surround sound, DVD player, and much more. Inside all the love that graced the beautiful truck, were bug devices. Ferrell wasn't searching for disappointment in his friend, he desperately wanted to be proven wrong, but since his old dude got caught up in the game, he had to be careful.

Well El got disqualified, not because Ferrell felt he was untrustworthy to the game, but because of something else he heard

190

on them tapes...Tyeisha and El gettin' their groove on! Words couldn't convey Ferrell's anger behind the humiliation. He didn't play around when it came to his family or freedom. After that, it was hard for anyone outside family to get within two feet of him.

In spite of all that, Tyiesha was still his little sister. He felt compelled to take care of her, protect her. She's spoiled and self-centered, and Ferrell has come to a point where he has to let her grow. He's tired of loving her too much.

So when Black came into play, he lost it! Ferrell knew his kind because he dealt with guys like him on the daily. Black was trouble; and definitely nothing he would approve of for his sister. At one time, Ferrell contemplated killing Black, but now he has a different outlook on things. Ferrell hoped that one-day, if not too late, Tyeisha would open her eyes to the conniving human being that Black was. Now, learning of her pregnancy, the fall was soon to come...

THIRTY-SEVEN

NAÏVE

*****

"Oh, Tye! I'm about to cum!" Black was jamming his flesh down her throat ready to explode.

His legs were gapped open; on his back he laid like the punk he was. He had her face smothered in between his thighs, gripping her head tightly.

"Swallow it Tye!" She couldn't do anything but accept his sperm.

"Mmmm," she mumbled, from the salty taste in her mouth. She swallowed the majority, but the after taste still remained in the depths of her throat.

"Good isn't it!" He said, laughing as she pulled away.

Black ass nigga! I hate...I love you so much!

She glanced up at him, questioning herself about the love she has for this fool. *Why am I so caught up with this black muthafucka?*

Tyiesha fell for a fine chocolate nigga in a black 2004 convertible 'Vette. That's what caught her attention. Since then, she's been a victim of foolish love. She's been on lock with Black going on a year now, dealing with the same shit, same drama. And she thinks he loves her. Instead of waiting on him to propose to her, she initiated it. Like most dogs that wouldn't marry a ho, he told her she had to prove her loyalty; meaning more of your brother's money. Nothing she had already done was good enough for this greedy fool. Tyiesha loves him so much; she peels the dead skin off the bottom of his feet with her teeth.

After swallowing the remainder of what was left in her mouth, it was time to get hers. She made an attempt to crawl up on his face to assume the position. That didn't happen. Black had a surprise for her.

"What you think you're doing?" He twisted her around into a doggy-style position.

"Black! Ouch! You're hurting me!"

"Shut up!" He cut her off, pushing her head down in the pillow. "Assume the position!"

With force he held her from behind, lubricating his three fingers with her wetness across her anal.

"You know what I want don't you?" He pursued.

"Just don't be too rough, Baby."

"You can take this girl. Quit cry'n!" He said followed by a smack on behind, bringing his flesh back to life.

He was a freak like that. He got off on being aggressive with her; her screams for mercy turned him on. And this is love? Whatever Black did to her body was okay. His happiness was hers.

"Black wait! AUHHH! That hurts baby!"

Her screams didn't mean a thing. He continued to force himself deeper inside her tight anal. You could literally hear her flesh tearing. Tyeisha tried to use one hand, pushing his hips from up against hers and the other holding the headboard away from her head. He had complete control, leaving her with none.

"Don't run... ssss...UH! Come here!"

Black grabbed her hair, guiding her to lift up, still thrusting with vengeance. He had her breast clenched in his hands, while he sucked on the back of her neck until it became bruised. Then the feeling of pain faded, and she became more comfortable. The more she got into it, the better it felt.

"Oooooohhhhh...Black..." She cried out.

"Yeah baby! I'm about to cum!"

"Yes, yes...I want it baby, I want it now...mmmm..."

He began to aggressively push himself all the way inside, leaving no sight of his flesh. Then he let loose.

"Uuhhh Damn...Fatima!"

SILENCE.

"Fatima!" Tyeisha angrily yelled out, pushing Black away from her. Black was tongue twisted and confused.

"Hold up! Hold up Tye!" He held his hand up, while using a towel to catch the sperm that was running down his thighs. He tried to explain.

"Hold up my ass! What the fuck you call me Fatima for, Black?"

"Baby, listen to me."

"I'm listening…"

*Damn…*Black paused, releasing tension, trying to prepare his explanation.

"It's not what you think Tye…" He sat at the edge of the bed, looking away from her.

"And what the fuck is that suppose to mean! YOU JUST CALLED OUT MY GIRL'S NAME BLACK!!!! I'm gon' kill that Bitch!" She started snatching up her clothes! She didn't get far.

"Chill out Tye!" He hesitantly demanded.

He lost some leverage, and he knew he had to be careful. She grabbed an expensive statue that sat at the bedside and threw it at him! He ducked dashing toward her, restraining her against the wall.

"Is'u fuckin' crazy girl? I ain't fuck that bitch!"

"U'ZA DAMN LIE NIGGA!" She tried to bite, scratch, anything she could to get away from him.

"STOP TYE!" He was losing his grip on her. "LISTEN TO ME!" He grabbed her around her waist, picking her up off the floor, tossing her on the bed. "You're going to listen to me!"

"I don't want to hear shit you have to say!" She tried to crawl across to the other side of the bed, but he grabbed her by her ankles, pulling her back to the center.

"OH! So you want to let a piece of pussy come in between us?" He held her to the bed by placing his weight on her. "You're about to have my baby, girl. Quit trippin'!"

Tyeisha started crying as he kissed her neck, taking advantage of her weakness. It wasn't long before she gave into him. She was still in her feelings about what her girl did, and it wasn't over by far. But right now, with Black's head in between her thighs, all that other shit can wait…

*****

Tyeisha had fallen into a deep sleep while Black crept into the bathroom to call Fatima. He had to inform her about what happened. There was no doubt in his mind Tyiesha was going to tap that ass when she stepped into her spot.

He left Tyeisha in the bed and headed over Fatima's. Pulling up to her crib, taking his key out to enter her apartment. She was patiently waiting on him. That was one thing about Black. When it came to his women, he owes no explanation. Fatima requires very little, being that she's a grimy ho anyway. He just bent her over the arm of her sofa, busted a quick nut, gave her a couple of G'z to move, and then picked up the dope she cooked up for him, and was out. Fatima was down with whatever.

The following morning Tyeisha awoke with Black sound asleep beside her. She never noticed he was gone for the time he was. She had one thing on her mind and that was tracking down Fatima. She was unsuccessful due to the fact that Black had gotten to her before she could. Fatima never returned to the salon. Tyeisha even staked out her crib, not having any luck.

Fatima had leased an apartment out in the suburbs to continue her commitment to Black; being a loyal ho by helping him moves his dope. Tyeisha was completely unaware of this by Black being up under her the way he was after the bedroom incident.

His reason for acting so phony was simple. …He still wanted Tyeisha to give him the money she promised. He knew he couldn't risk losing the $80,000 she was arranging to steal from Ferrell. Tyeisha believed in Black so much that she was willing to stage a robbery at the salon to help Black with the unknown. Once that mission was complete, Black was out! …

Well none of these shenanigans ever went down because the Feds were on the case! They had been watching Black for over a year, not because he was large or doing something hellavah! It was only the fact that he was involved with someone the Feds considered vitally important to reaching their long-term goal of building a case against a young retired gangsta, Ferrell Holmes.

The Feds have wanted Mr. Holmes for years. Couldn't catch him...he was too smooth. Now with Black slangin' drugs, and Miss "Naïve" by his side unwittingly purchasing the dope, it made things a bit easier. She fell straight into the trap that was made for her. Through tapped phone lines, they learned that Black set it up for Tyiesha to pick up a shipment of drugs through a local rental car place. So there it was; the feds were aware that Tyeisha was just plain dumb, but none of that mattered. They allowed the drop to fall as planned. Tyeisha fell for the bait. They knew what they were dealing with, a young silly girl who couldn't do a prison term if her life depended on it. So with that in mind, she would be willing to do almost anything to gain back her freedom, including lying on her brother. That's all they wanted. And she was all they needed to make it happen.

As an added bonus, while arresting Tyeisha, during the bust they also arrested Black at the apartment retrieving 10 kilograms of cocaine and four machine guns. Unfortunately, the apartment was in Tyeisha's name, and Black had no problem making a statement that the drugs belonged to Tyeisha and her brother Ferrell.

Since the RICO laws, a person doesn't have to touch the dope or have any knowledge of it. These days, just being involved with someone who does is all they need to lock your ass up...For life...

THIRTY-EIGHT

BEHIND CLOSED DOORS

*****

SUMMER

"My Baby Boo!" Oops! I almost said, "My Nigga". I keep forgetting Michael's white.

I have to catch myself. He can't hear a word I'm saying anyway. He's knocked out! My lovin' was still powerful ; even after all I've been through.

I have to give it to him. Michael handles his business, for real! I never expected him to give up as much loot as he has. Ever since I had been playing out the Angela-look-alike role, he's been setting a sista out royally! With the short time we've been down, he's already offered me a space at his place. I took his offer without thinking it over. Hell, my bills were too damn high and I was sick of seeing the same faces everyday.

The other night we were sexing and he kept the lights on watching me like a lion in the jungle. I could almost read what was on his mind. And when he moaned out Angela's name, that confirmed it. But, what the hell, I was reaping the benefits. I made an attempt to locate more info on the dead chick by snooping around. I looked for pictures or anything that I could have possibly found on her. I wasn't successful at all! He didn't have anything laying around this big ass crib! And out of all the paintings he had on his wall; I thought Angela would have at least been one of them. That's strange as hell! Maybe it was the fact that the women all resembled one another and Angela didn't. Hell, I don't know and don't care, for real. I didn't even bother to question him about it. I just strategize by using some of the woman in the paintings identities and life's been grand ever since. And after seeing his bank receipts, I'm now considering changing my name.

I woke up the next morning alone. Michael wasn't in bed beside me. I got up, threw on my housecoat, and browsed through what would soon be ours...

This place is enormous! Beautiful! Still unbelievable! How did I get so lucky?

As I made my way through the house, there was still no sign of him. I assumed he must have gone to his office after I noticed his car wasn't in front. As I made my way to the kitchen, the paintings again caught my attention. "Ya'll ho'z coming off this wall!" I said out loud, giggling. I pulled open cabinets, looking for something simple to eat. No luck. I could tell he had a maid up in here before! Damn, can a sista get some Frosted Flakes or something? I just ate some strawberries from the fridge and continued my way through his space crooning, *"It's all about the Benjamin's baby! Uh huh, yeah... It's all about the Benjamin's baby!"* Making my way up the long hall, something grasped my attention. "Well what do we have here?"

I walked up on a room he had locked. It's shit like this that always arouses my suspicion. I tugged, pushed, shook, kicked; anything I could think to do that would land me on the other side of that door! It was something inside and "Inquiring Minds" want to know! Maybe something about the chick!

If I could somehow call a locksmith!

At one point, I thought I had just about made it through, until...

"Lost something?" He strangely asked, breathing down my back. His voice sounded deep and suspicious. That alone made me uncomfortable.

"OH SHIT! You scared me!" I jumped at his unexpected presence.

Before I could completely face him, he slung me around then repeated himself! He stared maliciously in my eyes. He looked possessed. He wasn't the same person I slept with last night.

"Let go! What the hell is wrong with you?!" I tried to break loose. I was just about to kick him in between his legs 'til he released me, coming back to earth. I just looked at him like he was deranged! I had to walk away from him, I was too aggravated.

"Summer! Wait!" He followed. I kept moving. "Baby, hold on." He reached for me and I jerked away.

"Don't touch me!"

"All right, Summer. I know you're upset, but would you please give me a moment to explain," he pursued.

I was confused and a little shook by his behavior. I had seen something in his eyes that made me feel uncomfortable in his presence.

"Look I-I don't know what's gotten into you, but I can't live like this. You're scaring me."

"You don't understand." He sighed with distress. "Just hear me out, please..." I sat on the edge of the bed, looking away from him. He kneeled down placing his hands on my thighs.

"Summer..." He pleaded. He had a desperate expression as he started to explain. "Th-That room is one of my worse nightmares. It holds something so tragic, so agonizing, something that I'm not yet ready to face in my life. When I saw you trying to get through that door," he pointed in the direction of the room. "I became extremely uncomfortable at the thought of it being opened. I was distraught, thinking of facing those painful memories that stand on the other side. Baby, please understand. Please."

"You didn't have to react the way you did by grabbing my arm like you did."

"I know." He rubbed the area he restrained. "I know Love. I realize I overreacted, and I'm sorry."

"I guess I owe you an apology also, invading your privacy like that. I guess I felt too comfortable."

"I want you to be comfortable. And in due time, I will be strong enough to share that part of my life with you. Just be patient with me. That's all I'm asking you, Summer."

He was easily forgiven, but that room was only temporarily forgotten.

Another time Mike...

He knew exactly what to do to take my mind off of it for now! Sent me shopping!

I love the glamorous life.

THIRTY-NINE

REVERT

*****

TREASURE

"BOOM! BOOM! BOOM!"

"You can knock till your knuckles are sore! GOOOO! AWAYYY!"

There was no doubt in my mind that Ferrell was the fool banging on my door. For the last three days, I haven't returned any calls, mainly his, or answered the door. Ferrell has been lingering around every other hour. He had just left several messages, calling directly from his cell phone while sitting out front. If he knew what I knew, he would never carry another cell phone for as long as he lives.

I tiptoed over to look through the peephole. To my surprise, it wasn't him; it was Jacqueline. They must have found my car. I've been parking it a few blocks over. She is not giving up. This must be an emergency.

"Hold on, hold on," I tiredly responded, unlocking the door.

"I swear if I didn't have respect for you Treasure, I would kick your ass!"

I left her standing at the opening of my door.

"Jacqueline, please. I'm not in the mood for any lectures." She came storming in behind me.

"Do you really think I care about your mood, Treasure?" She dropped her keys on my shelf, folding her arms.

"Listen," I began crying, "I am not feeling well, I've had a rough three days, and my mind can't take this; so please..." I was sobbing as I sat down. She followed, plopping down beside me.

"I'm sorry, kiddo." She placed her arm around me. "You just had all of us worried. I mean, exactly how did you think I was supposed to react to this. You had me scared to death! Jeraldine's been by here several times, and Mrs. Jackson...come on now. Don't you think you owe us an explanation?"

"I'm...sorry, I-I just," I said sniffling.

"Right now you don't have to explain, just take a deep breath and relax." She massaged my shoulders.

"Thank you Sis."

"I don't know what's going on with you, but you could at least keep some of these damn lights on." She stood up, flicking on some switches. I placed my hand over my eyes to obstruct the brightness. "Oh my God, you look terrible!" She kneeled down to try to face me. I was hiding from her.

"Leave me alone." I laid down on the sofa in a fetal position, placing a pillow over my head.

"No, I will not leave you alone until you tell me what's wrong." She snatched the pillow, throwing it to the side.

"I thought you said I didn't have to explain right now." I sat up, holding another pillow to my stomach.

"Quit pouting. You make me sick with that."

"Shut up."

"You shut up." She sat back down, pushing my shoulder playfully.

"I guess this hide-out situation with you has something to do with that man, Ferrell." I shot her an angry glare. The mention of his name made me sick.

"Damn, okay, okay; if looks could kill."

"He'd be dead, trust me. ...So, talk to me," I said, trying to change the subject.

"For what, you wouldn't talk to me. I didn't come here for a tit-for-tat. This isn't about me right now, Treasure, don't play. What did that man do to you?"

"I'm too embarrassed to say."

"Come on now, this is me, Jacqueline. You know you can always talk to me."

"He's a liar and a cheat!"

"Like every man on the planet. They're all dogs. I tried to tell you."

"See, that's what I'm talking about."

"Kido, the guy has been up at the office constantly looking for you, acting like he was concerned about your welfare. But, you know how I feel about him. So he couldn't get any info from me...although, I didn't have any my damn self."

"Whatever."

"Well, I'm sure you could care less about what's going on with him." She waved it off.

"What do you mean?"

"Well, I was kind of ear-hustling, and overheard him conversing with Mrs. Jackson. You know how nosey she could be. He mentioned something about his sister, Tyenisha? Tyeisha?"

"Tyeisha," I corrected her.

"Okay, whatever. Anyway, she's in Federal custody."

"She's what?"

"Mm-hum. They caught her with a load of drugs in her possession. I bet any amount of money it was his."

"Don't go there Jacqueline. Ferrell doesn't mess with that stuff anymore. I can't sit here and let you disrespect him."

"Disrespect him?! You're still defending the dog after whatever he's done to you. By the way, what'd he do? You still haven't told me."

"It's not important. I need a drink of water. You want something?" She was mumbling something under her breath

"No. I'm fine." She followed me into the kitchen.

"What were you mumbling Smarty?" I retrieved some water from the dispenser.

"Nothing. Not a thing."

"Yes you did."

"Treasure, grow up!"

"I'm going to let you have that, you lesbian." I passed her a glass of water, as we headed back to the living room.

"You enjoyed me." She smiled devilishly over the rim of her glass.

"In your dreams. Listen, if this is your way of trying to place a smile on my face, its working."

We shared some laughter, talking about no good men and the hilarious times in college. We sat back in my living room gossiping for over three hours. She told me what she knew about Tyeisha's situation. Ms. "Prissy" finally got what she deserved. Some people truly needed to be locked up. Prison could be good for the brat. She was moving too fast, and it may help slow her roll. But when Jacqueline told me that Ferrell was going out of his mind about the arrest, I became worried. In spite of the fact that I was disappointed with him, I still couldn't help the fact that I loved the man.

"So, how come I get the feeling that you don't like this Tyeisha person?"

"I don't care for her. She's a bitch!"

"Treasure? Did you just swear? It doesn't suit you Kido."

"Shut the hell up."

"Okay, now you want to fight." She placed her water on the table, smirking at me.

"I'm sorry. You win. Only because I heard you know how to throw some heavy blows," I said chuckling.

"Who told you that, my sister?" She was holding back the shame.

"No, I was just kidding."

Oops... I almost slipped. Jeraldine would kill me if I opened my mouth.

"Listen, I don't want to say I hate this girl. She's just, like I said, a bitch," I said with confidence. "Suit that!" We laughed.

"I want to know what the dog did."

Why did she have to bring that up again? I was on a roll of placing my thoughts elsewhere, temporarily.

"Well since you must press the issue, Ferrell's already cheated on me with his son's mother. We haven't even had two years together. Anyhow, my cell phone rang. I answered. There was a short moment of silence, and then I heard a woman's voice. I was able to make out that it was his son's mother, Keyonna. Then I heard Ferrell. They had been together! She was trashing him while he was putting his clothes back on. The no-good dog! Then they were arguing about some things I don't care to repeat."

"Where were you?"

"His place."

"You've been staying over there?"

"No, I fell asleep waiting on him." I was getting upset all over again.

"You see. This is the reason I chose the lifestyle I did. Haven't you ever heard of the saying, '*The one who loves the least controls the relationship*?' You can't be falling all in love these days, too many disappointments. Let them fall head over heels for you, so when they act up, you won't be the one at home sitting in the dark looking crazy. They will."

"I know one thing...if he comes near me right now, I will be in custody, fighting for my freedom. As a matter of fact, let me retain you, right now." I snickered trying to hide my pain.

"You know what? I really miss us. We used to have some good times, you know."

"I know. I miss you too. I'm sorry I've been a little distant from you guys. I had been swept away by this man who I thought was everything I needed."

I became emotional and began crying again. Jacqueline reached out and comforted me. Out of everyone in the world, Jacqueline loved me more than anything else. I began to feel the warmth of our souls reach a comfort that had been lost for years.

"Mmm, that feels good," I whispered.

"Yeah." Moments passed, and we were still holding on to one another.

Uh-oh!

I eased up some, preparing to break away from her hold. I expected for her to release me, but instead she began kissing my shoulder.

"Don't do this, Jackie, please…" It just wasn't right, although it felt good.

"I thought you missed me…" She continued to take advantage of me, easing her hand up my top, caressing my naked breast.

"Please, Jackie. This is not right, sss, this…" I found myself allowing her to have her way.

"Shh, just let me do this." Her hand slid up my shorts while the other caressed my perky breast through my tee. She lifted my shirt and started kissing my sensitive nipple, gently. I then knew that if I didn't stop her at that point, I would be living in regret tomorrow.

I absolutely couldn't go through with it. "Really…no, Jackie." I tried to push her away, but she held on to my breast like a hungry infant that was being breastfed.

"I know you want this as much as I do."

Do I?

I questioned myself. I was confused. Did I really want her, or was I allowing it to go this far in hope that the pain I was going through would subside? The way she was stroking her finger against my wetness was making me quiver. Then she entered me with two fingers. I moaned softly, tingling and imagining myself with Ferrell, the one I really missed and loved. It wasn't really what I wanted from her. I craved someone else. This was wrong! I couldn't have sex with Jacqueline, again!

"No! Move, Jacqueline. Stop it!"

"What is it? You can't say that you weren't enjoying this." She licked my juices from her fingers staring at me seductively.

Does she really believe that she has it like that?

I made my way over to my bay window, staring out. I was scared of what I might say to her at that point. I really didn't want to lose her as my friend, but if our friendship was strong, then the heart-to-heart talk I was about to give her would serve to bring us closer.

"Jaqueline." I faced her, "you just don't get it, do you? What happened between us in college was a one-time thing, and I mean that. I love you. You're my best friend. Why jeopardize that? When are you going to accept our friendship for what it really is? How could you play on my weakness?" She looked away, painfully. "Look at me. Look at us. You're like my sister. I need your support, your respect, not your fingers in between my legs. And you need to stop playing so hard. You're loving, kind, a very warm person...I know you Jacqueline. Don't be afraid to let that show."

"You're right. And, I'm sorry if I have wronged you, Treasure."

"Ay! I'm not looking for an apology, Jacqueline. Don't you get it? I just need you to realize that you have to stop mistreating and taking advantage of the ones who love you. It doesn't suit you."

When she looked at me, she had tears in her eyes. That was a first. She didn't carry her emotions on her sleeves, but it made me feel good to know that she, at this time, allowed them to show.

My intentions were to sob, rot, and stay confined to depression. My skin had started to pale. Jacqueline wasn't lying; I did look pretty bad. My whole profile had changed. I bet people that knew me would've walked right by me. Jacqueline persuaded me to go out with her to catch some fresh air. We ended up going to Boston Market. I devoured everything on my plate. It was hilarious, but embarrassing. I tried to tell her I hadn't eaten in three days. I was hesitant to reveal my secret, but she insisted that there was something else wrong. She kept watching me, not being able to put a finger on it. She harassed me until I confessed. She said she would've never guessed that I would end up pregnant, and she acted happy for me, in the beginning. Then jealousy took over... jealous of my joy...that I was about to have my own child. I figured it probably made her insecure. I mean, lesbians not only wanted to be a man for a woman, but they also had that mother instinct, the desire to have a baby. Go figure!

Our experience that day did serve to draw us closer, through her acceptance of my courageous heartfelt honesty about her aggressions, and my appreciation of all her love and support for me as I endured one of my first heartbreaking lover's quarrels. I realized I had not only neglected the people closest to me, but I also disregarded the fact that the baby needed nourishment. I was well aware that I had to make some vital changes to pull myself back together, starting with, not letting Ferrell interfere with my happiness.

FORTY

CONTRADICTION

*****

TREASURE

Jacqueline had just dropped me off, and before I could turn the key HE appeared from the side of my condo...

"You mad at me?"

The deepness of his voice was stirring my anger, so I didn't answer. I was placing my key in my door as he was approaching me.

How did he catch me?

On our way back here, I had looked around to make sure I hadn't seen his truck or 500 CL. That was Ferrell, the man with many ways of getting what he wanted. He had ridden a motorcycle that was parked right in front of my place, and because I had never seen him ride a bike before, I had overlooked it when I was walking up to the door.

"Do I have a reason not to be?" I snapped, as I opened the door and entered.

I blocked the entrance as I stepped inside. He wasn't invited, but I couldn't convince myself that he didn't look and smell good right then. He looked exceptional in this outfit that matched his bike. Ferrell always had taste when it came to clothing.

Stop it.

Denying him was hard for me. I missed him, true enough, but I had to be strong.

"Oh, so I can't come in?"

"That would be best, trust me."

"We need to talk."

"About?"

"What do you mean, *about*?" His face turned up. He was becoming aggravated.

Good.

"Listen. I have to go, I'm busy." That just set him off!

"Move girl!" He pushed his way through.

"Leave Ferrell, please!"

"You got some nigga up in here or something?" He snapped.

No he didn't!

"And if I did?" I clenched my teeth. I was pissed at him, accusing me of someone being in my place. He's the liar, not me! "I don't have to answer that."

He went off, walking through my place like he owned it! I knew then this was going to be serious.

"Listen, I'm not here to play any games with you, Treasure!" He was moving in my direction.

Now it's time to show him the dark side.

"Let me make this clear!" I placed my hair in a ponytail and kicked off my shoes. "This is my place! If I choose to bring another man up in here, I can. I own this. I pay the bills, and you and I are no longer together! Now get out!" I pointed to the door. He stepped up to me and I involuntarily reacted defensively.

"Who the fuck..." He attempted to ask before I smacked him. He reached for me in rage. I tried to run, dashing for my room to lock him out!

"Come here!" He grabbed my blouse tearing it from my body. "I want a muthafuckin' explanation from you girl!" He restrained me. I broke down at that point.

"Do you really? Okay, let's see. Where shall I begin? Oh, I know... right here." He stared at me, confused, slowly releasing his grip.

"The last time I heard your voice Ferrell...was when you had just got out of bed from fucking Keyonna! Remember! Do you! I'm sure you do."

His eyes read CAUGHT! I snatched away from him, walking over; pushing the picture we took together off the shelf!

"I don't know…"

"I wish the fuck you would!" I got up on him with my finger in his face.

"Lower your voice and move your muthafuckin' finger out of my face."

"What! Nigga are you crazy!" I lost it, trying to tear his face off! He knew it was time to confess. I wasn't trying to hear nothing other than the truth at that point.

"How did you…?"

"Get the HELL OUT!" I was yelling and fighting him. He held onto me to avoid my cat claws scratching him. I wanted some of his flesh! "How did I know? Your cell phone!" I said, crying. "I heard you two. I thought you loved me! You told me you loved me Ferrell. I trusted you!"

I was now crying hard. He pulled me into him, trying to hold me, apologizing. I didn't want that right then. I wanted to fight! But the longer he forcefully held me, kissing me, whispering to me, telling me how much he was sorry, I became calm. What made me let him in was when I saw him crying too.

After a few moments or so of listening to him explaining and apologizing, I fell, weak. He picked me up, kissing me passionately, slowly, carrying me to my bed, stripping me from what ever was left on my body. I gave in, totally contradicting myself. The strangest thing was, the way he made love to me was like no other time, it was different… intense. Good. He took my vagina into his mouth, forcing an orgasm so strong that I fought him to avoid the feeling. Then he kissed the tip of my clitoris after sending me to home base and rose up on top sliding his flesh inside my craving tunnel. I was lost in his strokes. He knew what he was doing, and I was sure he had done this many times before. Either way I enjoyed him and I forgave him. We cried together; we moaned together, exchanging 'I love yous' continuously.

"Wh-why did I…ss, mmm… let you back in?" I moaned.

"I love you." He gently bit my bottom lip.

211

"No you don't. You don't know what love is."

"Marry me." He was on his way, I could feel it. His orgasm was soon to reach its peak.

"No," I answered him, while pushing myself against him. He felt so good.

"Why?" He sucked my neck.

"I s-s-s-said no."

"I'll make it up to you."

"How?"

"You'll see....uhh...sss oh, Treasure."

"Ferrell..." I whispered in his ear. "I have something else to say."

"I'm getting ready to cum, what? You cumin' too?"

"No...I'm pregnant..."

"OOOOHHHHHHHHH!! MY GOD..."

FORTY-ONE

99 PERCENT CONVICTION RATE

✱✱✱✱✱

The federal agent slammed his fist down on the table. He was aggravated with Tyeisha's attitude. She wasn't cooperating with him at all.

"You're a stubborn little B...." One of the other agents held his hand up to stop the other from cursing. They had her hemmed up with no attorney present, in a tight interrogation room, trying to intimidate her.

Where the fuck is my attorney, Ferrell?!

She was upset with her brother. Tyeisha seen no reason why Ferrell hadn't retained her an attorney by now. As far as the agents, they knew this was the sister of Ferrell Holmes, the elusive one, the one they could never catch in the past. She was very arrogant and has a little common sense when it comes to authority figures. Not anything like the way she dealt with her men. They knew she wasn't a dope dealer. She was too naïve.

"If you Boyz will excuse me, I would like to be sent back to my cell. I have *no* love for you!" She sucked her teeth, winked, favoring the late, beautiful *Aaliyah,* as she stood to her feet.

"We are going to hang you Holmes!" The agent snapped.

"Oh yeah...something like what your ancestors been doing to my people for centuries."

"This Bitch!" That slipped.

"Milton, Milton, careful. You know how we deal with tough criminals like this."

"Yeah," he sighed angrily. "You're right. Call the guard! Get her out of my face! She might as well get used to her home

213

here, being that it's going to be her solitude for the rest of her life." He smirked.

"Is this the time when I'm supposed to break down? You know, like on TV?" She sarcastically inquires.

They just stared at her with a vindictive smile. She just folded her arms and returned the same stare and smirk.

The guard came and pulled her out, taking her back to her cell. There were three agents that were present. One was obsessed with taking down Tyeisha in particular; badly wanting to take her freedom was an understatement. No matter how long or what it took he was going to make her world crumble.

"She can act as hard as she wants," he said, clenching his teeth. "Just wait; as soon as she figures out whose running this show, she'll come around, begging and pleading for her freedom. It happens all the time." They sat back after Tyeisha was out of earshot so they could finish their conversation.

"Yeah, you're right," the other agent said, yawning. "But Milton, you're going to have to calm down. Your behavior is really bothering me. I mean, I know how you feel, but we can't let this one slip out of our hands, Man."

"I know." He looked away.

"Let's move on here gentlemen," another agent said, clearing his throat.

"Sounds like a plan."

"Gentlemen, as you know, Black Moore has been under surveillance going on a year now. He distributed small quantities of cocaine onto the streets of Detroit, nothing major. He's really state material. But Ferrell Holmes isn't; he's another story. Do you know how many years I've spent trying to catch Holmes? His sister is the closest we've ever come. This is the break we've been looking for," Agent Washington announced. "Miss Holmes' involvement with Black Moore couldn't have come at a better time. I'm here to make sure no mistakes are made on this one. This is personal. Hardly anyone ever escapes us, and once we've got you, we have a *99 percent conviction rate*. Gentlemen, I refuse to allow the likes of Mr. Holmes to interfere with that record. Are we on the same page here?"

They all nodded in agreement.

"So, what do we do with the snitch boyfriend?" Milton asked.

"We'll offer him immunity in exchange for his testimony. Then we'll release the scum-bag to the streets."

"He won't last long. You know how it goes. Someone will either kill him, or he'll commit another crime and return to us; giving us our time back that we placed on credit for him."

"Humph, snitches. They make our job a whole lot easier, don't they?"

FORTY-TWO

A GAMBLE

*****

TYEISHA

"TYEISHA HOLMES! YOU HAVE A VISIT!" The officer called over the intercom.

I rushed back to my square to wash-up and grab my nametag so they wouldn't sweat me once I got down to the visiting area. They've had us on lock down in our pod after what happened in the male unit above us. I was relieved they let us out for recount. I can't stand these Robo Cops up in this bitch. I could tell they were punks growing up. Now that they have a little authority, they on some control trip!

Damn, my head still hurts after I allowed this dike to braid it for me. She probably did it on purpose. She had been actin' a lil shady since I went off on her for coming on to me! I told her to chill though, because if my ass got life, I was gon' make her my wife.

Once I reached the booth, I was so happy to see my brother's face, I broke!

"Don't cry Shorty. Your brother is going to get you out of this shit baby. Hold tight."

"How?" I said, crying. "They wouldn't give me a bond. They said I was a flight risk!" I wiped my eyes with my sleeve.

"Look, check this out...I hired you one of the best damn attorneys out here."

"Who? Johnny Cochran?" I asked, sniffling, happily assured.

"Johnny Cochran?" He chuckled under his breath. "Naw baby, we talkin' better than him, much better. Listen Tye, let me tell you how most of these high profile attorneys are that have made a name for themselves. They charge you a high retainer's fee up front, especially if they know you got paper, then, depending on the circumstances and how bad the government wants you, they might work a deal on the side with the prosecutor and judge to railroad you. So they come back asking for more cheddar, enough to split it with the enemy. You feel me?" I nodded. "My opinion, keep it in the family. That way you know who you workin' with."

I don't know where all of this is leading to, but it better be good. Sitting up in this dump will have you pondering on the thought of snitching on your Mama.

"All right Ferrell! Who's the bad mutha that's going to get me up out of this hole?" He laid back in his chair and took a deep breath. Then he spat the deadly venom…

"Treasure…" He sighed, and I lost it!

"WHAT! Are you fuckin' crazy! You know that ho don't like me! How could you do this to me at a time like this?"

"You better calm your ass down girl! And quit trippin on her! You are trying to tell me what's in my best interest when it comes to your spoiled ass! I'm just going to save the argument by saying this! Right now you're facing some serious time!"

I was steadily pouting and half listening to him. His voice sounded far away at that point.

"And believe me when I say, the shit ain't looking good. Whether you agree or not, Treasure's the girl! I'll leave you with that resting on your dome. OFFICER!" He slammed his hands down on the small table, rising up, walking away.

I could tell he was upset with the fact that I showed no appreciation to his fucked up choice. I am not feeling ole' girl, word is bond. And I can't figure out why he's gambling with my freedom like this, for a piece of pussy? He must not know the consequences behind this shit! I could easily make a deal with these muthafuckas against his ass! I know that sounds grimy, but he might leave me no choice. The only regret I would have is lying on him. I know he had nothing to do with this, he truly didn't. But fuck all that! All that money that Boy got, and he wanna stick me with his boot-leg-attorney girlfriend! Hell Naw! He better move to plan B, or somebody's taking a fall and it damn sure won't be me.

FORTY-THREE

CONTEMPLATING

*****

TYEISHA

Days went by, and I was becoming weaker by the minute. I slept most of my hours away, eating very little and having nothing to say to anyone. I hadn't called home since Ferrell came up in here with that obnoxious idea of Treasure being my attorney. Something inside was pushing me to call them cocky ass agents to see what they wanted from me. But after the way I talked to them, I was too embarrassed to kiss ass just yet. Later on that night, I was happy I didn't make that decision. I received a letter from Ferrell through mail call. I cried through the whole time I was reading it. I had to have read it at least ten times already. As time went by, I found myself in a better mood. My brother hadn't spoke words like this since I slept with one of his friends. I guess I had really disappointed him. He lost trust in me, and I could tell he had painted a whole different picture of the person he'd once seen me as. I was his princess, his baby sis. I know I fucked up our relationship, our friendship, that special bond we had. Before that went down, I was able to get damn near anything I wanted from him, no matter what the cost. I know I used to do some of the shit I did in the past to get next to him, in spite of the attention he was already giving me. I wanted more. I was greedy. Ferrell must think he's Tony Montana or some shit! I can give this to who ever I want! I don't have to answer to him! And as far as his boy... no love lost, just lust. Anyway, the letter was deep. I had to share it with my bunky, Vicki.

"Vicki?" I called out to her.

She was on the top reading *"A Hustler's Wife."* I could hear her laughing and enjoying herself. That's all Vicki does, is read her time away. She also was reading this other novel called, *"Every Thug Needs a Lady."* I heard it was the bomb, too. Maybe one day I could build up the urge to want to read a book. But, right now, I got too much shit on my mind to find the time. I called Vicki again.

"Yeah," she responded, looking down at me, hair swinging off the side of the bed. She slept on the top bunk.

"I want you to hear this letter my brother wrote me."

"Go 'head."

Tye,

"You know I don't get down with the writing thing, but for you, it's worth your big Bro's time. You know I love you, and I don't want you to sit up in that place no longer than you have to, but you need to understand this baby, Treasure's going to look out for you. I know she will. Anything personal between you two needs to be placed aside. Can you do that for me? Stop wanting things your way all the time! You need to grow up and call Mom and Dad! Don't make me come up there and whup yo' ass! You know I will!

Love you… Rel"

"I guess he told your ass!" Vicki laughed.

I shared my letter with her because she's my dog. I let her get back to her book while I read my letter again. I can't say I fully agree to this Treasure thang, but his letter overall changed my mood some. I would be lying if I told myself Ferrells' decision to hire his girl will make my situation better. The only thing I have to say about all of this is…

I ain't doin' no time big Bro…

*****

"Tyeisha? Guess who just came through booking?" Vicki shook me up out of my sleep.

"Who? This better be good .I was in the middle of getting some from this rapper out of Cali!" The dream made me not want to ever wake up!

"Your snake ass friend, Fatima." My eyes widened.

"You lying right?" I raised straight up off the hard iron that they call beds up in this dump. I couldn't believe my ears. I haven't been able to catch that ho since Black called out her.

"Where is she, Vicki?"

"She's over on the B-Unit where they place all the snitches to protect them until trial."

"Snitches?"

"That's what I was about to tell you. There's more. You remember I told you about the guard I was fucking, Officer Dean." I nodded.

As she went on, I was amazed at the pull Vicki has up in here. She be cop'n all kind of stuff; perms, cigarettes, weed; damn near anything from the streets! Vicki has this exotic look that drives these Robo Cops crazy, women C.O.'s and all, which gets her damn near anything she wants. Vicki has this mole above her lip that symbolizes a beauty mark, complimented with dimples on her cheeks. She's trying to do her bit here, but because she got knocked with thirty years, she's considered federal property, which means, being shipped to a federal facility.

She continued, "Officer Dean put me up on what the grimy bitch was here for. She's getting ready to testify *against you*, Boo. Her and that dude Black you told me about."

My heart dropped. I couldn't believe what I was hearing. But then again, I guess I could. Shit, Fatima fucked my man! That bitch was never my friend! I wouldn't place anything past her snake ass!

"Vicki, are we dawgs?"

"You know I got love for you Tye. I'll take care of it Boo!"

FORTY-FOUR

THE CORE OF MY SOUL

*****

TREASURE

When Ferrell asked me to defend his sister, I thought it was some kind of trick question. I truly didn't know how to respond! He was desperate. Guess he really loved and cared for her. Sorry, I couldn't say I felt the same or ever would.

Ferrell had no idea I despised his sister, as I hid it so well from him.

I should have been despising him.

I thought I was changing until this incident. The desire to lock up criminals was creeping back up in me. I had to question whether taking this case would be in my best interest. I loved Ferrell and didn't want to shut him out of our child's life, but this business with his sister could damage our relationship, especially if I lost the case. I was worried. The idea scared me, but I couldn't turn my back on the fool I fell in love with.

Valencia R. Williams

FORTY-FIVE

THE UNEXPECTED

*****

SUMMER

Michael should have never given me his credit card. I hit every store I could think of, Nieman Marcus, Gucci, Louis Vutton, Lord & Taylor's. ...I got so much stuff, I had to repack the truck twice. I even had the nerve to take Storm and her girls Charlotte and Alicia with me. They tried to spend more than me off my man's money! I had to get rid of they ass, but before I did, they took me by this guy Dwright's crib. Dude be selling all kinds of designer wear out his spot. I couldn't believe the love he was giving me up in there. I bought up so much stuff.

"Good lookin' baby!" I told him on my way out the door.

I dropped my cousin and friends off, relieved to get rid of their hot behinds.

As I was pulling away from Grams' crib, I noticed Justin washing his truck.

Damn he looks good as shit!

I haven't paid too much attention to Justin since I moved away from here. Justin was my Grams' play-son. He used to give me head daily back in the day. He had his own apartment for a minute until his Moms died; leaving him her crib and some more assets. I was 14 and Justin was 21 when we creeped. On the real, I would have rather let R. Kelly take it, but I settled for Justin instead. I was noticing how much older and sexier he was. And dude was buffed! My Grams never found out about us because we were smooth with our little secret. He was the first guy that had made me cum; and had me turned out on it. He never sweated the fact that I wouldn't allow him to dick me down. I guessed he enjoyed tasting, just as much as I enjoyed getting the head. I could never fall in love with dude though; his money was too short to carry me. I wouldn't mind sittin' on his face right now for old time sake...

I pulled up along the side of him, checking out the rips in his body. No sooner than he saw me, he dropped the hose and jogged over my way. Only thoughts I was having, were of those lips pressed against my pearl. He looked like Alan Iverson, with his tall fine ass. It was a hot day and his muscles were bangin' under the sun. He was making me throb!

Come here Boy...

"Hey you..." he flicked water on me.

"S-t-o-p..." I seductively whined.

"What are you doing around this way, Ghost?"

"I just came from the mall. Why?" I smiled. He loved my smile.

"Turn that music down some." He reached in pushing the volume down on my CD player. I was listening to OB's new joint, "The Set Up."

"Come on, Get out!" He opened my door.

"I can't. I've got to get home to my Man," I purposely imposed, exposing the bling.

"Look at you, all iced out. Must be nice." He looked intimidated. "Keep in mind, no white man can lay it down like yo' boy!"

"Don't hate."

He's not lying. I asked Michael had he ever had oral sex on a woman, and he looked at me like I was crazy! Just to think, that's where giving head originated from. Brothas wasn't licking the twott back in them days. That's a white man's original.

"Well, come on and let me get a taste of that good shit before he locks it down."

"Never that."

"Never what?"

"No man can lock this down."

"That's because you haven't had the right one. If you would slow your roll and allow me to show you what it feels like to be loved, you might just change your mind and give Daddy a key to your ignition." He winked.

"Humph, I think not."

"Girl, come on!" He gently pulled my arm.

I already had it made up in my mind I was going with him inside his crib. But the harder you make a brotha work, the better the head.

"Nope."

"Oh, so you teasing me, coming over here looking all good and shit."

"Whatever, Jay."

"All right, when you're ready to tell Daddy how you want it," He snatched my keys out of the ignition, "I'll be in my room."

"Give me my keys Justin!" I pushed the door closed on my truck and followed him inside. From then, it was on.

"Give me my keys." He was lying across his bed with my keys on his chest.

"Come and get them." He demanded seductively.

I strutted toward him, attempting to grab them, but I was unsuccessful. He grabbed my wrist flipping me on my back. I had on this loosely fit mini skirt. ...It cost me $750.

"Boy..."

He kissed my neck, played with my tits, making moves like the freak he was. I didn't mind, I knew what I was getting myself into.

"Uuuhh, ssss...."

I was releasing sexual tension that had been bottled up for a while now. Michael hadn't been doing his job when it came to the bedroom. Justin went straight to it, taking my love whole in his mouth, handling it pro style. I like that about him.

"Summer, I don't want you with him. You don't love him...I know you."

"Shhh..." I pulled his head into my wetness.

Eat now, talk later.

225

I was just about to cum when he said that. He should know by now that I'm down for the paper chase. Justin can't touch the white boy at all. Michaels' bank was bigger. Justin's paper was no where near long enough to take care of me.

I was rocking my hips, again trying to get that nut, not at all expecting anything extra. It was sitting right on the tip of his tongue when...

"What are you doing to...?" He cut me off, pulling my thighs into him, making his way inside with his hard flesh!

"Ooooosss...Summer," he moaned out my name. "You know how long I've been waiting on this?"

I tried to push him away, but he forced himself deeper, locking my arms over my head during my attempt to push him off of me. The whole thing surprised me, being that this was a first time with us. It's been oral sex only, no penetration.

"Why...ssss, uh!" My hips were following his. We both had a rhythm so deep, neither one of us wanted it to come to an end.

"SSSummer...I love you, and I don't want you to be with that man."

I could feel his body preparing to climax with mine. This was not the time for pillow talk! I was gon' get mines! It didn't matter how at that point. I just wanted to come.

He loves me... please!

I know this boy is not trying to holla' for real.

Just bring down my nut so I can bounce.

The juice was on its way; I could feel it in his strokes. I almost counted each one, it felt so good. My body was wrapped in his strong hold and then came more of the whispering that *almost* had me under his spell.

You got some good sss mmmm...I love this shit...girl...

It felt so good when I came. He followed right behind me, releasing years of pleasure inside of me. He lay'd on top of me, holding me close. I was confused. It was time to go.

"Justin..." He didn't respond. "I have to leave..."

226

I left Justin without saying goodbye. He stared at the ceiling the whole time I got dressed, not saying a word.

I know one thing…I'm *not* ready for love.

*****

"Freak-a-leak Shamika, Kecia, Tara, Freak-a-leak, Christina, Crystal, Deronda, Freak-a-leak... THAT'S MY SHIT!" I was singing, dipping through traffic, trying to get back to Michael's.

It's late as hell, messing around with Justin. It was worth it though. The lovin' was the bomb!

My song went off and I was just about to drop in Alicia Keys, when...

"We interrupt this broadcast... Rapper Ol'Boy had just been admitted to a local New York Hospital after suffering complications due to the AIDS virus. O'Boy, who's known for his..."

"OH...MY...GOD..." I had to pull over to digest what I just heard. "That in-the-closet muthafucka! I can't believe this!" He had to have had that shit at the same time I thought I did.

Damn, you just never know. All these on the *down low* men... the shit is crazy.

FORTY-SIX

BLINDED BY THE BLING

*****

SUMMER

It was late in the evening when I pulled up to the estate. The light from the room he kept me restricted from, was beaming down on my car. A spooky feeling had me wanting to turn around and roll out, but there was an overruling greedy part of me that wouldn't part from the money. I used the key to let myself inside, placing my bags to the floor. I started to call out his name, but I decided to walk up on him. I wanted to know what was in that freakin' room! I made it to the top of the stairs, trying to creep up so he wouldn't hear me. There was the strangest noise coming from the room, like someone was crying or moaning. I didn't know what the hell it was, but I was sure as hell about to find out! The suspense was kickin' in, the closer I got. I peeked around the corner of the door.

"HI!" Michael popped his head out. He scared me so bad; I almost fell back on the floor! He pulled the door closed, staring at me, drenched in sweat from his face to chest.

"What the hell is going on in there, Michael?" I tried to peek around him.

I wanted an explanation. I was beginning to think Angela was in there and he was holding her hostage! But I knew that would have been crazy! She's dead! He was in there fucking, I know he was! He has on nothing but pajama pants, flesh hanging all out the fly! I know this fool wasn't disrespecting me!

"Calm down Summer..." He held his hand up, still blocking the entranceway to the room. He looks guilty of something.

"Open the door Michael..." I folded my arms, taking a step back. I was ready. Somebody is going down up in this bitch!"

"Let's talk about this."

"Talk about what? I said open the freaking door!"

"If you're wondering why I'm sweating, I've been working out."

"Naw, uh-uh, fuck that! I don't want to hear that shit." I waved him off, trying to move him out my way.

With one swoop, he lifted me up over his shoulder, carrying me away from his private room! I was throwing blows up against him, kicking and screaming! I knew after this, it would be my last night with him, but I was going to leave him with a touch of Summer Madness! He carried me down the flight of stairs, through the kitchen, around the side, out the back that led to the garage. I was really becoming uncomfortable then. I didn't know what to expect.

Was he about to kill me?

"I'm sick of this shit with you Summer! You don't know what I went through to bring us to this point! Now I'll just have to show you."

I was beginning to accept the fact that this fool was crazy! It was too dark in the garage to make out what he was up to. He dropped me down inside of something. I was yelling and screaming as he walked off. Then I heard a click noise. Everything was silent. It was over, my life flashed in front of me as my heart dropped. He lit the room up with a bright light. I was looking all around with a look of fake surprise, until I realized I was sitting inside of a 2005 400 CLK Convertible! ...White with tan interior fully loaded.

"Oh My God!" I held my hand over my mouth as I saw the engraving of my name on the seats!

Again he made me feel like the overly paranoid gold-digga I was!

229

"You like..." He stood at the hood; arms folded flashing me that Ben Affleck grin.

"I-I don't know what to say!" I was trippin' on my tongue as I slid my hand over the seats, admiring everything in the front and back of me.

I had to give it to myself, I was one lucky bitch!

"You don't have to say anything. Seeing the look on your face is enough. You know, there are not many of these around. I special ordered this one for you." He walked around the car as I sat, struck by amazement. "You should feel real special tonight Darling."

"I'm sorry Michael."

He paused, and then said, "I know..."

FORTY-SEVEN

IN THE BLINK OF AN EYE

*****

FERRELL

"Ferrell! You need to come home! Don't you hear your brat?" My little brother, Rodney Jr., yelled. He paged me 911, and I was returning the call.

"What's going on? And why is Marquis over there?"

"Come home and I'll tell you! I know one thing; I'm not your baby sitter, man!"

"Boy, shut up and tell me why Marquis is over there!" Rodney Jr. was pissing me off with his smart mouth! I'm in a bad mood, and this was not the time to test me.

"Your girlfriend, or what ever Keyonna is to you, was in a car accident. Now, come get your brat!" Marquis was whining in the background.

"A car accident? Is she alright?"

"I don't know! The only thing I do know is I ain't no babysitter. Don't you hear this boy screaming'?"

"Put him on the phone, RJ."

"He does not wanna talk to you! He wants to see you!"

"RJ!" I was losing my patience.

"Here man, talk to your Daddy," Rodney said holding the phone to Marquis's ear.

"Hey, Daddy's man! Why you cry'n', huh? Why you cry'n?"

On my way over to my peep's crib, I made an attempt to call Marianne, Keyonna's mother, and couldn't get an answer. Keyonna played so many games and lied so damn much, I didn't know what to believe. Last week she called my voicemail a zillion times, making all kinds of threats because I wouldn't call her back. Her ass probably ran into a tree on purpose; trying to get my attention. I'm sick of her! It's going on 2:30 in the afternoon, and I'm exhausted! I'm not feelin' all this extra drama right now! My sister's tripping on me about my girl defending her; my Mom is under pressure about all this shit; and now this! Why is all this happening to me right now?

*****

I played with my son for a minute, until my phone started ringing. It was my pops informing me that Keyonna's condition was critical. Never once did Rodney Jr. tell me Mom and Dad was at the hospital with Keyonna! I should go upstairs and kick his ass. He was pissed and heated when I left my son with him again. That's what his punk ass gets! This shit was serious! I was convinced at that point that Keyonna wasn't playing any games.

FORTY-EIGHT

PONDERED

***

TREASURE

I received a message from Jeraldine, reminding me about my sister and her new love situation. I almost forgot about the whole thing since this case. Summer was finally happily living her own life, and hopefully found someone that would never take that away from her. I was sure whatever Jeraldine retrieved from the detective would probably be nothing to worry about. The doctor seemed like a good man. Again, maybe I was feeling a touch of jealousy; that could be why I was prying into her business. Michael was a very attractive and successful doctor; any woman would have felt envious of Summer's luck. Now that I've admitted my real feelings, I can honestly say I am very happy for her. At any rate, I had other things on my platter at the moment, with little time to organize.

Ferrell and I had patched up our relationship. I was fighting the apprehension after having agreed to defend his sister. I was well over four months pregnant, and suffering mood swings as I tried to prepare myself to coach and question the enemy. In another hour, I have to sit across from Tyeisha with a fake smile and a humble attitude. I can't stand her and it's too late to back out now. Anyone else would have sent her sailing up the river without a paddle.

FORTY-NINE

DEATH COMES IN THREES

*****

FERRELL

"MY BABY!!! NOOO!!! PLEASE DON'T DIE ON ME!! LORD PLEASE DON'T TAKE MY ONLY CHILD AWAY FROM ME, JESUS, PLEASE!!!" Marianne screamed to the top of her lungs as she clenched tightly to her daughter's lifeless body, as the machine read flat line.

Keyonna died in her arms. There was nothing anyone could do. The doctors did all they could to revive her. She had been knocked unconscious from the impact.

Keyonna was on her way to pick up Marquis from Marianne's, where he stayed over the weekend. On her way up the Jeffries Freeway, she was driving at 97 mph when a car jumped in front of her, forcing her to lose control of her brand new convertible SL500; flipping over numerous times. It took the paramedics an hour to cut her from the vehicle. It was a multi-car collision, killing two other people. Keyonna happened to be driving alone during this time. The doctors found alcohol in her blood, above the legal limit. She never had a chance of surviving the damage.

By the time I made it through the emergency room doors, it was too late. Keyonna had died. I was the enemy in her mother's eyes, I could feel it. She didn't waste any time blaming me for everything. Keyonna was her only child. Marianne knew we were having some problems, and she also knew there was someone else in my life. In spite of her accusations, I held Marianne until she calmed down. I mourned with her. I was at a lost for words. The situation was completely out of my hands. The rest was up to God.

*****

Four days passed and the funeral rolled around quickly. I asked Treasure if she'd mind allowing me to go alone. She didn't. She understood my situation, and that's why I love her so much.

There I was, trying to disguise the love that was still there for Keyonna. I can't explain how beautiful she looked in her casket. It brought back memories, good ones. That was the breaking point for me. I had to pass Marquis to my Mom. I was weak, especially when he was trying to reach in the casket, calling out "MAMA!" It was a rain bath, and I felt like shit the whole day and thereafter. I couldn't hide the fact that I still cared for her in spite of what we've been through. That was my baby's mama, and can't no woman touch that, and no woman could ever understand. At first, when they asked if anyone wanted to pay respects, I hesitated, afraid of what people would say or think of me. Then it dawned on me, once my name was called, that I was on the obituary to recite a poem I wrote. That left me no choice. I stood after the Pastor called out to me, and made my way to the podium.

For you love, I silently said, staring over at her.

Then I read:

"In The Blink Of An Eye,
At any given moment the one you love is taken away...
Someone close someone special, something so dear...
I took advantage of her love, her kindness, her weakness...
I took her for granted because I knew she was near...
At any given moment, my number He could pull...
To fly away from here, God, He rules...
We live by the moment, never expecting death...
Then when it comes, it's too late to confess...
In the blink of an eye, this is solid, written in stone...
Here one day, gone the next, there is no more right or wrong...
We live by the moment, just as the sky is blue...

The Hottest Summer Ever Known

Loosing that someone special, someone that's true,
I stand here before you not ashamed to cry, WHY?
I just lost my Baby's Mama, In the blink of an eye
We love you Keyonna,
Ferrell & Marquis"

FIFTY

DAMAGE

*****

FERRELL

My sister was real messed up about Keyonna. That just added to all the other drama that was going on! Tyeisha wanted to attend the funeral, but the Warden never responded to her request. That just pissed her off even more. She was already dealing with a substantial amount of stress. And not to mention, not getting her way was something she truly wasn't used to.

Treasure finally took time out to go see her and she denied the visit! I had to damn near drag Treasure back up there to give it another shot. This time I went with her. I wanted to place my foot directly in Tye's ass! She thinks this here is some kind of game. It's not all about Tyiesha anymore and it's definitely not a game.

I was thankful my girl reconsidered taking her case. I refused to allow my sister to make her situation any worse than it already was! It's time for her spoiled ass to grow the fuck up!

Treasure and I were waiting for her to come to the visiting area. Once she made it, she looked a mess! Her hair was all over her head like she had been in a fight or something! Tyeisha was not happy to see me accompanied by Treasure. Her attitude off the bat was not acceptable. I wanted to jump through the triple glass on her, but patience was required, and an ass whoopin' can be placed on hold for now. She's lucky she was behind that glass.

"What…" She blurted out, slouching down in her chair.

"Nothing, Lil Sis. I just wanted to come get one last look at my girl before she went up the river to start her new bit. Life? …Isn't that what they're talking about giving you, Tye?"

Oh, so this nigga changing on me? He must don't know how easy it would be to get out this bitch. Test me Ferrell, go right ahead. And look at this pitiful looking ho that he calls his woman. This whole thang is a set up. They're trying to get rid of me. I can't let them see me sweat. Don't break girl, keep control.

"You don't have anything to say? You're just going to sit there and look stupid, huh?"

"I'm out!" Tyeisha jumped up, calling for the guard.

Stubborn ass! If only she could have played this hard when that punk-ass nigga she claimed she loved was getting over on her! I bet she wouldn't be in this shit now!

"Oh, so you hard now? Huh? You hard? Do your bit Tye!" I signaled Treasure to come on. I've done all I can do. This is too much for a young buck like me. I'm just going to allow time to make a way, fuck it.

Just as I was making my way to the door that would separate us for a long time, Tye ran over to the glass, pounding, screaming, and crying out to me!

"REL! Don't leave me! Please, I'm sorry!"

Her hands and face were smeared against the glass. I released Treasure's hand and made my way back to her. I placed my palms up against the glass to meet hers. I allowed my feelings to show. I was tired of hiding them. Tears fell, and years of pain had taken over. We cried together as people watched.

"I'm trying to get you out of here Tye, I swear! Just trust me Baby girl, just this once," I pleaded.

I had to admit, I didn't want Treasure to see this side of me once again, but I found the strength and courage to turn to her during the process. I was surprised to see *her* shedding a few drops as well. She's feeling a nigga, for real!

"Come here baby." I reached out for my girl to stand beside me.

After calming down some, it was time to get down to business. Tye was still a little distant while Treasure was laying out her strategy, but I knew it wouldn't be an over night process with them. There's still some bad blood between the both of them, but I know in my heart that whatever happens, Treasure will still do the best she can. That's all I'm asking.

FIFTY-ONE

HUMBLE

*****

TREASURE

Ferrell and I made our way out of the county jail, ready to face one of my greatest triumphs... or greatest defeat. He had some business to attend to while I made an appointment to see Mr. Trenton Daily, who was the prosecutor on this case. I had to make arrangements to go over Tyeisha's plea. Once we met up, I was upset that he wouldn't offer us a better deal. His offer was outrageous! He had her facing no less than thirty years, if she didn't take them to trial. And if she decided to take this case to trial, he's talking life. Her chances were looking very slim. This cocky prosecutor was probably working on a way to snatch Tyeisha's freedom with his ridiculous offer, and today he may possibly get his chance. We're going to trial...

FIFTY-TWO

THE CASE ON JELLY STREET/ DAY ONE

*****

TREASURE

"Today's the big day, baby!" Ferrell held me before we entered the courtroom, placing a kiss on my forehead.

He then brushed his hands down my belly. I wore a nicely tailored maternity suit. People could barely tell I had a bun in the oven. This is going to be stressful and irritating. I was nervous. I chanted my silent prayer...with the exception of Ferrell by my side. He was all I had.

The marshals had already seated Tyeisha when I approached my seat.

"All rise for the Honorable Judge Michael Scibana." We all stood to our feet as the judge walked up to the bench.

My hands were becoming sweaty, and my heart was beating fast. It was very stuffy; the air in the crowded courtroom wasn't circulating properly. I felt like I was suffocating.

Treasure, you need to calm down. Everything will work out for the best.

Through positive thinking, I had convinced myself otherwise. In reality, I was feeling as if I had already lost the case.

"You may be seated," the judge said, making himself comfortable in his chair.

"We are here today for the United States of America versus Tyeisha Holmes. Docket number B2E44 dash 098."

"Be serious now. The United States of America, against me? Please! How crazy does that sound?" Tyeisha scoffed, suddenly becoming uneasy.

I gave her a serious glare. She obviously didn't know any better. This government will snatch your freedom away in a heart beat!

The judge noticed her rude outburst. He lowered his gavel and said, "Order! Ms. Lewis, I trust that you will control your client during these proceedings. I will not tolerate any outbursts."

"Yes, Your Honor. Apologies to the court." I made an attempt to calm her down by placing my hand on her shoulder, but she rudely jerked away.

I didn't even bother to look behind me at Ferrell. I decided that I would handle this unruly "ghetto chick" from here on out! She would not embarrass me from this point on.

I don't want to be here with you either, Girlie.

We have one thing in common, Our Love for Ferrell.

"Ms. Lewis, I assume you have discussed the proceedings with your client, and that she is ready to make her plea. Am I correct?"

I stared over at Black Moore, sitting behind the prosecutors, prepared to be their witness. Before I responded, he caught my eye and winked. I would have preferred he threw something at me instead. He seemed as if he had no fear, what so ever.

"Yes, Your Honor," I responded nervously.

"And how does the defendent plea?"

"The Defendant pleas not guilty, Your Honor."

"Will the defendant rise...?" I gave her a hard nudge.

"State your name for the court please."

"Tyeisha Holmes." She was rolling her eyes as she spoke.

"Ms. Holmes, your attorney has entered a plea of not guilty on your behalf. Is that the plea that you wish to enter?" Tyeisha shook her head.

"You will answer, yes, Your Honor, if that is your plea, Ms. Holmes. If not, answer accordingly." The judge was already becoming irritated with her.

"Yes... Yo' Honor."

"Be seated."

"Counselors, are you prepared to proceed with trial?"

"Yes, Your Honor," I responded, still nervous.

"Yes sir, Your Honor!" the confident prosecutor said.

"All right counselors, let's proceed. Swear Ms. Holmes in please."

We stood.

"Raise your right hand please. Do you solemnly swear or affirm that the testimony that you are about to give, shall be the truth, the whole truth and nothing but the truth, so help you God?" The female clerk quoted.

"I do," Tyeisha mumbled.

"You have to speak up, so that the court can hear you," the judge said wearily.

"I do!" she snapped.

Her tone struck a nerve, not only with me, but the judge was clinching his teeth. I knew the prosecutors were enjoying this. They knew her attitude would debase our case, causing the judge and jurors to favor their argument even more.

"Is there a problem with your client, Ms. Lewis?" The judge asked sternly.

"Nothing I can't handle, Your Honor. I apologize."

"Let's continue."

He moved on as he gave Tyeisha an ugly glare. All she had to do was give him one more reason to lock her up. ...For good.

We were out-numbered by numerous witnesses that Tyeisha wasn't familiar with. Something wasn't right. She claimed it was her first time ever seeing the first three witnesses that testified against her. I was experiencing hot flashes, as sweat and anger combined to intensify my shifty mood swings.

Between Tyeisha and the prosecutor, I had to ask the Judge for a short recess. The marshals escorted Tyeisha to a room adjacent from the courtroom. I needed just a few moments with her.

"Look," I snapped at her.

"YOU LOOK! I'm..." SMACK! I slapped her without second-guessing.

She slowly turned to face me, holding her lip the best way she could with handcuffs on.

"I don't believe you just..."

"Believe it! Now! Like I was just saying," I had one hand on my hip, finger pointed in her face. "My time is sacred, and believe me when I say that I don't want to be here no more than you do! But I guess the dick got both of us here, and I don't know about you, but I'm ready to get back to mine."

"Is everything all right in there?" One of the marshals asked, through the closed door.

"Yes, we're fine," I responded, and then focused my attention back on her.

She stared away from me, but I'm sure she could hear me, loud and clear.

"Listen, I'm not here to try to cause you more harm than you're doing to yourself. You and I have had our share of problems, but this is neither the time nor the place to act them out. I'm here to help you and that's all I'm trying to do. Believe me; you couldn't have paid another attorney enough to have to put up with your bullshit! Looks like I'm all you got. But, if you continue with this attitude and rude behavior, you're on your own, cause I'm at the end of my rope with you."

With that, I left her there, opening the door to allow the marshal to bring her back inside the courtroom. Ferrell was standing outside the door the whole time. I didn't know what to expect from him after having to give his overprotected sister the third degree, but if he wanted some too...

Hey, bring it on...

"Treasure, let me holla at you for a minute." He pulled me to the side.

"Now is not a good time, Ferrell. We only have another two minutes before court is back in session."

"I'm aware of that, but what I have to say won't take that long." We walked outside the courtroom.

"I love you." He pulled me into him, kissing me. "It's about time you handled Tyeisha, and that's exactly what she needed, someone to stand up to her. You did that baby girl, and I ain't mad at 'cha. I'm proud of you."

"Only for you Love. This is ONLY for you."

"I know, Baby. Now, get in there and show them what you're made of. I believe in you, baby…and I believe in our love." He gave me one final kiss before I had to go.

Court was back in session, and I was keyed up off of his love! It was hard to focus my attention back to Tyeisha. I tried to avoid staring over at her, after just slapping the taste out her mouth, but when I did, that spitefulness had changed. She was "humble as pie." It was really amazing what a right hand can do to some people.

At long last, the heat was on! The prosecutor was shooting us down with his immoral tactics. First, he brought in three witnesses, looking for a time cut. They didn't even know my client! And after I finished with them, I proved that to be fact. They were coerced! Dirty dogs! With that out the way, I felt secure, like I had the ups on them. The government takes the law and uses them to their advantage. They shuffle these people like a deck of cards, gambling with their freedom, and to think, I was once on their side.

"Your Honor, we have another witness who was in custody with the defendant at the county jail. We found that this particular inmate was connected to the murder of one of our key witnesses on this case, the informant, Fatima Chandler, who was killed while in custody, awaiting trial, Your Honor." The mentioning of her name made Tyeisha uncomfortable. Her expression was unreadable. She appeared to be shocked.

"Let's hope she's nothing like the three witnesses before, Mr. Daily," the judge said.

"No sir, not this young woman."

Tyeisha dropped her head to the table. *Please don't tell me Fatima was the one that was killed when they shut the prison down. This can't be happening to me! They're going to pin her murder on me! I can't take this any more! I'm losing my mind!*

I knew something wasn't right about this picture. Tyeisha's hiding her face. *Please don't have anything to do with this murder, Tyeisha.*

"Who is this woman, Tyeisha?" I leaned over to her and whispered.

"Trust me, you don't want to know," Tyeisha uttered.

FIFTY-THREE

PIMPLE LIP

*****

SUMMER

Michael kneeled over me and whispered in my ear, as I laid on the bed half asleep.

"Summer?"

"Humm…"

"I'll return in a few. I have a few errands to make. Don't forget, we're leaving in three days. You need to finish your packing, okay?"

"Mmm-hum." I pulled the covers over my head.

Just as quick as I heard him pull off, I threw the covers back, racing toward that damn room! I was determined to get inside this time!

"What's in this room?" I screamed. Again, I was pushing, kicking and tugging at the door with no luck! I even went as far as trying to pick the lock! Nothing worked! "FUCK!" I released an aggravated sigh, and took my frustrated ass downstairs and fixed me a bowl of cereal! To take my mind off of that room, I thought about the vacation Michael and I were going on to Africa. I was so hyped! I finally met someone that wants to take me on trips around the world, buy me all kinds of glamourous shit, and love me unconditionally. Maybe one day I'll be able to force myself to love him. I doubt it being anytime soon. I'm too wild for love. I want your M-O-N-E-Y…

This trip was planned unexpectedly. I was kind of leery at first, because he seemed so desperate to get away. I confronted him about his anxiousness to go on this trip, and he changed the subject, telling me how much money he was going to spend on me once we reached our destination. He knew how to reroute my attention.

I popped on some cartoons while chow'n down on my cereal. Many things were going through my mind, such as,

I wonder how much money Michael has in all his accounts. If I marry him and he dies, I will get everything!

My thoughts and cartoons were interrupted when someone hit the buzzer outside the gate. I asked who it was, but the speaker sound was too distorted. I figured it couldn't have been anyone important. I hit the button, allowing the unexpected guest to enter *our* estate. I trampled over all the shit I had packed to go out of town, and made my way to the door to answer it. Once I saw who was standing on the other side, I couldn't believe it!

"What the fuck do you want?" I slung the door open.

"Humph, well, well, well…If it's not the trick from the clinic. So, did you get your results?" Tawaunna asked, sarcastically.

A part of me wanted to pull the ho inside and beat her ass until she lost consciousness, but the more I stared at the bitch, the more I realized I had the ups! Look who's standing on the other side of the door…I'm wearing the bling, bling! She's wearing the cubic zirconia! I wouldn't waste my time.

"Michael's not here. Try the clinic." I prepared to slam the door in her face.

"The clinic? Ooohh, I see. You don't know…"

"Know what?"

"Where your man has been for the last couple of months."

"Not with you, Bitch!"

"Ooo, such harsh words. Well let me say this before I leave. If you did know your so-called-man like I do, you would have known he doesn't work for the clinic anymore," she sarcastically said, clearing her throat. "Tell him to call me when he gets in." She swayed off.

Let her go Summer.

I didn't want to believe a word she was saying. I just wanted to take something and go upside her head! I let the bitch roll out, though. Michael and I were about to hit the sky! I ain't sweatin' Ms. "Pimple Lip", for-real' for-real'. But I damn sure would like to know how she knew where we lived! I don't need any interference at this stage in the game. I moved out of my place to be with him, and I didn't tell anybody where I resided. Not even my Grams! He claimed he wanted me all to himself until he built me a bigger house.

Build me a house?

He can have his way until I become the wifey in *my* new house! The way he looks at me, I know for sure he wants to marry me. That day is coming real soon.

I made an attempt to call him on his cell phone to discuss our unexpected guest. No answer. I took my chances and called the clinic against his request. After I hung up, I hated to say that the chick was right about him not working for them anymore. He was definitely hiding something from me. I didn't like that at all. Before I could page him, he was walking through the door.

"Hello, Sweetheart. You just about packed to head out?" He attempted to kiss me on my forehead. I moved before he could. "What's wrong now?" I was sitting on the couch with my feet tucked under me like a two-year-old.

"I don't know, you tell me." He stared at me.

"What have you been up to, Summer? Please don't tell me you..."

"Wait, wait, hol'dup... Don't try to flip the script. Tawaunna? Remember her? She just left."

He cut me off. "Listen, Sweetheart. I still have some things I need to take care of. Why don't you go shopping, or say goodbye to your family while I get some things together around here." He walked off, ignoring my concern.

"Are you ignoring me, Michael?" He pulled off his shades to show me his look of intense displeasure with me. I couldn't believe he had the nerve to be eyeballing me. His eyes were red and swelled. "What is up with your eyes? Are you tired or something?"

"I'm not feeling well. Just let me have some time alone. Do what you do best." I reached for him.

He took my hand and kissed it. "Pick me up a few shirts and ties while you're out." He walked off, leaving me there in bewilderment.

"Okay." I smiled at him.

Fuck Tawaunna. Fuck the office tip...I'm going to Africa sharper than a bitch!

FIFTY-FOUR

THE CASE ON JELLY STREET/ DAY TWO

*****

TREASURE

"I still can't get over what happened in court yesterday, Ferrell."

"I'm just as shocked as you are, Baby."

Court was a disaster yesterday. Trenton Daily had his plan all worked out. His witness happened to be Tyiesha's old cellmate at the county. All hell broke loose when that woman came through the double doors. A tear fell from Tyeisha's eyes, once the woman appeared. It was like, once she saw her, something about Fatima Chandler's death was confirmed.

According to the prosecution, Vicki was being charged along with a correctional officer for killing Miss Chandler. The prosecutor informed the judge that Vicki was willing to make a statement in exchange for a sentence reduction. Once the girl approached the stand, the prosecutor began his questioning.

"Ms. McDaniels...how long were you and the defendant friends?"

"We only knew each other for a couple of months."

"So you two never knew each other on the streets?"

"Nope."

"How did the conversation come about between you and the defendant in regards to Fatima Chandler?"

"What conversation?"

251

"You stated to me when I came to visit you that you had information in regards to the murder of Fatima Chandler, is that correct?" The prosecutor was becoming aggravated.

"That's correct. I'm not denying that. But what do you mean I had a conversation with Tyeisha about this Fatima Chandler? I never told you that!"

"Okay, calm down Ms. McDaniels. Lets go over this again." He exhaled.

"Okay." She responded with confidence.

"Did the defendant hire you to kill or have Fatima Chandler killed on the day of February 29, 2004, while she was in federal custody?"

There were a few seconds of silence and caught up stares between Vicki and Tyeisha. I could read it was something only they knew, and it was best that I didn't.

"Like I told you once before Mister Prosecutor... I ain't killed anybody, and Tyeisha ain't told me to kill nobody! Why are you putting words in my mouth? If you wanna know who the real killer is, he's sitting right behind you!"

She pointed out the correctional officer, she was sexually involved with while in the county jail, as the one who killed Fatima. Everyone turned to look at the suspect. The court became loud. Fatima's family was present, along with other irate people.

"Order in the court!" The judge demanded.

"And further more..." Vicki continued, as the prosecutor was trying to talk over her, "We discussed..." Her tone became louder, "This at the prison," Vicki insisted.

"THANK YOU, Ms. McDaniels. No further questions." He embarrassedly turned toward his seat.

"Ms Lewis?" The Judge looked over in my direction.

"Yes, I have a few questions for this witness, Your Honor." Mr. Daily shot me an undefeated stare.

I stepped up to the witness stand, preparing my line of questioning.

"Ms. McDaniels, I'm going to get straight to the point. ...Did my client have anything to do with the murder of Fatima...?"

"OBJECTION YOUR HONOR! THIS LINE OF QUESTIONING IS NOT APPRO..."

"Overruled, Mr. Daily...It is appropriate. Go on Ms. Lewis."

"Thank you, Your Honor. Ms. McDaniels... Did my client have anything to do with the murder of Fatima Chandler?"

"Like I said, the man himself is sitting behind Mr. Daily! And to give a direct answer, NO. Tyeisha had absolutely nothing to do with the murder of Fatima!"

"YOU A DAMN LIE BITCH!" The correctional officer, Mr. Dean, screamed out in his defense.

"Escort that gentleman out of my courtroom!" The judge gave an order to one of the Marshalls.

"That's all I have your Honor. I have no further questions. Thank you, Ms. McDaniels." We both nodded at each other, and I went back to my seat.

"You may step down, Ms. McDaniels."

After all was said and done, very little was said, and nothing was really done.

Well, we were able to get the murder part of it thrown out, but we still have to argue the 50-kilos, that they were now trying to involve Ferrell on. Before we could get out of there, Mr. Daily approached both Ferrell and I.

"Excuse me, Treasure. Can I have a word with you please?"

"No." I kept walking past him.

I didn't care for him too much, bringing witnesses in to perjure themselves on the stand; all for his own personal agenda.

Mr. Daily continued, "Well, I guess the indictment on Lover Boy holding your hand here is not important to you." He caught both of our attention, and we paused.

Ferrell released my hand, then walked over to Mr. Daily and said, "The name is not Lover Boy, Player, and if there is an indictment on me, you can talk it over with my attorney. Here's his card. The only thing you should be bringing to my fiancé's attention..." Ferrell reached toward me, "is a better deal for my sister."

He tossed the card at him and took my hand, leaving him standing in the middle of the hall outside the courtroom.

"I knew they would try to attack me Baby, I knew it!"

"Don't worry Ferrell. Everything's going to be all right."

"Do you truly believe that Treasure? Can you honestly say it will?" He stared at me as we both sat in his truck, still parked at the courthouse.

We were like sitting ducks, waiting on what they would come up with next. This here is what I called drama!

FIFTY-FIVE

THE INVESTIGATOR

*****

JERALDINE

"Did someone page Jeraldine?"

"Yes, I did."

"With whom am I speaking?"

"A desperately waiting investigator, looking for the perfect opportunity to take you out to dinner."

"Oooo…Hi Darrion?" I giggled.

"Hello beautiful. What does your schedule look like? I have something for you."

"You do… and what could that something possibly be?" I asked seductively.

"Mmm. Me."

"How I wish I could take you up on that offer, but you know there's a significant other in my life."

"If you don't scream…"

"I'll holler!" We laughed.

"Jeraldine, I have something I would like you to take a look at. This is in reference to the guy you had me to check on, Michael Tice, the Doctor."

"Yes. When and where would you like to meet?"

"Whatever is good for you… my office, of course? I have a three o'clock open tomorrow afternoon."

"Let me check my schedule and get back with you in 15 minutes. Darrion, is this something serious?"

"Well, what I have now is nothing really, at least not enough to go out and arrest him. Then again, I really didn't have a lot to work with. A photo of him just got in my hands about an hour ago. I have a friend of mine doing a more detailed search. I should have something on my desk by tomorrow afternoon."

"You're scaring me."

"Oh, it's nothing like that, I'm sure."

"Good. That makes me feel a little better, I guess."

"I'm sure we'll find nothing. He looks pretty clean so far."

"I'm happy."

"Go ahead and check your schedule. I'll wait for your call."

It was good hearing from him. I kind of wish it was under different circumstances though. I would hate to take bad news back to Treasure. She couldn't handle it right now.

I called the office. "Mrs. Jackson, I need you to check my schedule."

"Well, hello Jeraldine. How are you this afternoon?"

"And how did you know my voice? My Mother can't even distinguish us when we call her."

"You're the only one who doesn't say *hello* first."

"Oh. Hello, Mrs. Jackson, I need you to tell me if I have anything scheduled for tomorrow afternoon."

"Sure, Dear. I have your appointment book in front of me. Ummmm... No. All of your appointments are for the morning."

"Good."

"Everything okay?"

"I hope so. How've things been going in court with Treasure?"

"I can't hear you; your cell phone is breaking up."

"Never mind! Talk to you later!" I said louder.

I returned Darrion's call.

He answered. "Lieutenant Darrion."

"Now that's a man who loves his job."

"And you're a woman who would cause me to lose my job."

"Ohhh Darrion,...why do you say that?" I was tickled.

He jumped straight into business, ignoring my question.

"Jeraldine, what I'm doing for you is illegal. I'm going into someone's personal life here, but you're worth it, so it's all good."

"The loving is even better."

"What about your significant other?" He asked, with interest.

"What about your wife?"

"What they don't know won't hurt."

"And whose philosophy is that?"

"Men."

"I'll see you tomorrow at three," I said giggling.

"Confirmed."

FIFTY-SIX

DEATH BEFORE DEADLINE

*****

Michael was kneeling over the toilet throwing up, feeling nauseous after Summer left. His illness was becoming more evident each day. He had his own troubled reason why he hadn't told Summer yet, but in due time, she will know more than she anticipates in a lifetime. His main focus now was getting out of town with her before the authorities caught up to him. Tawaunna had been threatening Michael for a couple of days now since he's been avoiding her. Somehow Tawaunna was able to track him down. That could be dangerous for the both of them at this point. He knew Tawaunna got her hands on some vital information that could mean his life, and if killing her would avoid exposure to his dark secret, so be it.

Michael was using all the strength he had left to pack his suitcases. He couldn't afford to leave a trail. Time was running out, there was no time left to waste. As he was removing articles from the drawers, he knew he had very little strength to go any further. He headed up to his secret hideaway, where he stored all types of experimental medications that he takes for his illness. If Summer had ever made it through to the other side of that door, his secret would have been exposed. He simply couldn't risk that. Losing her before her time would have been death before deadline. It's amazing what money can buy. Michael had access to drugs that hadn't been approved through the FDA. That's what's been keeping his appearance up till now, but this disease is serious. You can only hide from it for so long before it reaches the surface. You simply can't run from the truth.

As he reached the top of the stairs, his cell phone rang.

"Hello?" He answered apprehensively.

"MICHAEL!" Tawaunna yelled, "You're going to talk to me!" She was irate at that point. Michael turned back toward the bedroom placing one problem on hold, to take care of another.

"Look Whore! Like I said before! I AM NOT RESPONSIBLE FOR WHAT HAPPENED TO YOU! DON'T CALL ME WITH THAT ANYMORE!" He made an attempt to hang up, until she said something that was going to place her in an early grave.

"Okay Doctor *Andrew Grey!*" He jumped.

"How did you…" He muttered in shock.

"You want to play with me? Then I guess you don't have a problem with me telling your little girlfriend who, by the way, I'm following right now, what I know about you! Yeah Michael, Andrew or whatever the fuck your name is! I know everything, ABOUT YOU! Your wife, the others! Do you think Ms. Lewis would like that! HUH?"

"Christ." He shook his head, annoyed by this set back.

Tawaunna had his undivided attention at that point. He knew he had to think fast or it would be fate for everyone involved. He sat in silence as she continued.

"HOW COULD YOU DO THIS TO ME? I LOVED YOU!" She cried, "YOU STOLE MY LIFE FROM ME!"

Michael continued to hold the phone, sitting down on the edge of the bed. He had no remorse for her. No emotions. He knew he was the one responsible for her disease. AIDS now dwells deep inside of her, and death soon waits for her soul, thanks to the devil himself, Michael Tice. Tawaunna wasn't a part of his plan. Michael tried to avoid her in all ways possible, but she was persistent, throwing herself at him in their work environment until he couldn't breathe! So instead of resisting temptation, he had sex with her, not knowing until after the fact that she was a virgin. Not that he had any regret. Virgin or not, Tawaunna wasn't what Michael was looking for. She looked nothing like Angela to him, but she had some of her characteristics; a gold digger she was, and that was all he needed to add her to his plate. Tawaunna was well aware of Michael's wealth. After their sexual escapade, she

259

became obsessed. Michael knew then, he had to wean Tawaunna away before things became difficult. Bad idea. She wasn't willing to just let him go; especially when she found out she was infected. That's when she knew she had to get to the bottom of her situation.

Ever since Michael relocated to Detroit, his goal was to find another victim who reminded him of his late wife, Angela. That day finally rolled around when Summer stepped into his practice. That's when things changed. He knew he had to have her, especially once he found out she wasn't infected with the virus. It was then that he knew she would be victim number three, not including Tawaunna.

There were others before Summer. The two other women that unfortunately shared relations with him resided in the Houston area. Michael started off as a family doctor before Angela died. After the nightmare she left him with, he began to specialize in gynecology to make it easier to lure his victims. As a result, one of the women died from pneumonia, (a complications from AIDS). The other later tested positive with HIV, shattering all her dreams. She couldn't handle the fact that she was going to die and chose suicide as an escape. Her father found her hanging from the ceiling in her bedroom apartment with a note she wrote gripped tightly in her hand. It blamed Michael for her illness. Her father turned the letter over to the authorities and the courts submitted a court order to have him tested for HIV. He avoided it, of course, fleeing to another state. The man was a chameleon. The Texas police are still looking for him, rounding up any evidence or leads that could lead to his arrest.

Michael's a wealthy white man which means he can hide damn near anywhere on the planet. He chose the Detroit suburban area, using an alias and bogus credentials to buy property, invest in stock, and purchase flashy things. He would only work in small rinky-dink clinics to lessen his exposure to the authorities. Michael knew he didn't need too much background information in those places. His plot was going smoothly, until he met Tawaunna. Once she learned of her illness, she went on a mission to find out the truth about Dr. Michael Tice, a.k.a., Andrew Grey. Now with Tawaunna on his case, and Jeraldine (in the shadows unbeknownst to him), time was running out. Michael had to think fast, because quick thinking was the only possible way, to get him out of this situation. Michael was convinced that his mission to kill would be complete after Summer was infected. That was his way of feeling that he could rest in peace, taking out his last victim. Killing women this way was his way of dealing with the pain of dying like this. It took him away from the reality of it all.

Michael made his way in the bedroom, pushing the door up. He continued to listen to Tawaunna, thinking of a way to get rid of her before she gets in his way and alerts Summer or the authorities. Michael walked over to his drawer pulling it open, finding the solution to his problem.

"Tawaunna... I need to see you so we can talk about this..." He massaged his temples. His head was hurting and he knew he had to get to his medication soon. "Honey, please stop crying...I never meant to hurt you. And I'm going to prove to you that I'm not the one responsible for this misunderstanding. I'm a doctor for Christ sake!" She continued to cry. "Come on Darling, let's try to fix this. We'll work it out together. Are you there?"

"Y-Yes Michael, I'm here." She was slowly falling.

"Can you meet me at the hotel off of I-94? Let's say tomorrow evening at 7?"

Without a response, Tawaunna busted a U-Turn, allowing Summer to disappear into traffic. Tawaunna wanted desperately to see him and look him in the eyes, to hopefully find her answer. *Why me?*

"Michael... Don't stand me up, please. I can't handle that right now."

"I'll be there." He started coughing up mucus, spitting in a napkin. "I promise."

"I'll be waiting, okay?" She said, crying and confused.

"Shhhhh...please, stop crying. Everything is going to be okay," he lied, taking a seat on the edge of the bed, placing bullets into his 357.

He disconnected the call, and stood up on his weak legs, dropping the gun to the bed. "I have to get to my medicine." He staggered, struggling to make it up to his hide-away. Michael knew he had to pull himself together before Summer came home. He needed to take his drugs in order to carry out his plan.

Tawaunna must die...

FIFTY-SEVEN

THE CASE ON JELLY STREET/ DAY THREE

*****

TREASURE

I dropped Ferrell off at Darryl's office. He was stressing about the possibility of catching a case. It's too early to say right now, whether Mr. Daily was serious about the indictment on Ferrell or just trying to get a reaction.

In the meantime, I wanted to lie down before I headed back to court. "What time do we have here...?" I glanced over at my watch.

Twelve forty-five? How much sleep can a pregnant woman get in an hour?

This trial is almost worse than carrying a child. I decided to go to Ferrell's place to lie down for a while. Well, mission not accomplished. There was an unmarked vehicle parked two doors down from his place. Ferrell lives in a predominately white area. So the way this person was observing me through his rearview called for my attention. I was in no mood for anything out of the ordinary. All of my energy was exerted dealing with this case. In less than two hours from now, I will be giving my closing argument to an overworked jury. To be honest, this case seemed like a losing battle. The prosecution's argument had some leverage. Now I'm facing another obstacle. I stepped out of my car, staring over at the unmarked vehicle.

That's a Federal Agent

The male stepped out of his vehicle, heading my way.

"Ooohhh Boyy…" I sighed. I hope these people don't try to bring me into this crap.

"Ms. Treasure Lewis!" The tall white male called out. He was wearing your common government suit, as he approached me, with his identification visible.

"Yes." I glanced over at his badge. He hastily introduced himself.

"My name is Agent Reynolds. I'm with the F.B.I. I'm on the case against your client, Tyeisha Holmes."

"Okay." I placed my briefcase to the ground.

"How many months?" He asked noticing my belly.

"I lost count." I smiled.

"I don't want to take up too much of your time. I know you have to be back in court soon, so I'll get straight to the point." He pulled out a folder. "Do you mind if I come inside? I assure you this won't take long."

"Sure." Once we made it inside, I led him to the study. "Make yourself comfortable. Would you like something to drink?"

"No thanks, Ms. Lewis. I have to get back to my office before court." He was making me nervous. "Have a seat next to me…please, while I go over some important information with you." He spread some photos and transcripts over the table. My eyes don't lie, so there was no denying what lay before them. I was stunned!

"Don't allow this to alarm you. What I'm doing is exceedingly infrequent in my work environment."

While he was talking, I was apprehensively fingering through everything.

A day late, a dollar short.

"I'm not here to offer an apology. I'm just trying to be fairly supportive and honest in this case. No one should have to go to prison for something they didn't do. I've seen that happen to innocent people too many times."

"Why…why are you doing this?" I stared at him.

"You know, Ms. Lewis. One person can set a bad example for all. That's basically all I can elaborate on at this time. But I will validate that you don't have to trouble yourself about Mr. Holmes being brought up on charges. I'm not going to allow that, Ms. Lewis. I'm one of the good guys in this game." He smiled casually. "I'm sure you're aware that in any position a person works in, they're subject to make mistakes. Some are knowingly, some, unknowingly. We're only human. What's expected of us doesn't always happen. What I'm trying to say is. …That I choose not to play with an individual's freedom because it has a way of coming back on you. Don't need that in my life."

I don't believe he just said that to me. Makes me wonder if he knows something about my past. I did lock up a few drug dealers on rationale.

"In this business, Ms. Lewis, things can get personal, you know what I mean?" I nodded. "Now'a days, it doesn't matter who you are; a police officer, a lawyer, a judge, an agent. Never place your trust in man… or woman."

Isn't that the truth?

"Only in God we trust. This here, Ms. Lewis is a little something for your case. I can't guarantee you'll win, but I do know it will help you with future attacks against Mr. Holmes. Good luck, and please be careful Ms. Lewis." He stood, shook my hand and left.

*****

Court was now in session, and I didn't know where to begin. It's like my mind went blank! I was zooming in and out of everything going on around me. Again, I felt conquered, not to mention I had not given my closing argument yet!

Well, Lord… Here I go.

Mr. Daily left me with very little breathing room. I could tell the jury was anxious to get this over with. Their expressions were unwavering. I've experienced this behavior many times in trials, especially when the jury had already made their decision.

"Look at the expressions on your faces," I said to the jury, approaching them. "Mr. Daily has a way with words. That's one of the smooth effects about this man. Way to go, Trenton! I couldn't think of any other prosecutor who could convict someone of a crime they didn't commit better than him. Ladies and gentlemen of the jury, look at my client. She's innocent! But after listening to Mr. Daily's closing argument, I'm sure your mental picture is indistinct...

Now, I'm sure all of you have children or know someone who does. Young teenagers and adults can be so naïve! They would go for anything, especially if the right predatory person gets his or her hands on them. That's what happened to my client. She is what I consider prey; a victim in this case. That's the story in a nutshell. Nothing but a fly caught in a web! I have an idea. Let's picture my client as a fly and Mr. Moore as a spider. Can any of you imagine the torment a fly caught in a web goes through before death? Picture this, a big black enormous, hairy, spider slowly crawling down, then sucking every inch of blood from its body. Mmm, has to be painful, has to hurt. Why couldn't the fly see the web? Was the web invisible? Did the fly not know what it was flying into? Couldn't have, I'm sure it didn't know. Who wants to die, slowly? Who wants to do 30 years? Ladies and gentlemen of the jury, Black Moore has been selling drugs for a long time. This is his game! A game he knows oh so well. My client had no idea she was even picking up drugs, let alone selling them! But Black knew! It was pre-planned! Yet, he denies it. Who wouldn't! My client was the perfect fall girl! A woman who loved her man and trusted him, even after he slept with her best friend! That's beyond love, and I'm sorry to say, that's blind! Like that fly that flew into that web! ...

Mr. Moore denies knowing anything about these drugs. He has no recollection of how they ended up in a trunk with my client. Oookay... I'm going to move on, leave you with an analogy some friends of mine in college shared with me. Hopefully it will shed some light on how quick someone will lie, even if evidence proved his guilt...

Here we have a single parent with three little girls. Mom comes home from work to find, JELLY on the floors! JELLY all over her curtains! JELLY on the counters! JELLY ALL OVER

THE PLACE! Mom was furious! She wanted answers! So she lined the children up and questioned them one by one. She wanted the truth! She asked the first child, 'Was it you that was playing in that jelly!' The child responded, 'No Mommy... I wasn't playing in any Jelly.' Same question repeated for the second child, 'Was it you that was playing in that jelly!' The child said with fear, 'No Mommy, I wasn't playing in your jelly.' The third child was too conspicuous. This child in particular had JELLY on her mouth! JELLY on her hands! JELLY all over her clothes! Jelly everywhere! The mother looked at the child straight in her eyes and asked, 'was it you that was playing in my jelly?' The child stared back at her mother with tears in her eyes and softly said... 'No Mommy, I wasn't playing in your jelly...' Ladies and gentleman of the jury! Take a close look at what I have here. These are pictures of Mr. Black Moore packing drugs in the trunk of the rental car hours before the bust!" I quickly passed the 8x10s' around while the judge and Mr. Daily were reacting.

"OBJECTION, YOUR HONOR!!!

The Judge lowered his gavel, "MS. LEWIS! YOU ARE OUT OF LINE! YOU KNOW WE DON'T WORK LIKE THIS IN MY COURTROOM!"

Everyone was out of control. Mr. Daily raced over to the jury snatching away the photos.

"Your Honor! This case..."

"Shut up, Mr. Daily! I'll handle this! ORDER IN MY COURTROOM!"

I knew I was in trouble for this, but it was my last chance to free an innocent woman.

"Ms. Lewis! That evidence will NOT be admissible! That goes for the jury also...You will NOT consider this evidence in your deliberations...It will not be allowed! Ms. Lewis. I will allow you to proceed, but when this is over, there will be consequences. Am I understood?"

"Yes, Your Honor."

"Continue."

"I apologize, Your Honor."

"Continue, Ms. Lewis."

I turned back to face the jury. They seemed baffled. I wasn't even sure if they were able to see the pictures good enough to find the truth. That was my last hope in reaching them. I continued with my closing argument.

"I apologize to you all. I just want you to understand how important it is to make the right decision here. Please don't allow an innocent woman to go to prison. It's imperative that you all understand the jelly concept. My client is as clean as a whistle! There's no jelly around her mouth! No jelly on her hands! Nor is there jelly on one piece of her clothing! Ladies and gentlemen of the jury, Black Moore sits before you today with jelly on his mouth! JELLY on his hands! JELLY ALL OVER HIS EXPENSIVE SUIT! And auh, J-E-L-L-Y all over the prosecution's case!!! This here ladies and gentlemen is a sticky situation... The final verdict rests in your hands. Thank you."

The entire courtroom was out of control. . People all around were applauding, screaming, crying and cursing. The judge lost complete control over his courtroom. I needed some water before I passed out. This is too much for me. After this, my days as an attorney were surely over.

FIFTY-EIGHT

DECISION

*****

TREASURE

"You were exceptional in court today, Baby! You never cease to amaze me. I'm proud of you." Ferrell came up behind me, placing his hands around my waist. "That's Daddy's little girl in there." He kissed me on my ear lobe, wandering around to the back of my neck. He knows that's my weak spot.

"Ssstop… before you start something you can't finish," I moaned.

I was standing in front of my full-length mirror, naked, admiring my stomach that stuck out like a fat whale.

"I'm fat," I pouted.

"I know…"

"You know!" I pulled away from him. "How are you going to agree with me, Ferrell?" I whined.

"I was just playing. Aww, come here Bay."

"NO!" I pursed my lips up, attempting to walk away, but he was in a playing mood. "Stop it Ferrell!" He gently threw me on the bed, tickling me. "Ferrell! I'm too big for this." I couldn't stop laughing. "I'm going to pee on myself! Sto-op!" He attempted to kiss me again, but I turned my head away. "Move."

"You mad?"

I was pouting like a three-year-old child. Ferrell didn't care at all. He was used to my mood swings. That's why he carries on with playing the way he does. He knows that in the end, he usually gets what he wants, in spite of my attitude.

"You make me sick!"

269

"Oh, do I really? Okay, let me see if this will make you feel any better." He pulled his flesh from his boxers.

"I'm not in the mood, Ferrell. Let me up. We have to get ready for court tomorrow. You play too much."

He ignored me. The more he stroked himself, the harder he became. I knew at this point he had won. He eased down gently spreading my thighs apart, rubbing his flesh against my pouring rain.

"I-I told you...mmm, to stop..." I couldn't fight the feeling. He was laying firm kisses against my neck, making his way inside me. The race was on....

*****

"Ferrell, are you awake?"

"What's up?" He placed his arms around me snuggling up against my body.

"After this is over, I'm not practicing anymore."

"What? Stop tripping girl. You're just stressed."

"No, I'm not Ferrell. I'm serious. I just wanted to share this with you before I made my final decision."

"Treasure, if you are serious about this, and it's something you truly want to do, I'm with you."

"Thank you, Ferrell. You just don't know what that means to me."

"Yes I do. There's something else, Treasure. I wanted to save this until after the verdict, but I can't wait that long. We're leaving the country after court tomorrow. I planned us a vacation in the islands. We both need to get away."

"What about Marquis?"

"Mom's keeping him until we return."

"I love you," I excitedly remarked

"And I need you." He said sincerely.

Ferrell keeps me sane. I'm blessed to have him by my side. As he drifted back to sleep, I stared out the window at the stars. There were two that sparkled beautifully at me. One was bigger than the other.

I have been so caught up in this case, I haven't checked up on my family. I've been keeping them close in prayer. I'll call once this is over.

FIFTY-NINE

I HOPE GOD IS LISTENING

*****

TYEISHA

"Lord... I can't remember the last time I prayed. I notice how people here in the county carry their Bible and pray everyday. I also heard others say that the only time people seek You is when they're in trouble. Well, Lord... I'm in trouble. I know I haven't called on You in awhile, but if You give me another chance, I promise I won't make another mistake like this again. I will do right by You Lord. I promise You, I will. I ask You Lord to keep me strong, and watch over my family. Oh yeah, and Treasure too... Amen."

SIXTY

HER LAST BREATH

*****

"Michael, I hope you're keeping our appointment," Tawaunna insisted, finally getting through on his cell phone after her eighth attempt.

Michael avoided her calls until Summer was out of sight. Summer was off to one of her expensive, full body makeovers.

"What did I say?" He gritted his teeth.

Michael had just taken his medicine. He snatched up all he needed to get rid of Tawaunna once and for all.

"It's going on three o'clock. I was just calling to confirm our appointment tonight at seven. You haven't changed your mind have you?" She impatiently asked.

"I'll be there, Tawaunna. You just don't forget."

"How could I forget, Michael? That's where my nightmare began."

"What are you talk... forget it. We'll discuss this when I get there." He hung up.

Michael placed everything in his leather duffle bag and made his way out the door. After the phone call, his anger was reinforced. He knew things would become easier once she was out of the picture.

In a couple of hours, he and Summer would be on their way to Africa, where he had set up a whole new life. Summer has no idea of Michael's hidden agenda. He has scheduled both their deaths, to take place somewhere in the African jungles. They received their passports yesterday; he's more than ready, and she's greedily anxious.

Summer wanted the gold and the riches this trip had to offer her, but he had other plans. He set it up that no matter what happens, she can never return to the states. It's amazing what money can do. In the process, Michael ordered plots for the both of them, side by side like husband and wife. In his sick mind, he truly believed Summer *was* his dead wife.

Angela destroyed him to a point of no return. The woman he loved and trusted with everything had betrayed him. She had been sleeping around on him from the day they were married. Angela wanted nothing more than his money, just like most women he had dealt with. Angela didn't love him the way he loved her. Just like Summer...out for one thing and one thing only. To him, Summer's a perfect match. She was easy to fall into his hands. He's a handsome, wealthy doctor that could buy her anything. She trusted him, just like men trusted her. And now her life's in his hands.

SIXTY-ONE

CLOSE CALL

*****

JERALDINE

"What can I do for you, Miss?" The officer at the front desk asked.

"I'm here to see Investigator Darrion Richardson please. He's expecting me."

"Hold up." He paged Darrion's desk. "Yes Sir, there's a... I'm sorry Miss, what's your name again?"

"I don't believe I ever told you. It's Jeraldine Chambers."

"A Jeraldine Chambers, Sir... up front to see you. Okay, Sir. I'll send her right back." He hung up the receiver. "You may proceed through the double doors. Lieutenant Richardson will be waiting for you at the end of the hall."

"Thank you...Officer Coley?" I noticed his name on his badge.

"That's correct."

He buzzed me through the double doors, where a fine tall chocolate brother was waiting patiently for me at the end of the hallway.

"Hi, Gorgeous."

"Hello, Mr. Richardson. You're looking rather fine yourself." I followed him to his office.

"Have a seat. You'll have to excuse the chaos. No matter how much I organize this paperwork, I can't find shit unless everything is a mess!"

"I understand. I think I would rather a man be a little messy, than too clean. That might mean something when it comes to his sexual preference."

"That's not a concern in my department. Trust and believe, I love the feel of vaginal walls, not colon intestines," he teased.

"Please, my young virgin ears can't take any more."

"What am I going to do with you?"

"Do you really want me to answer that?" I winked.

"I hope what I'm about to show you Jeraldine, doesn't change your mood."

That was all he had to say to prepare me for the worst.

"Let's get down to business."

His mood changed as he pulled a file from under some papers.

"Here we are... Doctor Andrew Grey." He passed me some pictures.

"Who? Oh my God." I held my mouth, dropping the pictures on the desk.

"I'm sorry Jeraldine. I should have warned you. I didn't mean to let you see those without explaining who the victim is in the photos."

I was confused. "Wait a minute Darrion...who the hell is Dr. Andrew Grey? And who is this dead woman?"

"Here, let me have those." He picked the pictures up off the desk, placing them back in the folder. "The woman lying dead on the floor with bullet wounds to her head and lower back area is the wife of Dr. Andrew Grey. Doctor Michael Tice is an alias name he's been using. But, there's something strange about it all."

"I'm listening."

Poor Treasure!

"Doctor Andrew Grey wasn't the one who killed her."

"Who...Why?" I stuttered.

"The woman's sister did. The deceased woman's maiden name is Angela Harris. She was having an affair with her sister's husband during the incident. Her sister claimed she didn't know it was Angela in bed with her husband. By the time she realized who it was she was shooting at, it was too late."

"Oh, God. Can I see a picture of her again, please?"

"You sure you can handle this, Jeraldine?"

"Please, Darrion. I have to know."

"Oookaay…"

He passed me a photo of this Angela woman, and I almost fainted. Her resemblance to Summer was identical! If I didn't know better, I would have thought it was Summer in this picture!

"Darrion, this woman looks exactly like Treasure's sister! When did this tragedy happen?"

I was becoming uncomfortable. My mind was playing tricks on me; I was sure the dead woman in the photo, was Summer! I needed reassurance!

"This happened back in 2000."

I felt a little secure to learn of the year. It was then that I could convince myself of the truth of the matter.

"Are you okay?" He asked.

"These photos are disturbing. They're hard to look at, Darrion."

"Trust me when I tell you, I've seen worse. Try looking at dead bodies of children, battered women and teenagers lying on our city streets daily. That's when your job becomes hard. Have you ever heard the saying, *don't go looking for something; you might not like what you find*? Well, here's the rest on the mysterious Dr. Tice. My advice to you, after I show you the rest… call your friend. I'm sure she needs to be aware of this."

SIXTY-TWO

THE ELEMENT OF SURPRISE

*****
TREASURE

"Why are you shaking so badly?" Ferrell asked me, as we reentered the courtroom. It was three o'clock, and the jury was finally ready to release the verdict. Now we're all present, waiting on something that could possibly change our lives forever.

"Has the jury reached a verdict?" Judge Scibana asked.

One of the jurors stood strong and sharp, and then said, "Yes Your Honor, we have."

It was extremely quiet in the courtroom. The only thing heard was paper unraveling. It was like time was moving in slow motion. I could literally hear my heart beating. The dryness in my throat felt like my tonsils were sticking together. Tyeisha's skin was pale. She hadn't said a word the whole time we sat. She was just as nervous as I was.

"Will the Defendant please rise for the verdict."

I had to assist Tyeisha up on her feet. She was truly scaring me at that point. Suddenly, as Tyeisha stood, Treasure looked around at a room that was becoming a blur. The voices sounded distant...far away.

"On the charge of Possession with Intent to Distribute... The jury hereby finds the Defendant... GUILTY..."

My hearing started to fade. I saw Ferrell fall to the floor screaming, cursing! Their Mom fainted! Tyeisha glared at me with evil eyes. Before I could say one word, she had her handcuffs bound around my neck, choking me until I couldn't breathe! I could feel my life being strangled out of me!

"YOU DID THIS TO ME BITCH! YOU LOST THIS CASE TO GET RID OF ME!! DIE BITCH! DIIIIIIIIIIIEEEEEEE!!!"...

"TREASURE! TREASURE!!" Tyeisha was screaming my name.

I turned to look at her, and then backed away. It didn't dawn on me at first that her hands were not around my neck. I felt like I was caught in a trance.

"WE WON TREASURE! YOU DID IT GIRL!" Ferrell and Tyeisha's family and friends congratulated me. Ferrell had to fight through the crowd to get to me.

"You did it wife!" He kissed me. That's when I realized that I blacked out while the verdict was being read.

"Tyeisha! You're free?" I said, still unsure.

"Yes, thanks to you Sis." She hugged and kissed me on the cheek. "I owe you, Treasure."

"Just promise me you'll be a better judge of character the next time!" I pushed her hair off her shoulder.

"I know riii-ght..." She wiped the tears from her eyes, hugged me again, and then fell into her Dads arms.

I was so happy when all the hugging ended. Ferrell and I couldn't wait to leave that courtroom. We didn't hesitate to prepare for our trip to the islands.

Thank God, it's over...

SIXTY-THREE

RUNNING OUT OF TIME

*****

TREASURE

"FERRELL! .... Marquis wants his Sponge Bob toy!" I had to scream down the steps.

He had that loud obnoxious rap music playing, and it was driving me nuts! I am not in the mood for listening to this after all I've been through. He must be crazy!

Get on my level! WHAT! Get on my level! YOU CAN'T! Get on my level! YOU CAN'T! Get on my level! You can never-ever, never-ever, never-ever, never, never-ever! GET ON MY LEVEL!!!

My head is already spinning. I feel nauseated, and Marquis is whining. I've played a major role in Marquis's behavior. I spoil him, picking him up every time he cries. Now look what I've done. He's holding on to my pants leg while I'm trying to pack. At first, I thought it was my pregnancy that has him tripping, but now I know whose to blame... me. I love the attention though. Since Keyonna died, we've become closer. He's accepted me, and I will continue to do my best on her behalf. He will always know that his biological mother loved him just as much as I do.

I found out I was having a girl a couple of days ago. I was elated! Ferrell was just as happy as I was, being that it's his first girl. But the most important part of this pregnancy is our baby being healthy.

"Here boy, you are getting on my nerves," Ferrell said giving Marquis his toy.

"MINE! Daddy!" He snatched it and stumbled off.

That boy is going to be something else, with that attitude. I couldn't help but to laugh at him. He was serious about that toy. The fact that Ferrell took his time bringing it to him, made it even worse.

"Treasure, how much longer are you going to be Baby Girl? Our flight leaves in three and a half hours. You know I have to make a few stops along the way."

"Stops? Oh no, I know of *one* and that's to drop off Marquis."

I stood in front of the bathroom mirror looking over my eyebrows that I had waxed. They were swollen and irritated. Everything irritated me!

"I'm not going to stand here and argue, Treasure. Hurry up," he said walking off.

"I'm coming baby. Did you load the luggage into the truck?" I asked trying to buy more time.

"I got this." His voice was slowly fading as he walked away. "Now come on Treasure! Beauty doesn't take that long, Baby!"

"Whatever." I exhaled.

Before we left his home, I made an attempt to call my Grams and Aunt Kim. Neither was home, so I left a message letting them know of my whereabouts. I also informed them that I should return in a couple of weeks. Other than that, I've avoided all other calls from friends and associates. I needed to get away to relax. I'll return all calls as soon as my vacation is over.

SIXTY-FOUR

LOOSING PATIENCE

*****

JERALDINE

"UNFUCKING BELIEVABLE! This can't be happening! I have left several messages on Treasure's answering service, and she still hasn't called me back! What's it been, two, three hours now! She's not at home, and Grams and Aunt Kim are nowhere to be found; I have no idea where to begin to find Summer! My tolerance right now is zero! I'm perspiring through my very expensive blouse, and I'm holding enough evidence to bring the doctor to justice! I feel like I'm in a damn movie! Or even worse! A chapter in someone's book! My phone rang. I just knew it was Treasure.

"Hello, Treasure?!"

"Treasure? Sweetheart, Treasure is probably on her flight right a bout now. Didn't I mention it to you yesterday, Jeraldine? Treasure and Ferrell are going on vacation," Mrs. Jackson said.

"Oh no, Mrs. Jackson, please, tell me she's not gone. How could this be? Didn't she have court today?" The chips were starting to fall. I knew it was too late for everyone at that point.

"Yes, she did. Not guilty. Treasure's really…"

"Mrs. Jackson, I don't have time for the praise, where is she?"

"Did you try her cell phone? What's wrong, Jeraldine?"

"I can't explain right now." I was trying to drive and find something to write with at the same time. "The only number I have here is this voicemail number, 555-6809. Is this number still valid?"

"She doesn't respond to that number as fast as she does her cell phone...Tell me what's going on Jera..."

"Mrs. Jackson, no disrespect, but WHATS THE GAH-DAM NUMBER?"

SIXTY-FIVE

THE DARK SIDE

*****

Treasure sat in the truck, impatiently waiting on Ferrell to re-appear.

Another stop? I can't believe he was rushing me!

She pulled the mirror down, focusing her attention on a blackhead that was annoying her. Treasure's phone started ringing, taking the attention away from the change of her appearance. The last thing she wanted to do was to be bothered with family, clients, and friends. She made a commitment to relax on this vacation. She ignored the call, throwing the phone to the back of the truck. By then, Ferrell appeared.

"It's about time," she snapped.

"Chill out Treasure. I know you gon' let me handle my business." He backed out the parking lot. "I didn't rush you when you were focusing on your swelled eyebrows, now did I?"

She decided not to feed his comment. Treasure realized she had been riding Ferrell's nerves since the beginning of her pregnancy. Ferrell was used to this kind of behavior, being that Keyonna did the same thing. With only eight minutes away from the airport, timing was perfect. Well, almost that is.

"Ferrell, pull over in that restaurant over there. I have to pee."

"Let me ask you this…we have less than an hour to catch this flight, and you want me to pull over? Why didn't you do this at the salon?"

"Boy!" She threw her hand up.

Ferrell had to bite his tongue on that one.

She is lucky I've changed my philosophy, because there is no doubt in my mind that I would of broke her wrist for throwing her hand up in my face! He thought to himself.

Like usual, Treasure didn't care about his attitude. As bad as she had to pee, cursing him out would have came easy. When she left the truck her phone went off again. It slipped her mind to tell Ferrell not to answer it. The thought of turning it off didn't arise either. Ferrell looked for the phone, finding it on the backseat of the truck. He contemplated on answering it. Ferrell didn't want any interference that would keep them from reaching their destination on time, but Jeraldine was persistent. She would hang up and call back continuously.

"Hello?"

"I'm sorry, is this 555-3223?" Jeraldine asked desperately.

A man's voice made her feel distracted. She had doubts that this was the right number.

"Yeah, who is this?"

"OH!" Jeraldine remembered. Her voice was so loud, that he had to pull the earpiece to readjust the volume. "You're Ferrell, right?"

"That's correct. Now can I ask who you are?"

"I'm Jeraldine, where's Treasure? I need to speak with her, please!" She breathed harshly into the phone.

He knew it was something important by her tone. Possibly something wrong with Grams, he thought.

"Hold up, Baby. She's in the restroom."

"Please tell me you guys are still in the state."

"Unfortunately, yes. You know how slow your girl is."

"Thank you Lord!"

Ferrell didn't ask any more questions. Sensing the urgency, he hurriedly went to get Treasure so she could answer Jeraldine's call.

"Treasure!" he yelled, banging on the door. "Here! Get this phone!" Ferrell was frustrated. He knew their little vacation was out of the question. Exasperation was slowly setting in.

"OOOO! I can't believe you answered my phone!" Treasure shouted through the closed door.

She was upset. She felt he should have known she was avoiding people. As bad as he wanted to make their flight, not answering her phone was self-explanatory. Treasure swung the door open flashing him a goaded stare.

When I get off this phone, I'm going to let him have it! Her eyes read. He passed the phone to her and made his way back to the truck.

Calm down boy! She's pregnant. Don't back slap her, he said to himself.

"Hello…" Treasure spoke rolling her eyes.

"TREASURE! Thank God I caught you! Where are you?" Jeraldine was hysterical, but relieved that she had finally caught up with Treasure.

"Jeraldine. Calm down. What's wrong?" Treasure felt a little uneasy with Jeraldine's tone.

"Calm down! I think you better be sitting down for this!" Jeraldine insisted.

Treasure slowly made her way to the truck. Ferrell couldn't help but to wonder what necessitated their conversation. He watched Treasure as she made her way toward him, stepping out and opening the door for her. The look on Treasure's face definitely read something was truly wrong.

"You alright, Baby girl?" He asked as she stepped inside.

Treasure was so immersed with what Jeraldine was saying, she didn't respond. Ferrell pulled off, making his way toward the airport, hoping against all odds to make their flight. He hoped that the situation wasn't serious, but now Treasure's crying. He knew then the vacation was sure to be cancelled.

"Oh my God, Jeraldine, please tell me what you're saying is not true. Please. Please." Ferrell kept his eyes between the highway and Treasure.

"OH NO! FERRELL! TURN AROUND! JERALDINE WHERE ARE YOU!!"

SIXTY-SIX

NOT A CARE IN THE WORLD

*****

SUMMER

"What could I possibly pick out to wear that I don't already have?" I found what I could for Michael. Now, it's my turn. This will be hard. I have just about every designer outfit out here. I guess I'll just snatch up a few Baby Phat pieces and be on my way. This mall has had enough of me for one day.

I thought my nails were still wet, but I see they're dry now. The massage was the bomb, and I feel like a new woman. I'm just ready to go! Get up out of here for a while. Africa... here I come baby!

I called Michael not too long ago, and he mentioned he had some business to take care of. Too much of that has been going on lately. I'm beginning to wonder if something is up between him and Pimple Lip. I'll have to kill that ho if she fucks with *my* steelo, fo' real! I've come too far and put up with too much shit to go out like that. I know I sound selfish right now because I'm sure as hell about to go get me some more of that good lovin' Justin snuck me before I hit the sky.

I'm on my way baby boy...

SIXTY-SEVEN

BLINK

*****

"Baby, calm down," Ferrell made an attempt to console Treasure.

They were making their way to meet Jeraldine. He was only able to get bits and pieces from Treasure about what was going on. With the little that he did know, things will get worse before it gets better.

"OVER THERE FERRELL!" They pulled up at a restaurant that was connected to the Ramada, not too far from the airport.

Jeraldine ran up to the truck while it was moving. She knew she had to get to her friend. Treasure jumped out, big belly and all.

"Hey, Sis." Jeraldine hugged Treasure. "Don't cry," she said wiping the tears from Treasures eyes.

Ferrell looked lost, but Jeraldine took him out of the dark with the evidence that she had. She passed the file to Ferrell, and allowed him time to look over the self-explanatory information. Jeraldine was hesitant in sharing any other information with Treasure. She knew Treasure couldn't handle too much more, especially, when it came to the ones that she loved. Ferrell's eyes widened, as he looked at the photos, and everything else that the evidence revealed.

Treasure looked over at him and asked, "What is it Ferrell?"

She jerked away from Jeraldine. Treasure wasn't going to allow Jeraldine and anyone else to withhold anything from her. Ferrell tried to place the file behind his back, but she fought to see what he was hiding.

"Don't play with me! This is about my sister!" Ferrell knew then that he had no choice. He passed the folder and watched her unfold.

"OH MY GOD!! NO! SUMMER! GOD NO!!!" Treasure dropped everything to the ground, falling in Ferrell's arms.

"Treasure." Jeraldine tried to calm her down, "The deceased woman in the picture is not Summer. Listen to me, Sweetheart."

Treasure was crying uncontrollably. Jeraldine had to force Treasure to understand her. Treasure didn't want to believe otherwise, because of Summer's resemblance to Angela. Jeraldine finally calmed her down.

"Hey!" Ferrell called out for their attention. "Isn't that my man over there, pulling in the parking lot?" Ferrell pointed over at a dark midnight blue Lexus convertible.

Treasure didn't hesitate making her way over toward the direction they pointed in. The closer she got, the more she convinced herself it was Michael. He was heading inside the Ramada Inn. The whole picture didn't look good to any of them. Accompanied on his arm was Tawaunna. They both turned toward Treasure as she approached.

"WHAT THE HELL DO YOU THINK YOU'RE DOING! AND WHERE IS MY SISTER, YOU SICK BASTARD!" Treasure was vexed.

Michael couldn't believe who was standing before him. He knew in her tone that she knew something more than he anticipated. He prayed he was wrong.

"Excuse me?" He tried to sound unnerved.

"Come on Treasure. Let's allow the police to handle him." Ferrell reached for Treasure, but she snatched away.

"Let go of me! I can handle this!" Ferrell knew he would have to pick her up and carry her to his truck. He contemplated on the perfect time and move, but drama had taken over, making it too late to even consider it.

"POLICE?!" Michael's face wrinkled at the threat. "What are you people talking about?" He acted astounded, releasing a small chuckle. Tawaunna made an attempt to speak, but he shut her up quick.

"Michael…" Tawaunna called in a meek voice.

"Stay out of this!" Michael snapped.

"You're pathetic! I can't believe you're standing here looking like you don't know what's going on… Dr. Andrew Grey…"

Tawauna caught a wit of surprise as Treasure sized him up. Treasure showed no fear toward this predator. His expression told it all, but he continued to hold his ground.

"I don't know what you're talking about! I would advise you…"

"YOU ADVISE ME TO DO WHAT! HUH!! ADVISE THIS!"

Treasure snatched the folder from Jeraldine, and threw it at him. The pictures of Angela's lifeless body and the other victims fell to his feet. He was dismayed. He felt disrespected. Now there would be consequences.

"How dare you!"

He bent down to pick up the pictures from the ground. Tawaunna couldn't believe what stood before her eyes. She covered her mouth at the gross encounter of the photos. None of the information she had on Michael revealed pictures of dead women. It was at that point that Tawaunna knew her life had been knowingly snatched from her.

One by one, Michael placed the dreadful memories in the folder as he stood to his feet.

"Look man, you all…" Ferrell intervened.

"FUCK YOU, YOU LOW LIFE PRICK! YOU DON'T…" Michael pointed his finger in Ferrell's face.

Nothing at that point was open for discussion. Ferrell was all over him, beating him like the animal he was. Tawaunna screamed, and took off to get help in the hotel. Michael tried to fight Ferrell back, but he was too weak. Jeraldine held on to Treasure, trying to calm the situation. It was useless. They were like two men fighting to the death. Treasure couldn't stay calm.

She wanted to break them up. Blood filled Michael's flesh. He was doing all he could to avoid being hit anymore. Treasure was able to loosen Jeraldine's grip, and make her way to Ferrell. She reached for him, pulling at his shirt! She screamed for him to stop! As Ferrell tried to push Treasure away, the opportunity presented itself for Michael to get a hold of his gun.

Jeraldine yelled, "OH MY GOD! FERRELL!"

Ferrell's first reaction was to jump for the gun. Michael held on to it tightly as they both fought to take possession. Jeraldine attempted to pull Treasure away but she was too hard to handle at that point. Jeraldine regrets she didn't place more effort towards helping her friend.

"POP! POP!" The gun went off. There was complete silence... then sudden screams, as Treasure fell to the cement with a bullet lodged in her chest...

Treasure was fading in and out. Her vitals were at their highest point of no return. The EMS technicians were doing all they could to save her.

Ferrell cried, holding Treasure's hand, leaning over her.

"BABY, DON'T DIE ON ME!!! OH GOD NO!!!"

The ambulance fought through traffic to get Treasure to the nearest hospital. Ferrell was emotionally distraught. Attempting to calm him down wasn't possible at that point.

SIXTY-EIGHT

A PREDATORY MAN

*****

"You have the right to remain silent. Anything you say can and will be held against you. You have a right to an attorney..." The officer read Michael his rights, while escorting him to the back of the police vehicle.

"SUCK MY COCK PIGS!"... He spat a mixture of blood and mucus on the ground. "and your rights!" He continued, coughing.

Jeraldine was too upset to go into details with the authorities on what had just taken place. She left what she could with them, and followed the ambulance to the hospital.

Michael continued, "I should have the right to die, but you bastards locked Dr. Kevorkian up, leaving people like me to suffer on the streets!"

He continued to cough. The officers became uncomfortable after reading over the paperwork that revealed his deadly attempts on women.

"What on God's earth would make a person do something so evil?" The female officer asked her partner.

"Pretty Whores like you," Michael rudely intervened.

"One more word out of you and..." The officer retorted before Michael cut him off.

"OR WHAT?! You can't do any more harm than what's already done!"

With that said, the officers proceeded to the station, anxious to get rid of him before he became the victim of police brutality.

SIXTY-NINE

ALL IS FORGIVEN

*****

Summer pulled up to Justin with only one thing on her mind...

The diznick.

Before she could turn back her ignition, Justin was tumbling over the hood of her truck!

"Whaat the fuuck..." She muttered.

Summer had no idea what she was about to endure. She thought he was just overly excited about the Piston's winning the championship. She had witnessed people acting like damn fools all night.

"MOVE OVER!" Justin yanked the door open, forcing her to the passenger side!

"Nigga is you crazy?!" Summer asked in awe.

Justin knew he had to be careful how he informed Summer on what was going on. He was still in shock, himself. Justin released a nervous exhale and backed out of the driveway. He tried not to show too much emotion, but the pain was hard to hide.

Jeraldine finally caught up to Grams and Aunt Kim, relaying the tragedy to them. They rushed off, leaving word with Justin to contact Summer the best way he knew how. Summer had called Justin before this had taken place, making arrangements to stop by. After Justin heard the breaking news, their plans changed.

"Are you ignoring me Justin? Tell me what's going on?" Summer stared at him like he was crazy. She was becoming uncomfortable.

293

"Summer… it's your sister…" He attempted to hide the tears that were forming in his eyes.

"What about her?" Summer lay back in her seat, brushing his behavior off. In her mind, anything about her sister wasn't important. "What is it? She had the dope dealer's baby?" Summer chuckled in disgrace.

"No, no… Summer"… He breathed uncontrollably. Justin could no longer hide his tears.

"WHAT?!" She sat up. Fear of the unknown came over her.

"Su-Summer… Treasure's been shot." Justin was crying a river by then.

"She what?" It took a moment for what he said to register. She truly didn't want to believe what Justin had just relayed to her. "Repeat that to me again." Her voice shook. Summer became nervous, not sure she wanted to know the truth…

Justin didn't have the strength to repeat himself. He just made his way to the hospital. The silence made Summer lose control. Her heart jumped. All the bitterness towards Treasure vanished. She wanted nothing more than to get to her sister right away! It was then that Summer realized life wasn't worth living without her. Justin had very little information to offer. He was speechless.

Not my sister…

They pulled up to Oakwood Hospital. Summer didn't waste any time jumping out of her vehicle. Justin hadn't even parked before she was sprinting inside the hospital to see what was going on with Treasure. There were several police cars, and everyone from family to friends was there in the emergency room. Justin double-parked, and ran in behind her.

Summer was out of control! She was blaming herself for Treasure's situation. She felt that if she would of spoke up when she saw Ferrell, her sister would not be in the middle of his shit. Summer was convinced that Ferrell was the one responsible! She had no idea that this situation was one caused by the one she trusted.

"WHERE IS TREASURE, AUNT KIM? WHERE'S MY SISTER!"

Summer ran inside of the waiting room where everyone was in tears and out of control. There was emotional turmoil filling the waiting area. Everyone was dreading the unknown. No one could utter a word. Ferrell was in the arms of his mother and sister.

"Which one of you ho'z did this to my sister?!"

Summer made her way over to Ferrell. Justin snatched her up before she could cause more damage to a disgruntled man. Ferrell ignored Summer. He was too out of it to feed her accusation. Aunt Kim, Tony and their kids were trying to hold themselves together. No one had the strength to deal with Summer's sanity... or lack thereof. Justin did all he could to keep her calm. The police were even trying to calm her, but she fought for answers!

"Summer, baby please calm down, please," Grams cried.

Summer fell into Grams arms. At this time, Summer still wasn't aware that it was Michael who had caused all of this.

The police pulled Justin to the side and explained the situation. Justin couldn't believe his ears. He was ready to kill or be killed. The officer warned Justin about his behavior, and told him that it would be safer for the family if he would please calm down. Justin agreed. The officers also wanted to question Summer, but Justin explained that she wasn't aware of the situation, and that now was not a good time. The officer agreed to allow Justin to bring Summer down to the station for questioning once she was made aware of the situation, and had calmed down.

"GRAAMMSS! WHYYY! WHY TREASURE, GRAAMS!" Summer cried.

She became so unstable that the doctors thought they would have to sedate her, if she continued.

"Ma, let me go over there and talk to her," Ferrell said to his mother, feeling sorry for Summer.

He himself wasn't in any shape to be offering anyone support, but he wanted to do all he could to maintain his state of mind by trying to help others.

"No baby." Ferrell's mother grabbed his wrist. "Let her mourn."

He agreed, breaking down again himself. The pain was unbearable. Even the strongest person would find it difficult to handle a situation like this one.

"Treasure didn't deserve this Mom, she didn't. What am I suppose to do now? I can't see life without her, I can't Ma, I know I can't...dealing with Keyonna's death was one thing... but now Treasure?" He would never be the same if he lost her and his unborn child, never...

The doctor appeared in the waiting room. The room became silent. You could almost read his eyes. Whatever he was about to say wasn't good news. Ferrell and Summer were so traumatized, they couldn't bare hearing what the doctor was about to say.

Summer ran over to him, falling to her knees, crying and begging for the doctor to save her sister.

"PLEASE DON'T TELL ME MY SISTER DIED! I CAN'T HANDLE IT! SHE DOESN'T DESERVE TO DIE! I DO! TAKE ME! PLEASE!"

Summer pulled at the doctor's pants leg. Justin tried to pull her away. She was kicking and screaming.

"I'm sorry. I don't know how to tell you all this..." The doctor dropped his head in desperation, as he relayed the bad news...

SEVENTY

GOD WORKS IN MYSTERIOUS WAYS

*****

Ferrell's mother was overtaken by all the turmoil that rested on her son's heart.

'The boy can only take so much Lord," she continued to pray, pleading with God.

She knew God doesn't give you more than you can handle. That was one true factor in Silvia's life. She was stern about religion, always had been. Even when her husband and son were involved in the game, she stayed in prayer over them. Her belief goes deeper than anyone could ever imagine.

It was not too long ago that she sat in a theatre, watching a new movie called "Passion.". That movie touched her in a way that changed her life forever. It answered many questions.

If Jesus could go through so much for us, and that was His purpose here on earth, then what makes my son any different?

It made her think about death and how it comes at such an awkward time in one's life. Thinking about the death of Keyonna, and her present situation, reminded her of a parable she read last Sunday; about two angels that traveled from town to town through the night. These angels approached a home of a family who was extremely wealthy. Instead of this family offering love and support to the tired angels, they were cruel and selfish human beings. They forced the angels to sleep in a cold basement that had a big hole in the wall.

A couple of hours passed and the angels moved on, passing through another town where they came to another home to rest. This home was warm, filled with love and affection. Even though this family was poor, they offered the angels their bed, a warm meal, and a comfortable setting. The family survived off of their livestock. It was the only income that placed food on their table.

The following morning the angels were awakened by loud screams and cries from the husband and wife. Their whole livestock was wiped out! Every single animal that fed them had died.

The one angel looked at the other and asked, "Say? How could you allow this to happen? This family was good to us. They welcomed us into their home. Why didn't you stop this from happening?" The young angel was upset.

"My little one, I need you to understand this. The first family we visited was so greedy that I didn't inform them of all the gold that sat behind that hole in the wall. Instead, I sealed it up. They will never find it. Last night while this family was asleep, the *angel of death* came for the wife. Instead, I gave him their livestock."

Ferrell's mother thought the same about Keyonna, Treasure and her son's unborn child. And just to think, Marquis could have been in that car when Keyonna was killed. God works in mysterious ways...

SEVENTY-ONE

WONDER WOMAN

*****

The doctor continued, "We were unable to save the child. Believe me; we did all that we could. As for Treasure, she's in a coma right now, and her vitals are critical at this point. We will continue to do all we can. If anything should change, that is, if she should improve within the next few hours or so, you can thank your higher power. If not, then she will be on a respirator and the rest is up to you. Again, I'm sorry." The doctor stared carefully over at Ferrell, and said, "Are you the fiancé of the victim?"

"Yes sir." Ferrell tried to be strong in his words but he couldn't. He lost his baby, and possibly his wife-to-be. Ferrell was slightly incoherent.

"If you would like to come back and see her now, you can. I will only allow one at a time."

"Thank you. Mom?" Ferrell looked over at his mother. "Hold this for me."

He stood; passing her his shirt that was covered with blood from Treasure's wound. His wife-beater t-shirt was all he had to cover his chilled naked skin. He began to follow the doctor to the back, but something stopped him where he stood. He could hear loud sobs, but the one that stood out the most grabbed his attention. It made him think about Treasure and the one thing she always wanted... Summer. Ferrell knew how much Treasure had struggled to just receive an inkling of attention from Summer. To the death is where Treasure was willing to go to be with her.

"Son?" The doctor gently touched Ferrell's shoulder, noticing his disturbance. "Are you okay?" Ferrell never responded to the doctor; instead he turned toward Summer.

"Yo, Summer! Go see your sister."

He gestured for Summer to come toward him. She slowly rose from her knees and looked around at everyone. They stared in silence and approval.

"What are you waiting for? Come on." Summer didn't hesitate. She rushed past the doctor, anxious to see the sister that had been lost to her for so long.

Ferrell walked back over to his mother. She stood up and hugged him whispering in his ear, "You did the right thing Son."

"I know Ma." Everyone that was present seemed to be more at peace as they watched Summer disappear behind the swinging doors.

Summer tiptoed over to Treasure's bedside and placed her hands over her mouth trying to silence her cry. The scene took her back to their Mom. It made her nervous, uncomfortable…helpless. She didn't want to leave Treasure at that point. Summer didn't want to risk hearing those same traumatizing words that she heard on the day their Mom died… *"Summer, your Mother passed this morning at four o'clock."* …

Inch by inch, Summer approached Treasure. She could hardly think straight. She stood there staring at Treasure, thinking about all the degrading and hateful things she had said and done in the past.

"I could have lost you. I'm so sorry Treasure. I'm truly sorry." She carefully sat beside her. The heart monitor was clashing with the respirator, making her feel uneasy.

"Hey you," Summer whispered softly in Treasure's ear. "I'm here. It's me, that stubborn sister of yours. I love you and I hope you get better soon. Do you think you will ever be able to forgive me for the way I've treated you?" She asked through her tears. "I would understand if you didn't…forgive me... No one deserves to be done the way I did you. Just promise me you won't die on me, okay?" She sniffled and wiped the tears that fell from her eyes. "Please Treasure. If I lose you, I'm lost. Don't go." She whispered in Treasure's ear, placing a kiss on her forehead.

"Listen." She tried to compose herself, "Remember when you used to tie that sheet around your neck when we were young." Summer chuckled, trying to find a loyal sense of humor. She continued to hold Treasure's hand as she reminisced, "You wouldn't even let Mom wash that thing!" She forced out a giggle. "Wonder-Woman, that's who you were, you loved that show. You had the panties and the bra. You had it going on, girl, yes you did." Summer again wiped her eyes. "There are no words to explain how much I missed Wonder Woman."

Treasure's finger twitched on her right hand. Not noticing Treasure's movement, Summer kept hold of her left. She felt comfort being by Treasure's side after all these years.

"You know, Sis, I've always wanted to know why you stopped playing Wonder Woman with me. I was maaad at you. I wish Wonder Woman was here now... I wish I had her powers. I would have been there for you. I would have never let anybody hurt you and the baby. Listen, I know you remember the time I used to keep you up at night singing, *'You can ring my be-e-ell!'* You threw pillows at me, and told Mom on me! WO! You were heated because you couldn't get any sleep! You blamed me for you being tired in your first hour class. I loved aggravating you with that song! I told you I could go on 'Star Search', but you didn't believe me. That's why I did you like that." She started chuckling and crying at the same time. "I need you Treasure." Summer started singing the song in Treasure's ear, fighting through her tears.

"You can ring my be-e-ell, ring my bell," Summer crooned. It was then that the machines attached to Treasure went haywire!

The unexpected noise startled Summer! Within seconds, the room was filled with doctors and nurses, moving Summer to the side.

"It's my fault. Oh no. What have I done?" Summer held herself close as she watched the nurse inject medication into the I.V.

"It's okay. Treasure's fine," the nurse consoled. Summer stared at the nurse in guilt. "You didn't do anything wrong. She must have heard your voice," the nurse gently said, stroking Summer's hair.

"Huh?"

"Shhh... Go over there and be with your sister."

The doctor told Summer that he didn't know what she said, but whatever it was, stabilized Treasure's vitals, and brought her out of the danger zone. Summer knew in her heart that it was the love of God that brought her sister through. She lay back beside her, stroking Treasure's hair, singing, talking, and kissing her forehead. Time was escaping Summer. She knew she had to allow others to visit, but when she made the attempt to unravel her hand from Treasure's, Treasure weakly gripped Summer's hand, making her aware that her presence was all Treasure needed at the time.

"It's going to be okay, Treasure, I'm not going anywhere. I love you and I will never leave your side again...

Wonder Woman."

SEVENTY-TWO

DEATH IN DISGUISE

*****

"NOOOO! NO!" Summer screamed, falling in Justin's arms after hearing about Michael's involvement. "THAT BASTARD! WHERE IS HE?!" she shouted, breathing harshly.

Justin had taken Summer down to the police station to give a statement. The authorities waited until they got her inside their office before they disclosed all the information they had. Justin told her he felt that it was best if she waited on the investigator to explain what happened. Of course, Summer didn't agree. She wanted instant gratification, but Justin refused, making Summer even more discontent with him. Even Justin wasn't aware of Michael's disease until the investigator told them! Justin had no idea he was also in for a rude awakening. That's when all hell broke loose!

"WHAT! What the hell you mean he has AIDS! What is this man talking about, Summer?!" Justin pointed over at the investigator, while staring over at Summer, demanding an explanation.

Summer cried, "I don't know Justin, I don't know."

The investigator didn't hesitate to call for medical assistance for her. They ended up transferring Summer to a psychiatric unit for further evaluation.

In the meantime, Justin was in an uproar. He didn't want to believe that the one time he allowed himself to have unprotected sex, could've been his last.

Justin sat in with one doctor, while Summer sat with another. Summer stared at the woman as she asked questions about her and Dr. Tice's sexual involvement.

"Summer, how often did you and Michael have sex?"

Summer ignored the question, as she verbalized her thoughts.

"You know. ...What you do to others come back double. And when it does. ...You won't even see it coming. It's invisible. It could be standing right beside you, sleeping with you...misleading you. It never exposes itself until it's too late. Death...in disguise..."

Justin and Summer were on the same wavelength. The psychologist questioned him and Summer's sexual contact. He had very little response also.

He said, "It's not like other sex I've had. With Summer, it was different. I trusted Summer. I love her. This is not fair."

"Mr. Holland, you haven't been tested yet. Don't take this situation and turn it into a death sentence. You..."

"Let me say this, Doc. Summer had sex with a man that has AIDS. I had sex with Summer. Even though, we've only done this one time, it's more than likely that I do have the disease. I've practiced safe sex in the past, Doc, always have. But I felt I could trust Summer. It was my pleasure to share something so precious with her. She has my heart and my love, and she doesn't even know it. I realize more than ever now that Love has its own mind. It can't be controlled. If you allow your heart and one's beauty to lead you, you're at risk of making wrong choices. Love walks alone; it conquers you. Love is blind. It's selective. I love Summer, and I was blind to anything other than that."

Justin scheduled an appointment to be tested. Summer, on the other hand, asked for more time. They wanted to test both of them right away, but they both refused the immediate medical attention. Justin prepared himself for the worst-case scenario, but he knew it had to be done. Summer decided to give it to God. For now, she realized that *HE* was all she had.

SEVENTY-THREE

PREMONITION

*****

After Summer calmed down, Jeraldine asked her to accompany her on a small trip to retrieve some additional information on Michael Tice. Janet, was the district attorney on the case and Jeraldine had to get all she could to help support it. Summer agreed to go along. She was very anxious to learn *anything* about Michael and…

Why did you choose me?

Their destination was to meet Angela's sister, Melonie Ganther. She was being held in a maximum-security psychiatric ward at Cincinnati's Women Penitentiary.

As they pulled up to this enormous, bricked facility, Summer received chills, "WOW! The only time I've ever seen something like this was on TV." Summer stared up at the walls surrounding the prison.

"And look at the gun towers" she said, amazed.

"I know. This is no place for humans, girlfriend."

They checked in, calling Ms. Ganther out on an attorney visit. The correctional officer escorted them to a closed room.

The officer called over the radio, "Inmate Melonie Ganther has an attorney visit."

He glanced over at us, placing his radio on his side, and then said, "The inmate will be here shortly."

"Thank You Sir," Jeraldine said.

They took their seats and waited patiently.

"You okay, Summer?" Jeraldine placed her hand on Summer's thigh.

305

"Not really. In the next 48 hours, I will have my results. I'm scared Jeraldine."

"Give it to God, Summer. Give it to God."

"Treasure still doesn't know, right?"

"As far as I know, I haven't said a word about it. Everyone knows to keep quiet."

"I want her to get well. I don't want her to have any other setbacks because of me."

"You're going to be okay,"

Jeraldine didn't believe what she just said herself. She knew the chances of Summer's being infected were highly likely. The only thing she could offer Summer was a prayer.

The correctional officer entered the room with the semi-sedated, Melonie. She looked to be in her early forties or so. Summer stared at her, feeling no remorse. Anything that had to do with Michael gets no love. Melonie kept her head down as she sat.

"You behave," the officer said, leaving them all alone.

"Hello, Melonie. My name is Jeraldine. I'm an attorney, and this is a friend of mine, Summer. I need to ask you a few questions in reference to Dr. Andrew Grey. "

Melonie slowly lifted her head. She was weak, but once she laid eyes on Summer, she reacted as if she had seen a ghost!

"AN-GE-LA?" Her eyes squinted, staring at Summer.

"No. Let me set the record straight. I'm Summer. This is Jeraldine. You might be playing crazy up in here with these people, but we have no time to…"

Jeraldine interrupted touching Summer's shoulder, "Let me take it from here Summer."

Melonie continued to stare heavily at Summer. She didn't feel threatened by Summer's tone or attitude. That was all too familiar. Summer's voice and attitude convinced her that she was Angela.

"What is this, some kind of freaking joke?" Melonie snapped out of her sedation.

"Not at all. We're here to ask you a few questions about your late sister's husband," Jeraldine replied.

"Why ask me when she's sitting right in front of us? Ask her," she said staring deeply at Summer.

"Look! Now I've told you!" Summer retorted.

"Summer! Please! Let me handle this."

"Is everything okay in there?" The officer asked.

"Yes Sir, we're fine. Please give us a little more time."

He turned away from the door.

"Summer, if you want to step out..."

"No. No. I apologize, Jeraldine. I just..."

"You don't have to explain. Just let me handle this, okay?"

Summer nodded.

"You're really not Angela?" Melonie said as she stared. Summer stared back just as hard.

"Melonie. Give me the opportunity to let you know why we're here. ...Your brother-in-law was involved with Summer because she resembled your sister."

"I don't get it."

"He has AIDS. He was trying to kill anyone that reminded him of Angela. That's why we're here. ...To see what happened between you and your sister? Why would someone do another human being like this? What provoked him?"

"I don't believe this."

"Please Melonie. We need to know what happened," Jeraldine pleaded.

"He was a turn-out! Angela never cared about nobody! Andrew was at the wrong place, at the wrong time. He was more than good to Angela. *I* was good to Angela! She didn't appreciate it, it was never enough for her. I loved Angela so much."

Melonie slowly started to relive the nightmare.

"She didn't want anything to do with me and I never knew why. She just hated me. Everything I had, she could have had even more. I would've given her the world! But that wasn't enough. Angela had to go and sleep with my husband. That old dirty dog, he was. I didn't blame my sister! ...In spite of *HER* motive to give *him* AIDS, I blamed him! If I had the chance to do it all over

307

again, I would've kept my eyes open while I was shooting. I didn't mean..." She broke down, crying, "...To shoot Angela, I swear."

"Take your time," Jeraldine reassured.

Summer just continued to stare. She wasn't at all touched by the performance.

"So, Angela tried to give your husband AIDS intentionally?" Jeraldine questioned as she passed her some Kleenex over the table.

Melonie continued, "Yes, *intentionally.* That was Angela's only way to get back at me. Angela and I were like oil and water. We didn't mix. But I didn't want to give up on her. No matter how bad she treated me, I just couldn't turn my back on her."

As Melonie continued on, Summer was slowly letting her guards down. The more Melonie revealed about what happened on the day she killed her sister Angela, the more nervous Summer became. Summer felt like she was there during the murder of Angela, like she witnessed the whole thing between the two...Déjà vu. That's when it clicked,

"The nightmare...You were in my nightmare. You're the face I couldn't distinguish. It was you," Summer said as a tear trickled down her face.

Both Melonie and Jeraldine stared at Summer as she revealed a nightmare that prophesied Angela's fate. It was then that Summer realized that *all* dreams have meaning. She wondered where her life would've been if she had paid more attention to that nightmare.

Damn...It was a premonition.

But, it's too late now. The damage is already done...

SEVENTY-FOUR

FACING THE TRUTH

*****

SUMMER

I pulled up at the clinic. Today was the day that I'd get my results. This time I went to one out in the suburbs. When I looked over to my left, I couldn't believe who was staring in my face.

"What are you doing here?"

"I came to support you," Justin said with a concerned tone.

"I need to do this alone Justin. I've already hurt you enough. I can't deal with the situation as it is."

"Summer, please. I want to be there for you." He walked over, opening my door. "Let's do this, together."

"I'm scared. I don't know how to handle the truth, Justin."

"You'll get through this. And if it makes you feel better, I'll be there for you every step of the way," he consoled me, holding me as I feebly walked toward the entrance.

"I can't go inside Justin. Please don't make me do this."

"You have to face this Summer. You're Grams and Aunt told me you didn't want anyone going with you. Why?"

"It's too much pain for me. I can only imagine what it will do to my family."

The nurse was waiting on me. My case was high profile and *everyone* knew exactly who I was! The doctor came to the front, meeting Justin and me, before I signed my name on the clipboard.

"Hi, Miss Lewis. You don't have to sit down. I'm ready to see you, now. You can come on back with me."

I stared at Justin. He nodded in support.

"You must be Justin Holland. I'm Doctor Lynn." She kindly reached her hand out to greet him, "You both can follow me to my office."

As bad as I wanted to run at that point, Justin constantly reminded me of my reason for needing to know the truth.

"It's going to be okay." He kissed my forehead as I walked in the office with the doctor. He took a seat on the outside of the door.

"Have a seat Ms. Lewis."

I nervously sat, staring away.

"I know you're probably nervous, but I need you to understand something. Your situation is not the end."

My heart was trying to come out my chest! Hot flashes covered my body and sweat was starting to form.

"Can... Can we get this over with please?"

"Sure." She opened my file and started to read off my results...

SEVENTY-FIVE

FAITH

*****

JUSTIN

I can only imagine what Summer's going through. I was there just the other day, when I received my results.

"Okay Mr. Holland." The doctor opened my file, "I've reviewed your results."

My heart raced and my hands were cold. ...I rubbed them together until I felt a burning sensation. I'm sure he could tell I was nervous, as I sat there waiting, it seemed like forever.

"Your test came back negative."

"Yes! ... Thank you Sir!" I shook his hand.

"Well, you're not quite out of the woods yet. You will still have to make an appointment in six months to be tested again. It can take up to six months for enough antibodies to build up in your immune system, for the virus to become evident. If these tests come back negative as well, then I can safely say that you are free of the disease. I would suggest that you be more careful in the future Mr. Holland. Do you have any questions? "

"No sir. I'll see you in six months..."

"AUUUUUUUUUHHHHHHHH!" Summer cried out, interrupting my thoughts.

She screamed so loud that it startled me. I jumped up and burst into the office. She was on the floor crying. I fell down on my knees, taking her into my arms.

"What should I do, Doc?" I asked, desperate and confused.

311

"There is not much either of us can do at this moment, Mr. Holland. Just console her for now."

*****

Summer's results were positive. She is now HIV infected. This was one nightmare she couldn't escape. Although she expected it, it was still a shock to actually hear the words, 'Your Test for HIV came back *Positive.*'

As hard as this whole situation has been on the both of us, I made a vow to myself to be there for her. I don't want to ever leave her side. I can't hide the fact that I love her.

Summer regained her strength within a few days. It was time to face her reality. Now, with me in her life, she made a decision to receive counseling and use her own experiences to counsel others.

We're practicing safe sex. Even though I love the feeling of a woman's warmth, I have to make healthy choices with the one I love, even if it means sacrificing the full benefit of enjoying my self sexually. I'm aiming to please my future wife.

Summer found the courage to tell Treasure. Surprisingly, she didn't handle Summer's situation like a death sentence. Treasure had educated herself about the disease. As she explained to Summer, their mother's speedy progression to AIDS was brought about by her denial. Now that Summer has accepted the fact that she has the disease; Treasure had faith, her sister could fight this set-back head on. They have become closer, and we have become a family.

For this I am happy, not only for them as sisters, but especially for Summer. Her family and social support was what she needed. It will help slower the progression of the disease. That is very important... because I want her around for a long time.

Available Now!!

"Vindictive Wo-Men"

ORDER YOUR SIGNED COPY NOW
BEFORE THEY HIT THE SHELVES!!!

hottestsummerever@hotmail.com

**FOR
ADDITIONAL COPIES
OF**

*** THE HOTTEST SUMMER
EVER KNOWN *
By Valencia R. Williams**

Send a check or money order for
Book Price $16.95 + $4.95 S&H
Talking Book Price (Cd Only) $29.00 + 4.95 S&H
Book Qty _____ CD Qty _____

Name _____
Address _____
City _____ State _____ Zip _____

Fill out and mail to:
The Williams Sisters' Publication Group
P.O. Box 48541
Oak Park, MI 48237

HIV/AIDS STATISTICS
Estimated number of diagnoses of AIDS through **December 2002.**
For additional or updated information,
You may request a free copy of the
HIV/AIDS Surveillance Report by calling:
The CDC National Prevention Information Network at
1.800.458.5231 or www.cdc.gov/hiv/stats.

Age	# of Cumulative Aids Cases
Under 13	9,300
Ages 13 to 14	839
Ages 15 to 24	35,460
Ages 25 to 34	301,278
Ages 35 to 44	347,860
Ages 45 to 54	138,386
Ages 55 to 64	40,584

United States

Estimated numbers of diagnoses of AIDS through
December 2002, by Race or Ethnicity.
For additional or updated information,
You may request a free copy of the
HIV/AIDS Surveillance Report by calling:
The CDC National Prevention Information Network at
1.800.458.5231 or www.cdc.gov/hiv/stats.

Race or Ethnicity	# of Cumulative Aids Cases
White, not Hispanic	364,458
Black, not Hispanic	347,491
Hispanic	163,940
Asian/Pacific Islander	6,924
American Indian/ Alaska Native	2,875
Unknown or Multiple race	887

Exposure Category	Male	Female	Total
Heterosexual contact	50,793	84,835	135,628

Exposure Category	# of AIDS Cases
Mother with or at risk for HIV infection	8,629